Desire by Blood

A Vampire Alliance Novel

Melissa Schroeder

I0662328

Dedication

To the one person who would never leave me alone about this series: Joy Harris. Thank you for your support, even if it did border on stalking. I treasure our friendship more than you know. Oh, and now will you shut up and leave me alone?

Mel

Acknowledgments

This book was had a long road to publication, and if I did not take a chance and publish it myself, it would not have happened. So many people helped me make that decision.

First, Brandy Walker for helping me set up the schedule and urging me to do it. It would not have happened without you.

I cannot ignore the fantastic cover art done by Kendra Egert. Even after I decided to do a different marketing plan, you stepped in and did the work, and my how lucky am I?

And of course, to Les and my girls, all four of them. I complain a lot but without you, I wouldn't amount to much. Thank you for always believing in my dream.

A Passion they could not deny

"It works better if you kiss me back."

His voice was deep, resonant, filled with something she could not discern. It did not matter if she did not understand, her body responded. Heat shot through her veins causing her to shiver. Without another word, he swooped down to capture her mouth again.

Every worry she had dissolved as he slanted his mouth over hers. This time she responded the best she could. It was her first true kiss, for she did not count the few stolen kisses early suitors had subjected her to. If they had been as skilled as Blackburn, Cordelia might have been tempted to break the rules.

Cordelia willingly opened her mouth, allowing Blackburn to slide his tongue in. Little bursts of heat crackled over her nerve endings. Slowly, she skimmed her hands up his chest, over his shoulders, and behind his neck. He took the opportunity to pull her closer, into his warmth. His hands slid down to cup her bottom, pull her tightly against him. Even through the layers of clothing she could feel the beat of his heart.

Her head spun, her body rejoiced. Tentatively, she slipped her tongue into his mouth, sliding it along his as he had to her. The taste of him burst through her, tart lemonade, a touch of brandy, and Nicodemus Blackburn...that was the most intoxicating part. Every reservation she had dissolved into the glorious passion he was building,

Praise for Melissa Schroeder's Harmless Series

A Little Harmless Fascination" is one of my favorite of the Harmless series. It has some incredibly hot moments as well as some wonderfully tender ones. It is a great romantic read.
Jennfier, RNN

A LITTLE HARMLESS SUBMISSION was just about perfect to me. It had the perfect mix of sexual tension, eroticism, suspense and cheekiness that I've come to associate with Melissa Schroeder's writing.
Rho, TRR

INFATUATION is an awesome contemporary, erotic and military romance that was such a joy to read, I finished it in 24 hrs while having to work. It was sizzling hot and emotional.
Pearl's World of Romance

Praise for Melissa Schroeder's Cursed Clan series

First thought when finished: Holy Cow! This is going to be a fun series to read---just the right combo of story/romance!
Felicia, The Geeky Blogger's Book Blog

This is a great Paranormal Romance novel! The dynamics of the McLennan clan are remarkable, the characters are impassioned and compelling, the plot is riveting and the delivery is faultless.
Smitten with Bad Boys Heroes

Prologue

Late in Queen Victoria's Reign

"He was Made?" Malik asked.

Nicodemus Blackburn did not look at his friend, but nodded and continued to clean the blood from beneath his fingernails. The only sound in the dank room was the splashing of water.

"How old?"

"I would say less than two months. Definitely not completely transitioned."

Silence. When Malik didn't respond, Nico glanced at him. The passive expression and cold gaze told Nico everything he needed to know. They had learned long ago Malik would be the whipping boy for every damned Made vampire.

"He was completely out of control. The woman..." Nico closed his eyes and swallowed back the fresh wave of nausea that threatened to bubble up. In five hundred years, he had never seen anything so brutal, so bestial. He had killed Mades before, but never happened upon one of their kills. He opened his eyes to find his friend with a knowing look on his face. "She did not die easily."

If possible, Malik's expression grew colder. "Meaning he raped her to death."

There was nothing to be said, for nothing would stop what was going to happen, what was already happening. Nico grabbed a linen cloth and started to dry his hands.

"We need to find out what the bloody hell is happening. This one had no connection to family. There has to be a reason for the Made vampires to be popping up all over the countryside."

Malik nodded. "I've heard more rumbling amongst the Borns. Not to mention the Carrier woman they found dead in London two nights ago. There might be trouble for my kind again."

Nico shrugged and retrieved another shirt. "I don't think you need to worry."

"Don't lie."

"You are always exempt from these witch hunts. You trace your roots back further than mine. Anyone who has made it through transition has no problem. They never lose control."

A cynical smile curved Malik's lips. "True. And so I shouldn't have to worry at all. But the youngest generation doesn't remember the Inquisition...they don't remember how many of us fought on your side. They will be out for blood—so to speak."

Nico faced him. Irritation and worry gripped his stomach in a cold, hard fist. What Malik said was true. Before the Inquisition, Borns regularly hunted for Mades, killing them before they gained control of their new powers. He could not defend what had happened in the past, only work to fix the present.

But that would come later. Nico could still smell the corpse's blood on his body. If he closed his eyes, he could remember everything. The mutilation of the Carrier woman. The sickening feel of shoving a piece of wood into the vampire's flesh. The word *Suprema* still echoed in his ears.

It was worse than it had been almost four hundred years ago. God, he did not want to do that ever again. But he would...he knew that down to his core. There was no way to avoid it. If he allowed someone else to lead the hunt, it would become a massacre of every Made vampire in England.

He opened his eyes and looked at his best friend. They had seen the worst mankind could throw at them. Nico feared they were about to see things neither of them were prepared for.

"The trail leads to London," Malik said.

"Yes. My father agrees."

"Your father is the only family leader with any intelligence."

True, for he was the oldest of the four family patriarchs that comprised the Vampire Alliance of England and Scotland.

"In father's mind, he is the only one who matters. But, in this case, he is correct. London would be easier…the maker could resort to the lower classes, and it would not attract any attention."

"Do you have any idea who it might be?"

Nico shook his head. "Not a clue. All I know is the sightings in the country have dwindled, and those clues we have found all lead to London."

"I hate London."

Nico smiled at his friend's irritation. Both of them hated London, the *ton*, and all of their idiocy. But his father had asked him to go, and Nico could not refuse. "We go to London."

Malik studied him for a moment, and then nodded. "We go to London."

Chapter One

He was avoiding her again.

Lady Cordelia Collingsworth searched through the milling crowd in the Smythe's ballroom as irritation shot through her blood. This was the third night in a row she had lost him. The mysterious man was making it impossible to discover anything about him...or his shady businesses.

"Lady Cordelia."

She grimaced before she could stop herself. Viscount Hurst. She had been dodging his steps at every event for the last fortnight. He always appeared at her side, a genial smile on his face and pretty compliments. Drat the man. She smoothed her expression and turned to face the viscount.

Cordelia understood why he had been labeled "The Catch" by the ladies of the *ton* early this season. Just thirty years old, he sported a strong physique. Blond hair and deep brown eyes had all the women sighing, or so she had been told. He was pleasant enough with that square jaw and all his proper manners, but there was something about him she did not like. Something that made her blood chill every time she came in contact with him. Even in the overwhelming heat of the ballroom, she could not seem to keep herself warm in Hurst's presence.

He smiled down at her, and she fought the shiver of dread that raced along her flesh.

"I hope you are enjoying yourself tonight."

She forced her lips to curve into a welcoming smile as she offered her hand. He bent over it. Even with her skin protected by gloves, the top of her hand grew cold. Bile rose in her throat as she watched him. Most women—especially women decidedly on the shelf and with no dowry—would kill to be this close to him. The idea that she wanted to flee whenever she spotted him made no sense.

"I always enjoy the Smythe's ball. It is very amusing."
She tugged on her hand, twisting it to free it from his grasp.
"And you, my lord?"

"I thought to ask for your hand in the next dance." The
moment he said it, the first strains of a waltz filled the
massive ballroom. Dread filled her stomach. "I assume you
are free?"

His smirk told Cordelia he knew she did not have one
dance on her card. She rarely did. She was not on the
marriage mart, far too old and poor to grab attention—except
from the viscount. Now she regretted not securing a dance
partner for the first waltz.

"I—"

"Lady Cordelia." A strong masculine voice filled the air
around her and sent a rush of heat along her nerve endings.
Even without turning she knew who stood behind her. The
man she had been chasing for three days straight. The man
she was positive ran illegal businesses in London. The
subject of her now-due article.

Nicodemus Blackburn.

She turned to face him, her heart beating hard against her
breast. As blood rushed out of her head, she felt a bit
lightheaded. Where the viscount and his patrician features
were attractive in a very English-gentry way, Mr. Blackburn
was dark and dangerous. If women sighed over the viscount,
they fainted when Blackburn gave them his attention.
Cordelia wanted to be the exception to that rule…but he was
heady indeed.

"Yes, Mr. Blackburn?"

"I believe this is my dance."

For a moment, she didn't respond. She couldn't. Her
mind simply could not formulate a reply. Blackburn, who
rarely danced and had been known for disdaining most of the
ton, had just asked her to dance. No. He lied and said she had
promised him the dance.

One black eyebrow rose as she said nothing. The curving of his lips was enough to pull her out of her trance.

She offered him her hand and turned to Hurst. "If you will excuse me, my lord."

Hurst tossed Blackburn a nasty look before offering her a pleasant smile. "Of course. Perhaps the next waltz?"

She merely smiled but said nothing. Cordelia would make sure not to be in sight of the viscount again. Blackburn led her out to the floor and pulled her closer, swinging her into the rhythm of the dance. She drew in a deep breath. The scent of bay rum filled her senses. That lightheaded feeling returned.

"A bit of advice, my lady."

She looked up at Blackburn, trying to keep her wits about her. Everyone sought information on this man, especially her editor who had told her to dig into his character and find out just where he got his money. There were more than a few rumors, one being he was a moneylender. And he was here, like a ripe peach for the picking. She had a list of questions memorized. Unfortunately, she found herself staring into his mesmerizing eyes and could not gather her wits long enough to ask him anything.

It was Blackburn's fault. His attractiveness did not come from a trained valet who knew how to dress his employer. He possessed the most remarkable gray-blue eyes and blacker than midnight hair—worn ruthlessly short and not a strand out of place. He was put together well, solid. She could feel his muscles flex as he guided her through the waltz, maneuvering around couples with ease.

His attractiveness turned heads, but there was more to it than that. It was the strength she sensed beneath the surface of the polished veneer. Something about him, dangerous and male, seethed just beneath his polite façade. It almost made her giddy to be this close to him.

"Lady Cordelia?"

She blinked. "Yes? Oh, you had advice."

"You should stay away from the viscount."

She nodded at his comment. No, not truly a comment. A command. She didn't know Blackburn, knew nothing of his family—and he only could know of the gossip surrounding hers. But for some unknown reason, he felt the need to tell her what to do. Of all the cheek!

"Whatever do you mean?"

His eyes flashed with irritation as they narrowed. "I mean the man is trouble. I fear that he is after but one thing in his pursuit of you."

Where was the tact Blackburn was famous for? Everyone in the *ton* knew her situation, or thought they knew. It was much worse than she let people know, otherwise she would never be invited to these functions. And while everyone attending knew that her brother was drinking away her inheritance, none of them knew she was so close to living on the street.

People may gossip about her, but they did not do it in front of her. Did Blackburn realize he insulted her? Looking at his serious expression, she thought not. The man actually believed he was helping.

She adopted her most innocent look. "What would that be, Mr. Blackburn?"

His expression blanked as he studied her. "I beg your pardon. I was led to believe you were somewhat of a..."

"What, sir?"

Oh, he did not like being put in the corner, but she was happy to shove the man there. The gall of him to insult her so. Granted, she was positive Hurst was after her for the reason Blackburn implied, though even that was odd because the viscount could have his choice of most women of the *ton*—married and unmarried. Why would he want the Lady Fionna's bastard daughter, who had no dowry and a penchant for books? His pursuit made little sense. But most men of the *ton* had little sense.

With an aggravated sigh, he maneuvered them through the French doors and out onto the patio. Light from the ballroom spilled over them as the cool night air hit her skin, chilling her anger and desire.

Blackburn hesitated, then released her. The dark night surrounded them, the tension in the air rising. She walked away from him to the edge of the terrace. "Why ever are we out here?"

When he did not answer, she turned to face him. He placed a hand on each of his hips and frowned at her. Again. "Stop playing the simpleton."

She blinked. "Playing?"

"Lord Hurst is not a well man."

That was not what she expected to hear. She dropped all pretenses. "Not well?"

He hesitated. "There have been rumors about him."

"Indeed. There are rumors about almost every eligible man here tonight, including you."

He nodded in acknowledgement. "He has certain...tastes that would shock you."

"Do you mean he frequents the House of Rod?"

That had his eyebrows rising. "You know of that?"

"Why do you think I accepted your dance? I didn't have to. After eight years in the *ton*, I am well aware of how men behave. I know there is something wrong with the viscount."

His gaze sharpened. "You do?"

His intense study suddenly made her very wary. It was as if she were a specimen he was trying to decipher. Blackburn's attention filled her with an unusual flash of warmth.

"Y-yes. He...well, he was acting just a bit strange." She could not come up with another way to describe it.

"Strange?"

She nodded. "Quite."

He sighed. "Well, thank goodness you have some sense. Most women swoon over him."

"Yes, but as you said, he isn't after my hand in marriage. Many ladies have set their cap for him. *I* am not one of them."

"Indeed. I do apologize for my insensitivity."

She waved it away. "You are not the first, and you will not be the last."

With a smile, he offered her his arm. "If you would allow me to walk you back into the ballroom?"

"Before you do, could you answer one question?"

He dropped his arm as his brow furrowed. "That depends."

"I understand you are in the shipping business?"

"Yes."

She bit back an irritated sigh. He was not going to make this an easy task. "There have been some questions about the nature of the shipments."

His expression darkened, his eyes narrowing again as he studied her. His gaze moved over her face, but she did not allow her own to waver. Breath clogged her throat; her pulse doubled.

"I import many things, Lady Cordelia."

She opened her mouth to ask another question, but Blackburn stepped closer. He towered over her, but she did not feel threatened as when other men did it. She felt…hot. Her whole body shimmered with heat.

"My company is known for its fine silks. I understand they are in demand by many ladies. Have you ever felt truly fine silk?"

She could not answer. His voice had dipped lower, caressing her like the fine silk he spoke of. Cordelia knew she should step back, but she could not make her feet move. He inched closer, his legs now brushing the front of her dress.

When she did not answer, Blackburn continued, leaning down to place his hand on the stone wall behind her. He was now much closer than propriety allowed, and her heart threatened to beat from her chest.

"Fine silk slides against flesh," he murmured.

His breath heated her earlobe. Cordelia inhaled deeply, trying to regain her wits. But her breasts brushed against his chest and tingles shot through her body like shooting stars.

She shook her head. Other questions swirled in her brain, and she knew that Blackburn was trying to divert her attention. Her body did not care. Need coursed through her veins, urging her to move closer, into Blackburn's heat.

At that moment, a group of younger people came out laughing and talking, their excitement of the season easily heard in their voices. Blackburn's head whipped around, and a growl rumbled in his chest. For a moment, she thought he might attack them.

"Mr. Blackburn."

She whispered the words as not to gain the others attention. He hesitated, then looked down at her. Fierce hunger darkened his eyes. Cordelia was not sure he even heard her, but a moment later, the harsh lines of his face smoothed. He drew in a deep breath then stepped back, the cool night air replacing his heat. She shivered as goose bumps rose over her flesh. Cordelia should be thankful he had pulled back in time. With her background, she had to be careful. There was always a chance that she would step over the line. And at that point, her invitations would stop, and she needed them to earn money.

He offered her his arm once again. "May I escort you back to the ballroom, Lady Cordelia?" He pitched his voice just loud enough for the group to hear.

She nodded, laying her hand on his arm. "I do thank you, sir, for your help. Hurst is a nuisance, and I could have deflected him. Your help just made it much easier."

He guided her over to a group of matrons. "I trust you will be able to avoid him in the future."

It was not a question, but an order. Odd, because before tonight, she had barely spoken to him. She sent him a sharp stare to tell the man he had overstepped his bounds. Little shock that he ignored her.

Instead, he bowed. "Thank you for the dance, Lady Cordelia." His voice was loud enough for the group of nearby matrons to hear.

She had been in his company for the last five minutes and had yet to ask him more than one question about his finances. As she stared at him, that eyebrow of his rose again. Mr. Blackburn knew she had questions for him…which was why he had avoided her for days. Now that he was dumping her with the matrons, she had no way of asking anything else. She was stuck—and he knew it.

She offered him a smile she reserved for the most vapid of young misses. "You are most welcome, Mr. Blackburn."

His lips twitched as if he repressed a smile. After a nod to the matrons—watching the whole scene as if they were at the theater—he turned and walked away.

And Cordelia cursed herself again. She still didn't know if the man earned his money legally or not. She thought back to the dance, the way his body pressed against hers, the heat she saw in his eyes, and sighed. She had to learn how to keep her wits about her the next time she encountered Mr. Blackburn.

Her livelihood depended on it.

* * * *

"You look ready to faint, Blackburn," Grayson, Duke of Queensbury, said, amusement threading his voice. "Done in by a little mouse of a woman?"

Nico threw him what he hoped was a nasty look and grabbed a drink as a waiter passed by. Bloody hell, his hand was shaking. "You are treading on thin ice."

"I've never known Lady Cordelia to have this effect on anyone but Hurst, and seriously, I cannot understand why he is interested."

Without knowing or caring what the drink was, Nico tossed back the contents in one huge gulp, wincing as the warm lemonade slid down his throat. God, he needed to get out of there, find a woman. The moment he thought it, he caught sight of Lady Cordelia. His body responded as if he'd been struck by lightning.

"So, tell me, how did Lady Cordelia ensnare you? Was it her modest gown or her discussion on anything political?"

How could he explain it? Not once in society had he come so close to losing control. How could one petite, blue-eyed miss have brought him so close to the edge? Even now he had to grind his teeth together to keep his incisors from descending. He had been moments from taking her, and she would not have resisted. It was in her makeup to respond to him—even if she did not understand. His plan to divert her attention had gone horribly awry. He could remember the feel of her hardened nipples as they lightly brushed his chest. The need to drink from her had doubled.

Damn! He pulled his attention away from Lady Cordelia and back to Gray, who was now studying Nico with enjoyment.

"She's a Carrier."

Gray's face lost all emotion, and his body turned to stone. "You must be mistaken. I know every Born in the *ton*. She is not one."

Nico glanced around, looking to see if anyone had overheard. He quickly realized that the only attention they had was from a crowd of eligible young women across the floor. With a sigh, he motioned with his head and turned, not even waiting to see if Gray followed. Nico knew the duke would. He found the library easily and was relieved to discover it empty. Gray shut the door quietly and leaned against it.

"Do you really think she is a Carrier?"

"I don't think. I know. At age five hundred, I think I know the difference between a Carrier and a normal human female."

"She is not descended from any line I know. Her mother was married to the Earl of Collingsworth."

"He must not have been her birth father."

The look of comprehension slid over Gray's face. "Of course. Only the oldest is his, the son. The daughters were said to have different fathers, all four."

"Yes, and the youngest, Cordelia, is treated as an outcast by the others."

Gray sneered. "That brother of hers is a bastard in deed if not in birth. Owes everyone in town, which is why he isn't here."

"You mean she is in town alone?"

Gray crossed his arms over his chest and frowned. "Indeed. I think she stays in the family townhouse, but with little staff. Truthfully, I have no idea how she affords it. Her father...Collingsworth left her barely anything to live on from what I heard."

"And there is no rumor of impropriety. She has no protector?"

"Not that I know of. And I assure you, with the notorious Lady Fionna as her mother, if there was a hint of scandal, it would be all over the *ton*."

Nico shoved that aside and moved back to the subject at hand. "Regardless, she is a Carrier."

"Again, I point out that my family has kept track of all the noble families. She isn't on that list and neither is Lady Fionna."

Irritation turned Nico's voice sharp. "Think. When the church attacked us during the Inquisition, many families hid. We scattered to the winds, and I am positive we have yet to find everyone. There are probably several dozen Carriers in the *ton*, and they have no idea. Why would they unless they have mated with a Born?"

He had known about Lady Cordelia for days. Something about their first meeting, the way his body had reacted, had told him she was not just a simple bluestocking. He had immediately responded to her despite the fact she was not his type of woman. He usually liked females tall, lithe, and definitely experienced. Cordelia had none of these attributes, but she was a Carrier. So he was predisposed to respond to her.

Though in truth, he had never reacted even to another Carrier so strongly.

"You may be right," Gray surmised.

"I am. It's easy to scent a Carrier. But her pull is stronger than any other Carrier I have come in contact with. It also explains why Hurst is after her."

The young duke crossed his arms over his chest. "Hurst is not one of us."

"Indeed. He's Made for sure."

With satisfaction, Nico watched Gray's eyes widen in alarm. He was the first Made vampire to hit the *ton* in recent times. "Bloody hell."

"Precisely. He has shown little to no interest in Lady Cordelia until recently. We need to find out where he was before his fascination arose. If he has not left town..."

He let his words trail off, allowing Gray to draw his own conclusions. "And a nobleman at that. This is not a good development. The Alliance is not going to be happy about this."

"No. I need you to find out where he was, discover any of the places he frequents and who he's spent time with. We also might want to put a man on him."

"Do you think we need to warn the other noble houses?"

Nico snorted. The other vampire families were notoriously stubborn. "Would it do any good? They refuse to believe there is a problem. My father is the only patriarch who is worried. No one else but the three of us seems to understand the gravity of the situation." He thought about Lady Cordelia and her role in everything. "I say that Hurst's attention started just over a week ago. Something must have happened then. He does not appear to have gone completely into Blood Lust, but there is a good chance he is not far from sinking there."

"How do you know he isn't already there?"

Sometimes Nico forgot that Gray was too young to have seen Made vampires and their terrible descent into murderous madness. "If he was in Blood Lust, you would have seen more than just a slight altercation when I asked Lady Cordelia to dance. It is very likely the bastard would've challenged me on the spot—possibly even attacked me."

Shock crossed Gray's face. "Truly? That would have been a sight."

Nico ground his teeth again, but this time not to keep them hidden. Gray was a good sort, but he was young, especially for a vampire. He was not around for the last purging, and he did not know just how bad this mess could end up.

"He probably doesn't know I am a Born and has no idea what is going on. His body is telling him to pursue her. And since she has no protection, like your sisters and others in the *ton* do, he knows she would be easier to prey upon."

"I'll get a man on him, and I'll talk to father about his connections, where he has been before. I hope this doesn't end up like that bit of business you had to handle up north."

With that, Gray left Nico alone.

There would be no way out of it; Hurst would have to die, but not before they got some information out of the bastard. The one he had to kill three weeks ago had been too far gone to question, but Hurst seemed to still be functioning surprisingly well. Nico didn't expect that to last. If they could grab the viscount off the street, they might be able to persuade him to talk. He'd make plans tonight with Malik. Time was precious when a vampire had been Made. If they were not handled properly, they would turn into craven beasts, searching out the nearest Carrier to consume. If the woman didn't die, she would wish she had.

Now Hurst had apparently set his sights on Lady Cordelia. And that bothered Nico. Exceedingly.

With a sigh, he straightened away from the desk. His body was still humming with anticipation of a joining. While he could not satisfy the mating call Lady Cordelia had nearly wrested from him, he could find a woman to slake his lust.

He walked to the door but it blew open, bringing Lady Cordelia with it. His body responded immediately. His blood heated with the need he had tried to ignore. The normally perfectly coiffed curls that dangled over her ears were in disarray. A look of irritation marred her usually smooth features. She slammed the door shut behind her and then leaned against it much the same way that Gray had. Clearly, she did not notice him in the room.

"Stupid man." She locked the door behind her and then patted down her hair. "He is becoming a real trial."

"I hope you are not referring to me," Nico said.

She started and then peered in the shadowed corner where he stood.

"Mr. Blackburn?"

He cursed himself the moment he realized she could not see in the darkness. If he had stayed quiet, she would not have seen him. She had not mated yet, so she possessed only human abilities.

He stepped out of the corner. "It is I. I take it from your comments that you did not follow me here?"

She sniffed. "Of course not. I am trying to avoid that idiot Hurst. Why on earth he has decided to bother me now is beyond me."

Bloody hell. Hurst's constant pursuit could herald the coming of his Blood Lust. If the viscount touched her, he'd likely sink into madness. Something would have to be done—tonight.

"Come, now, Lady Cordelia. You could easily attract his lordship's attention for any number of reasons."

She mumbled something under her breath that sounded

like "not bloody likely."

At least she understood there was danger. Unfortunately, it did not help his protective instincts. The need to shelter her, keep her safe, coursed through his blood along with a healthy dose of lust. He did not speak for fear of revealing the depth of his need.

Silence loomed several moments, then without any warning she flashed him a brilliant smile. He blinked as he watched her approach, amazed at the change in her expression. And wary. No woman could be trusted, especially a Carrier. Those with the ability to birth vampires were frighteningly clever—they had to be to survive. He knew without a doubt, Lady Cordelia was working something out in her brain that would only bring about disaster for them both.

"Mr. Blackburn?" She stopped in front of him, her scent wrapping around him, tempting him. It was a mixture of musky woman and innocence that had his incisors threatening to descend. The woman was too bloody tempting for her own good. No wonder Hurst had been after her.

"Yes?" he asked, surprised that he hadn't started panting. Or done something far more aggressive. Even now, as she gazed up at him as if she worshipped him, he reacted, his lust in full bloom. He wanted—ached—to throw her across the desk and strip her naked. Nico knew it was primal; it had nothing to do with the woman. The urge to feed from her sang through his blood.

But he'd never had such a strong reaction to a Carrier.

"I wondered…" She pulled her bottom lip through her teeth, and he inwardly groaned. The woman was going to undo him with her innocent gestures. He curled his fingers into the palm of his hands.

"Lady Cordelia, what do you need?"

She blinked and hesitated. He did not blame her. Even he could hear how his voice had deepened, roughened. The earlier altercation still thrummed through his blood. Maybe she would flee the room, and he would be free of her long enough to ease his desires elsewhere.

He should have known better.

She raised her chin. "Can you explain a bit more about your shipping business?"

"W-what?" He could not concentrate on her words, but rather watched the way her lips moved in the slant of moonlight that illuminated her face. They were pink and wet.

Cordelia cocked her head to the side. "Are you unwell?"

He shook his head, his attention still on her mouth. Her tongue flicked out over her fuller bottom lip as she took a step closer. Bloody hell, he craved to taste her, to feel her mouth move beneath him. He wanted to feel her flesh beneath his, and he wanted to sink his teeth into her neck. With every bit of his control, he pulled his mind away from the image of her wearing nothing but the moonlight.

He needed her to go far away. He made one last attempt.

"Lady Cordelia, I think you should leave." He bit out each word, the lust he felt dripping from each syllable. Unfortunately, the woman apparently was oblivious.

She stepped even closer, determination stamped all over her face. Passion darkened her eyes. She was magnificent.

"I will not be deflected again."

Good God, the woman smelled of heaven. He could imagine rolling with her on a bed, the scent of her surrounding him, the tangy taste of her on his tongue. His incisors descended, primed for feeding. He did not even try to stop it. He knew it impossible.

Without another thought, he grabbed her. She gasped, the sound erotic in the darkened library. He had the satisfaction of seeing her eyes widen as he dipped his head.

"Mr. Blackburn, whatever do you think you are doing?"

"Shutting you up."

Then he bent his head and took possession of her mouth.

Chapter Two

Everything in Cordelia stilled; every thought flew out of her head. It was as if time stopped. Then in a rush, reality blazed back to life. Nicodemus Blackburn was kissing her. *Her.* Bluestocking Cordelia Collingsworth. *Why?*

Before she could puzzle that out or contemplate the oddity of Blackburn's actions, he slid his hands up her arms, cupped her face, and deepened the kiss. His tongue skimmed over her lips. She gasped, and he used the moment to dip inside of her mouth.

Cordelia knew she should be shocked to her toes. This was everything she had avoided. She did not want to be saddled with her mother's reputation. But at the moment, her heart was beating so fast she couldn't think. The masculine scent of him surrounded her, intoxicated her. Blackburn pulled back just a bit, cool air replacing the heat of him. When she slowly opened her eyes, she found him watching her, his gaze brilliant.

"It works better if you kiss me back."

His voice was deep, resonant, filled with something she could not discern. It did not matter if she did not understand, her body responded. Heat shot through her veins causing her to shiver. Without another word, he swooped down to capture her mouth again.

Every worry she had dissolved as he slanted his mouth over hers. This time she responded the best she could. It was her first true kiss, for she did not count the few stolen kisses early suitors had subjected her to. If they had been as skilled as Blackburn, Cordelia might have been tempted to break the rules.

Cordelia willingly opened her mouth, allowing Blackburn to slide his tongue in. Little bursts of heat crackled over her nerve endings. Slowly, she skimmed her hands up his chest, over his shoulders, and behind his neck. He took the opportunity to pull her closer, into his warmth. His hands slid down to cup her bottom, pull her tightly against him. Even through the layers of clothing she could feel the beat of his heart.

Her head spun, her body rejoiced. Tentatively, she slipped her tongue into his mouth, sliding it along his as he had to her. The taste of him burst through her, tart lemonade, a touch of brandy, and Nicodemus Blackburn...that was the most intoxicating part. Every reservation she had dissolved into the glorious passion he was building,

He growled, the sound vibrating deep in his throat. She shivered at the primal sound. Easily, he walked her backward. Before she could even discern what he was about, she found herself beneath him on the couch. Blackburn tore his mouth from hers only to set about attacking her throat. His tongue slid over her flesh, and the scrape of teeth followed. She heard a moan filled with lustful longing. It took her a moment to realize the wanton sound had come from her.

Her lungs seized the moment she felt his hand move over her breast. For a moment, sanity tried to take hold. She opened her mouth to tell him to stop. This was insane, and again, it could ruin her. Somewhere in the back of her mind a voice told her to resist, to push him away. In the next instant, his thumb moved over her nipple. It responded, tightening immediately, aching for more attention. Again, he growled, a sound that should have shocked her, but it did not. Something in her reacted immediately. An ache tightened her belly then feathered out over her body. A demand for completion battered her, urging her to ignore everything else. She could do nothing but fall into the morass of lust he was creating.

Nico gave her bodice a quick, hard tug, causing her full breasts to spill out. He pulled back, and she had a moment of trepidation. Cool air replaced the heat of him. She opened her eyes to find him looking at her. Not at her face, but at her chest. Heat spread from her breasts up into her face as he continued to stare. His eyes were brilliant, his breath coming out in short, choppy bursts. It was the only sound in the room.

Embarrassed, she moved to cover her bosom, but the rumble from his chest stopped her. Once more, it brought to mind a feral animal. Without moving his attention from her chest, he captured her hands and pulled them back.

"Sweet Jesus." Lust deepened his voice as his hungry gaze moved over her.

Her mortification melted as she realized there was admiration in his tone. He swooped down and took a turgid tip into his mouth as he caressed the other. This was beyond anything she ever imagined, almost as if she could not control her reactions. Delirious with the heat he was creating within her, she speared her fingers through his hair, allowing the dark tresses to slip through her fingers. Closing her eyes, she moaned as he moved to give her other nipple the same treatment as the first. His breath was hot against her flesh. Her heart galloped.

Nico pulled back slightly. Cordelia allowed her hands to drop from his head and opened her eyes. He was gazing at her again, his face like stone, his nostrils flaring with each breath he took. Without breaking eye contact, he blew on her wet nipple. A tidal wave of need crashed through her. Moist warmth slipped down further as the craving grew within her. She wanted—needed—him in a way she could not understand. Everything in her being called out to him just as it had the first time she had met him.

She couldn't comprehend why this man...when so many before him had tried and failed. Before she could contemplate why or how, he was moving down her body. When he pulled her skirts up, she protested.

"Mr. Blackburn."

He stilled and looked up at her. The harsh lines of his

face were more prominent, his appetite easy to see there. It should scare her, should send her running from that room. Instead, want surged through her, thundering through her blood. She did not even know what she craved, but she knew she wanted it from him.

"Nico."

"W-what?" she asked.

His jaw moved, telling her he was grinding his teeth. "Call me Nico."

"Nico." Was that her voice? All breathy with desire? What had the man done to her?

He smiled in response. "I like the sound of my name on your lips."

Before she could respond to that, he shoved her skirts to her waist, situating himself between her legs. She felt his hot breath on her most private area.

"Mr. Blackburn!"

His head whipped up, an untamed look in his eyes. "Nico."

"Nico."

He smiled, but it was something close to what she imagined a pirate's smile resembled when he was about to capture a booty. It transfixed her, and he used her hesitation to dip his head and place his mouth on her most private parts.

Shock came first. It held her frozen as an ice sculpture. But soon the shock dissolved into wicked pleasure. His heated breath warmed her sex before his tongue swept inside. Even with pleasure rushing through her, she tried one last move to dislodge him. She moved her hands to his hair to pull him away, but instead she found her fingers molding to his head, encouraging him. She had never before experienced anything like the sheer delight spiraling through her.

Cordelia shifted, spreading her legs further apart to allow him more access. He hummed in admiration, the vibrations against her skin shooting throughout her entire body.

He shifted his body as he kept his mouth on her. When

she felt the tip of his finger pressing into her, she stilled
again...then shuddered. Thrusting in and out with his finger,
he continued to assault her with his tongue. Everything in her
tightened, reaching for something she did not comprehend.
He added another finger. Her inner muscles tightened on it
with each thrust. Heat burst through her, circling her
stomach, dropping lower.

Aggravated, she pulled her legs up, planting her feet on
the cushions and lifting up. Another growl rumbled in his
chest. Cordelia writhed against his mouth, begging for him to
end the torment he had built within her. She had no idea what
she was asking for, but she knew he was the one to give it to
her.

With the flick of his tongue, he pushed her over the
edge. Delight coursed through her as some unknown dam
broke. She convulsed as she burst into a thousand
shimmering pieces, screaming his name. Delicious heat
swept over her flesh as she felt herself drain of every bit of
the tension he had created.

As she drifted back down from bliss, she registered Nico
crawling back up her body, covering her once again. She
opened her eyes and found him watching her as he had
earlier, the untamed look in his eyes even brighter now. He
braced himself on his hands and lowered his mouth to hers.
This time there were no tempting kisses, but complete and
utter possession. When his tongue swept into her mouth, she
could taste herself there. Her body still shimmered with her
release, but he was already building another with his kisses.
He pressed his groin against her, allowing her to feel just
how aroused he was.

He pulled away, his eyes still closed, and growled.
Unbelievable, she wanted that bliss again, wanted to feel the
tension build then explode. Cordelia knew it was wrong, but
she didn't care. Something deep inside her, in the deep
recesses of her soul, begged for the completion, to become
one with him. It would ruin her, but her morals apparently

dissolved the moment he touched her. He moved away, pulling himself up to his knees, his hands on the top of his breeches.

With greedy eyes, she watched, waited, yearned. But before he could even undo one button, the door crashed opened.

* * * *

Wood splintered, blowing into the library with a force so strong it broke pottery. Every predatory sense Nico had went on alert. The lust he had built with Cordelia transformed into anger. When he rose from the couch and saw that it was Hurst, it turned into white hot possessiveness. The beast within him knew the viscount was here to claim Cordelia, that he had sensed Nico in here with her. The civilized part of Nico understood that Hurst did not comprehend his actions. The viscount could not control his behavior, but Nico's primitive soul did not give a damn. He had not gained completion or even mated with Cordelia, but she was his, and no man would have her.

The woman in question tried to sit up to see what was going on, but he pushed her back down.

"Mr. Blackburn!" Her voice was no longer soft and breathless. Now she sounded like a shocked-to-her-toes bluestocking. He would laugh, but he could not find it in him to do so. He glanced down at her, hoping she would read the danger in his eyes. Unfortunately, she was still exposed, her breasts spilling out of her dress. She gave him a disgruntled look, but it was lost because of her dishabille.

A feral growl came from the doorway, and Nico pulled his attention away from Cordelia. He knew now they had no time left to lose. The stark look of need stamped on the viscount's face told Nico he was sliding into Blood Lust, Cordelia as his subject and prize.

Without taking his gaze from the approaching man, Nico

said to Cordelia, "Stay down." Hoping she would listen to him, he braced his hands on the back of the sofa and jumped over, swinging his legs to hit the viscount in his groin.

The Made vampire went down with a grunt, but not two seconds later he was back up and charging. Nico braced himself as the younger man rushed toward him. Nico punched him, his fist scoring a direct hit. The crack of bone filled the air around them. He heard a gasp behind him, and glancing back over his shoulder, he saw Cordelia, still on the sofa, her bodice pulled up, but her hair hanging in silken waves down over her shoulders. Momentarily, he could do nothing but stare. The taste of her was still on his lips, the scent of her calling to him. He could hear her blood pulsing through her body, seducing him. He needed to feed from her. Rustling sounded behind him, and he realized Cordelia was looking over his shoulder. Her eyes widened with alarm.

"Nico!"

He turned and found the viscount charging him again, but this time, Nico did not have time to prepare. They both went tumbling over the sofa, Cordelia jumping out of their path and moving behind a chair. Once he registered she was out of the way and unhurt, he went about subduing the viscount. It was not easy as they toppled over onto the floor. Nico landed on his back, and before he could react, the other man's hands were around his neck, his fingers digging into Nico's flesh.

"Mine!"

Hurst screamed the word. It echoed through the chamber, the meaning of it not lost on Nico. Hurst thought of Cordelia as his. The scent of her arousal hung heavy in the air, easy for any vampire to smell. Since she was a Carrier, the younger Made vampire would become homicidal, seeing that his prize, his possession, had been stolen from him. He could see that Hurst's teeth had already descended. He lowered his head to Nico's neck.

A crack sounded and pieces of porcelain cascaded over

Nico. The fingers around his neck slackened as Hurst turned to look over his shoulder. It gave Nico enough time to push the viscount back and reverse their positions. Hurst's head slapped against the corner of the marbled table as they went down. The younger man's body went limp beneath Nico. He felt for a pulse and found it beating hard against his fingers.

"What the bloody hell is going on?"

Nico looked up and found Gray staring at them. The young duke's face went quickly from shock to recognition when he noticed Hurst lying on the floor.

"What the hell does it look like happened?" Nico asked as he picked himself up. His attention was on Cordelia who stood staring at Hurst, her eyes dilated with shock. Even though she had pulled up her bodice, there was a tear along the neckline. Her hair was completely undone. The soft, golden curls lay tangled over her shoulders. Just looking at her made his body ache, and it was not the sweet ache of desire. The need to comfort her stirred within him. He rose to his feet and walked to her, wanting nothing more than to soothe her worries. Hurst had not gotten his hands on her, so she was safe in that quarter. But Nico had taken advantage of her...seduced her without a thought of what he was doing. He had never done so with an innocent. Before she had time to recover from that, Hurst had burst in ready to kill.

"Cordelia?"

She looked up, but more through him than at him. A shiver danced over his flesh and cooled his blood. All the color had drained from her face, and she looked like she might start crying any minute.

"Are you all right?" he asked, amazed at how gentle his voice had turned.

"All right?" She blinked, her eyes finally focusing on him. She glanced down at the viscount then back up at him. "No, I am not all right. Bloody hell."

A muffled snort came from the direction of Gray.

"The man is insane," Cordelia said.

"Yes. Hurst—"

"I am not talking about Hurst," she spat out. She stalked over to him, anger vibrating off her in waves. "He has always been odd. You, on the other hand, have a lot to answer for. Just what was that about and how did Hurst make it through the door?"

For a moment, he didn't respond. He could not. It took him a second to comprehend she was not angry because he seduced her. Cordelia seemed more upset by the fight afterwards. And she spoke to him as if he were a naughty schoolboy who had misbehaved.

He ground his teeth together. "I'll explain all of this later."

She poked him in the chest, color flooding back into her face. Her eyes blazed with angry passion. Her body shimmered with indignation. By God she was something. His blood heated, and his teeth began to descend again. If he did not gain control of the situation, he would lose himself to passion once more.

"You will tell me now."

"We have no time *now*."

She crossed her arms beneath her breasts. "I'm not moving from this spot until someone tells me just what is going on."

God, she was going to drive him crazy. His body begged for relief. One more word from her and he might just lose control. He drew in a deep breath, trying to calm his temper…and his lust.

He stepped closer to her, so close he could feel her heat, smell her arousal. "Any moment, we will become fodder for gossip."

Her eyes widened, comprehension sliding over her face. She opened her mouth, but another high-pitched voice interrupted her.

"My gracious. What is going on here?"

All three of them turned and found the lady of the house,

Lady Francis Smythe, the most notorious gossip in the *ton*, gaping at them.

"Is that Hurst?" She squinted, looking through the darkness. Her gaze rolled over all of them, then focused on Cordelia. Her eyes sharpened, and a look of astonishment moved over the lady's face then dissolved into evil pleasure.

"Why, Lady Cordelia, your hair is a mess." Her gaze slid down further. "Whatever happened to your dress?"

Chapter Three

"You will have to marry her," Malik said as he watched Nico pace.

Nico threw his best friend a threatening look but did not stop walking. "I know. It is not as if I do not understand the implications."

"If you do, then what the bloody hell were you doing in the Smythe's library with her?" Gray asked.

Irritation crawled down his spine and had him growling at the duke. Gray may be a peer of the realm, but Nico did not have the patience to deal with him—not tonight. "I did not plan that. She came into the library trying to escape Hurst. By the way, where is the viscount?"

"Down in the dungeon," Gray said.

Nico stopped and looked down at the floor then back up at Malik. "Gray has a dungeon in his townhouse?"

Malik's lips twitched. "Not so easy. Gray over there might be easily led astray, but I am not. What are you doing about the Collingsworth chit?"

Nico sighed. "I'll marry her. Even if I had not ruined her reputation, it goes beyond that. I cannot leave her without protection. She's a Carrier."

Surprise lit Malik's light green eyes. "I did not know of it."

"I looked at father's list." Gray shook his head. "There is no mention of her mother being a Carrier."

"Bloodlines?" Nico asked.

"That will take a bit more research. I've dispatched a message to my father about it. It is definitely his area of expertise. He might know who her birth father is, but that means nothing. The Carrier gene runs through the female line. Her father did not have to be a Born for her to be one."

"You say that you had no control with her in the room?' Malik asked.

Nico frowned. "I would not say that, precisely. There is a chance that her mother's bloodline was very pure. Or…her sire might have been a Born. That would explain a lot."

"So that is how you are trying to explain your behavior?" Malik's voice dripped with sarcasm.

Nico ignored him. They did not have time to fight amongst themselves. And he was not ready to deal with his behavior. He still didn't understand it himself. He definitely could not explain it to his best friend.

"That is certainly why Hurst was after her. She has a strong pull."

Again, Malik watched him. "Indeed?"

He nodded. "Have you ever known me to lose my head like that?"

Malik shook his head. "Never…for obvious reasons."

He tossed Malik another warning look. He did not want to talk about the past tonight. There was too much at stake. "I don't think there is a need to go into family histories at the moment, do you?"

Malik said nothing.

Nico glanced at Gray, who watched them intensely. "What kind of state is our prisoner in?"

Gray winced. "Beyond any reason. The man kept shouting about Lady Cordelia being his. He would not let it go. We poured enough laudanum down his throat to put out half of London."

"Keep a lot on hand. We actually might be able to save him from himself." Nico glanced at Malik. "Do you agree?"

The cold, shuttered expression in his friend's eyes was one he had seen before. Both of them had their demons to deal with…only Malik had to relive his any time he tried to help a Made vampire through transition. "I have not seen him, and you know it varies from person to person. If the man was of strong character, we might be able to save him—

if he hasn't progressed too far. I need blood, all from Borns."

Gray stepped in. "I already put out the call. Father will want to discuss this with you after you are finished. I know that he has never heard feeding them Born blood helps them through transition."

Malik nodded. "I need it from a variety of sources. It will help pull him through and cut off his connection to the Born who made him. We also need to factor in that there might be others who will object to my presence and methods."

Nico shook his head. "You are always exempt from these witch hunts. They know you fought on our side when the priests came after us."

"You know the younger generation does not understand," Malik said. "I will try to help him, but there will be no promises. I will not kill him."

Nico said nothing because he knew Malik was right. There would be some among the Born vampire families who would always look down on Malik for being Made, no matter how old he was.

With many Made vampires came trouble. There was always the occasional Made popping up, but the number that had appeared in the last six months was alarming. Still, as they always had, the Vampire Alliance did nothing. They wanted to wait to see if it would just blow over. Samuel Blackburn thought differently. His father was more than likely right to worry, especially now that they knew someone had turned a member of the aristocracy. It was true they'd found nothing concrete yet…but Nico knew something deadly swirled in their midst.

Malik rose from his position on the sofa. "Where is this dungeon of yours?"

Gray called in a servant. "Please take this gentleman to see our guest."

With a bow to Gray, the young man held the door open for Malik, but Nico saw the look in his eyes. Disgust. Sadly, many in the Born bloodlines had an irrational hatred of any Made.

"Now, explain to me why I would not understand about Malik?"

Nico glanced at Gray then wandered over to the window. A smudge of red filtered through the grime of London. The sun was rising.

"Nico?"

Without turning around he said, "Malik is Made."

"And?"

Nico faced the young vampire, thinking Gray had been lucky to have missed the vampire genocide. It had been four hundred years since the Spanish Inquisition. So many of them had perished...especially their Carriers. It had almost wiped out all of their kind.

"Many want to kill any Made for fear of their behavior—thanks to the memories of Vlad the Impaler and his army."

A look of pure astonishment passed over Gray's face. "But Malik is always accepted. The man is a legend. Father speaks of him in such awe, I will admit I expected him to be a sword-wielding giant."

Nico chuckled at that. "He saved your uncle's life."

Gray nodded. "Yes, along with many others. But I do understand that there might be a witch hunt...which means we need to discover who is making vampires before it comes to that."

"One of the reasons my father sent me down here. The rest...well, they would prefer not have to deal with another Vlad if they don't have to. They would rather pretend this is all just rumor. The Quad refused to send in anyone officially, and let's not even start with the Alliance. To get a qualifying vote from all the different factions would be impossible. Pretending there isn't a threat is easier than facing death. Especially for Borns who think they will live forever. But with the viscount..."

"We know better." Gray blew out a breath. "The problem is many of them are too old, too set in their ways. Your father is the only intelligent one on the Ruling Committee. My father said that if needed, he and mother can return."

That surprised Nico. As with the rest of their predecessors, the older generation would "die," allowing the next Duke of Queensbury to take over. They usually lived on the continent, away from court. To offer to come back to support Nico's father on the council meant that the old duke knew just how grave things were.

"My father would hate for that to happen, but I will let him know."

"Father knows the situation is bad." Gray grimaced. "There have been a rash of murders near our Scottish estate...similar to the one you spoke of."

In that instant, the scene from a fortnight ago came rushing back in stark clarity. Nico had to close his eyes, but when he did, the image of the damaged woman, the stench of her blood, appeared. He swallowed the bile that rose to the top of his throat. He would never forget that image or the feel of thrusting a stake into the heart of another living vampire.

"But on to more important matters...I can get you a special license if needed. I assume you want to conduct your business as quickly as possible."

Nico opened his eyes and wanted to smack the smug expression off the man's face but knew better. Gray allowed a lot of things, but that would be stepping over the line.

"Yes. I require one. My problem is actually proposing."

Gray's eyebrows rose to his hairline. "You think she might refuse? I would think Lady Cordelia is smarter than that. She knows the consequences of her actions. More so than others, I would say."

"Why?"

"Her mother. The woman's reputation would make a courtesan blush. It is said she had more lovers than the prince regent did. Except for the present earl, her children have lived by strict guidelines."

The memory of their interlude came rushing back to him in vivid detail. Cordelia must have iron control of her emotions. He must have just tapped the surface of her passion. She would be the death of him.

"All girls, correct? It stands to reason they would be held to a higher standard."

Gray chuckled. "I would love to hear your soon-to-be betrothed's ideas on that, but you mistake what I say. Not one of the girls was presented...none had a season."

That gave Nico pause. "But Lady Cordelia..."

"Is here because she did not want to stay with her drunkard brother...or he turned her out. I would not put it past the bastard."

"All the others are married?"

"Yes, one widowed. All to local gentry, and they had dowries. What little Lady Cordelia had is probably gone. From what I understand, the bastard of a father left her with nothing but a pittance."

"That is beyond odd."

"The whole family is odd."

Nico threw him a warning look. "Stupendous. And now they will be my family."

"Look at it this way. She's a Carrier at least. You have a way to mate. It is difficult enough to find a Carrier these days...and most leave much to be desired. Besides, it seems that you two are compatible."

The duke shot him a mocking smile. Nico glared and tried to fight off memories of Cordelia against him, her flavor on his tongue. Impossible. His body responded immediately, his blood quickening, his fangs stirring. He ground his teeth together. He had to keep his inner beast in control or he would be no better than a newly turned Made.

"Who knows, you might want to bond with her."

Those words threw cold water on Nico's thoughts of his

bride. He had seen what bonding did to a vampire, how a simple mistake could take away everything precious...including your life.

Noticing the younger man staring at him, Nico shook off those thoughts and smiled. "At the moment, I am not convinced the woman will even allow me in her house."

* * * *

Cordelia took a sip of her tepid tea and winced. She could not abide tea and would rather have coffee, but that was much too expensive...as was chocolate. Living on her meager earnings from her articles in the *The Daily Inquisitor* did not allow for luxuries. She could not complain since she still had a roof over her head—for now. If her brother heard about her mishap, Alex might throw her out on the street.

With a sigh she leaned back in the chair. She was out of sorts. Any sane person would be after last night's events. Closing her eyes, she remembered the way Nico's mouth had tasted, the way it felt to have his long, lean muscled body pressing her into the couch. She shivered, her body warming at the intense memories. Cordelia opened her eyes. In one action she lost her reputation and proved to everyone, including herself, that she was no better than her mother.

Fionna Bentley, the Countess of Collingsworth, had lived life by her own rules, which apparently had been at odds with society. By all accounts, her brother was Collingsworth's son, but she and her three sisters had no real idea who their fathers were. There were rumors about Amelia, Sophia, and Diana's fathers, but no one had any idea who Cordelia's birth father might be. The truth had died with her mother in the early morning hours the day after Cordelia's birth. And now she had proven she had a lustful streak like her mother.

She was ruined in so many ways. She cared not a whit about society, except that it was her meal ticket. And without access, she was one week away from begging for food. There was a way…if she dared. It would require ignoring the loss of her reputation and allowing society to think she was truly like her mother. She shook her head. That just would not work. Cordelia would never enter the *demimonde*, even if she were pretending. It went against her nature.

Wells, the Collingsworth town butler, opened the door to the breakfast room. He sniffed in disapproval of her meager breakfast, but she refused to give in. She would not have Cook make breakfast for a family of one. Porridge and tea was enough for Cordelia and all she could afford.

"A Mr. Blackburn is here to see you, my lady." His voice dripped with censure.

At the mention of Nico, her heart turned over. Heat filled her face at the thought of seeing him in the daylight.

"My lady?"

She glanced up at Wells and realized their old retainer was staring at her with interest.

"Y-yes, please show him in. We will need another setting for him."

The look of horror that crossed over Wells' face almost made her laugh. "Just bring the tea service out. I doubt that Mr. Blackburn will be here to eat."

With another sniff of disapproval, Wells left. He returned a moment later and announced Nico.

Nico stepped into the breakfast room and everything that had gone on the night before came rushing back to her. If possible, her face grew even hotter. She had no idea what kind of conversation a lady had with a man who had done such shocking, wonderful things to her…person.

She rose from her seat as he approached her.

"Lady Cordelia." He took her offered hand and kissed her fingers. The brief contact had her head spinning.

"Won't you have a seat, Mr. Blackburn?"

His lips quirked. "I believe I will, Lady Cordelia."

Wells appeared with the tea service.

"I will serve, Wells."

He hesitated, his narrowed gaze telling her he was not happy with leaving her alone with Mr. Blackburn. Cordelia was positive Wells would include this in his report to her brother—not that Alex cared enough to stop drinking. She did not waver her gaze. Wells sighed then bowed, leaving them alone, though he left the door open.

"Sugar or cream?"

"Neither."

Setting her cup aside, she squared her shoulders and faced him. "I know you did not come here for the refreshments."

The smile he offered her told her he had been testing her. He placed the cup back on the saucer. "No. I have come to discuss our situation."

"Situation?"

He studied her for a moment. "Indeed. By now, what happened in the Smythe's library has been recounted to every nosey dowager and debutante in London. If not, it will be by sundown."

"Every detail?"

She watched as his jaw flexed telling her he was grinding his teeth again. It seemed he was always doing that around her. "Well, not everything. Just...the particulars."

She could not help the snort that came out of her. "I'm sorry, but I find that unbelievable."

He frowned. "You do not think that Lady Smythe did not tell every gossipy hen she knows she found us in the room, your hair a mess, and your dress...well, it did not look as it had earlier."

She waved that away. "No. I expect that to be making the rounds this morning. It will probably end up in the gossip pages. Most people expected that kind of behavior out of me a long time ago, if you must know."

A look of understanding lightened his eyes. "Yes. It is hard to live up to society's expectations."

Her throat closed up, and tears burned the back of her eyes. His voice had turned so gentle, as if he knew exactly what she spoke of, of what it felt like being an outcast in your own family.

Cordelia cleared her throat. "I was speaking of the fight."

"Oh, that." He sighed. "More than likely Lady Smythe will tell everyone he was fighting for your honor."

She rolled her eyes. "If anything he was trying to replace you."

Nico's eyes widened then narrowed as he studied her. "Indeed. But he is no concern of yours."

She opened her mouth to respond to that, but the icy look in his eyes told her not to pry. She would let it go, but only for now. She would find out just what was going on with the viscount's strange behavior.

"Now, to get on to the business at hand. Gray is going to make sure we have a special license."

A strange combination of relief and irritation twisted through her. He meant to marry her, but he was not planning on proposing. Granted, their situation—especially hers—was perilous. Without a marriage, she was ruined. They both knew it. It did not mean she didn't deserve a proposal.

"Is he?"

The foolish man did not hear the warning in her voice and continued his explanation.

"I assume that we can get married any time after that, and we can actually have the archbishop oversee it, thanks to Gray again."

When she said nothing, he turned to her. "Is there something wrong?"

"No."

Finally, he truly looked at her. "Yes, there is."

"You seem to have everything planned."

He nodded. "Yes. That way you will have no worries."

"You have every detail taken care of." He smiled at her.

Stupid man. "You, however, do not have a bride."

He frowned, confusion clearly stamped on his features. "You are my bride."

She cocked her head to the side and studied him. "Am I?"

"Who the bloody hell do you think I am going to marry?"

She pursed her lips as if in deep thought. "Maybe a woman you asked?"

His face blanked then flushed. Seeing Nicodemus Blackburn blush was somehow endearing.

"I beg your pardon, my lady."

"It was not as if I expected poetry, but I did expect to be asked."

He cleared his throat. "My apologies."

It took every bit of her propriety not to laugh. He was being subservient but he did not like it, not one bit. It went against everything she knew of his character. He stood then came to her side. Her nerves jumped to life, her heart beating faster. She stared up at him, wondering what he was about now. He sighed as he took her hand, signaling that he expected her to stand. With an arched eyebrow, she stood and he dropped down to his knee. Mortification filled her.

"Oh, for goodness' sake, get up."

He gave her a knowing smile. "Will you do me the honor of becoming my wife?"

She looked down at him, the clear intent in his eyes, and knew that no matter if he asked or not, they would be married. Blackburn had an impeccable reputation...not even the whisper of a mistress, and he took great pride in that fact. There was no way this man would allow her name to be ruined.

"Yes, Mr. Blackburn, I would be," she swallowed, "pleased to be your wife."

He rose to his feet and, before she could stop him, pulled her hard against his chest. And just like that, her pulse fluttered, and her breath caught in her throat.

"I think we should seal it with a kiss."

His rough voice shivered over her flesh, caused her head to spin. He dipped his head and brushed his mouth over hers in an innocent caress. With a sigh, she leaned into him, into the kiss. He deepened his touch, slipping his tongue between her lips. The intimacy of the action had her head spinning. He pulled her tighter against him, his body surrounding her. She slid her hands up his arms and behind his neck and gave herself over to the kiss. He slanted his mouth over hers, again and again as he built up the heat that burned her the night before.

Everything around them disappeared, the sound of passing carriages, of the servants going about their work. Her nipples tightened as desire spiraled through her veins. It seemed not to matter where they were. He could dissolve any barrier she erected. She might have let him have her right there in the morning room if she had not heard the clearing of a throat. It took a few moments for it to register that they were being interrupted. She pulled away. With a growl, Nico tugged her back, but she placed a firm hand on his chest.

"Nico, we have company."

She whispered the comment. He finally opened his eyes and stared down at her for a few moments. The heated lust darkening his eyes almost had her leaning toward him again, but she fought the urge and turned to face the person who dared interrupt them. She gasped when she saw the woman standing there. She was dressed in a pleasant gray traveling dress, much too staid for a woman in her thirties, but this woman took her duties as a widow very seriously.

Her sister, Mrs. Diana Simpson, smirked at her, her cold blue eyes taking in the scene before her.

"Seriously, Cordelia, do you always entertain men in your breakfast room, or is this a special occasion?"

Chapter Four

Nico ignored Cordelia's attempt to disentangle herself from him. The primal demand of his body grew with each minute. It was a bit disconcerting that he seemed to have no control, but at the moment he didn't care. All that mattered was that she was there and he had to touch her. She had agreed to be his. That thought sung through his blood as he pulled her closer. Cordelia needed to understand what he wanted from her. Everything else dissolved as the image of stripping her naked took over his thoughts. Nothing but letting her know that she was his for now and forever blotted out any reasoning.

"Nico, please."

Her voice was strained and there was a hint of embarrassment threading her tone. The haze of lust started to dissolve when he saw her glance over his shoulder. He finally grasped at the reigns of control and pulled his needs back. When he turned to face the interloper, he was surprised at the diminutive woman in front of him. Dressed in a gray morning dress, her expression was cold, her gaze colder. She raked it over them as if she were disgusted by their presence.

"Diana," Cordelia said, her voice breathless as she tried to pull away from him. He would not allow it. If this was the sister, she would need to grow accustomed to him touching Cordelia in her presence.

"Cordelia, do you think you should introduce us?" he asked.

She gave a slight wiggle, trying to dislodge his hold. He tightened it. She gave him an odd look. The depths of her blue eyes seemed to be confused, but he never knew a woman as smart as his soon-to-be wife. She was not one of their kind or she would understand his need to touch her when he was near. It was something primal for all vampires. Their mate would become their life, and with that, it was essential to be in physical contact.

Cordelia sighed then pulled herself together.

"Nico Blackburn, my sister Mrs. Diana Simpson."

He nodded in her direction. "My pleasure."

The smile she gave him was filled with condemnation. "Of course. Cordelia, your staff is lacking in even the basic manners. They wouldn't even escort me back to the room."

There was a small moment of silence. "They are not my staff. They are Alex's," Cordelia said, her voice ripe with irritation.

Diana seemed to hesitate, and for the first time, he saw the woman was not as sure of herself as he'd thought. He knew there had to be friction in the family. There was in any family, but when the youngest was left to fend for herself without the help of anyone, there had to be something else going on behind the scenes.

"Mr. Blackburn and I are to be married. You should be happy."

"Indeed?" Diana said as her attention shifted to him. "And why, pray tell, would I be happy about that?"

He felt Cordelia's spine stiffen beneath his arm. He knew from his small amount of experience with his fiancée that she could stand her ground. That did not matter. As her mate, he was pre-engineered to protect.

"I would think a family member would be more accepting of one's spouse," he said. Only an idiot would miss the threat in his voice.

For a moment, there was another beat of silence, a tense few seconds that seemed to fill the air around them. He was not sure what Diana would do, but he did not care. Cordelia might be the bastard of their family, but she was to be his wife. It was best his sister-in-law understood the situation.

"Of course," Diana said eventually.

"You are just in time for some tea, Diana."

Diana turned her attention to Cordelia. If he had not been watching closely, he would have missed the way her eyes softened before her expression hardened. This was more than just an older sister showing up to berate the youngest for her behavior.

"Have a seat, Diana."

For a moment, he didn't realize his soon-to-be wife stepped away from him, and he didn't like it one bit. He knew it was part of her Carrier genes that brought on this need to always have her close. Mating was always a mystery to him. He had avoided innocent Carriers for this reason. Nico did not want to marry—correction—had not wanted to marry. He knew that the need to have her near him all the time was going to cause him more than a few sleepless nights until they married.

Diana nodded and took a seat at the head of the table, not allowing Cordelia and Nico to sit beside each other. Of course, she did it on purpose. He'd known his wife would be an obstacle, but now he was going to have to deal with her bitch of a sister. It did not matter. He would do the pretty until they were married. Once that happened, he would damn Diana to hell. She had allowed her sister to be left to survive on her own. That was something that he would never do, even if he hated the family member. English aristocracy was so bizarre to him, especially some of the women. Some of them seemed to have no empathy toward their own sex.

Cordelia did not give any indication that she noticed her sister's slight. Instead she spent her time getting their tea ready.

"I am surprised that you are here, Diana. You almost never come to town."

Cordelia's back was to Diana, but Nico noticed that look of panic before it vanished.

"I decided I needed some new clothes."

Cordelia said nothing, but Nico could tell that the clothes Diana was wearing were in the first stare of fashion.

"When did you arrive?"

"Late last night. I traveled all day to get here, and then I find the gossip rags all awash with the scandalous charades of my younger sister...well I came right over."

The disdain in her voice had his teeth threatening to descend. It wasn't for sexual need. A member of his family was being threatened, and his body took over. Of course, it might get better once they mated, but at the moment he had to keep it somewhat under control. He ground his teeth together to keep from baring them to Diana.

"This will be fun then. I will need some help with the arrangements."

Diana blinked. "Oh, but of course, your wedding. And when will that be?"

"The Duke of Queensbury is taking care of the arrangements for the marriage license. Once we have secured that, it will be a matter of days."

"Duke...you know the Duke of Queensbury?"

"Yes. He's an old family friend."

He couldn't keep the smugness out of his voice. He might not be royalty in the eyes of the English *ton*, but his family had more clout within the Vampire Alliance than any one duke had in regular society. In his world, Gray and his family were a few steps below his.

"I would think we could do it quite fast. Something conservative," Cordelia said. Her voice was small, her demeanor one of being defeated. He did not like it. This was not the woman who demanded an answer from him the night before.

"I would like to wait at least a week. My family would love to attend. And I wondered if your brother would be there to give you away?"

"Oh, no. I would rather he not attend."

"Cordelia." Her sister admonished.

"You don't want your brother to come?" he asked, completely happy with the situation. He didn't want to deal with a man who had virtually abandoned Cordelia to survive on her own the last few months in London. That made him less than a man in Nico's estimation.

"Of course she wants him to come," Diana said.

"No, not particularly."

"You have been living in his house for the last few months."

"So nice of him to allow poor little Cordelia to live in a house and not on the street. He deserves an award," Cordelia said, sarcasm dripping from every syllable.

Diana glanced at him, and he surmised she did not want to air dirty laundry in front of a stranger. Yes, he was going to marry Cordelia, but they didn't know him. There was also a part of her that probably thought he would break off the wedding if he heard the rumors about Cordelia's birth.

He didn't want to leave, but he sensed he needed to allow the sisters to talk. He finished his tea and set it on the tray.

"I must be off to the newspapers to set the announcement, and I need to send a message to my parents so they can prepare for their journey."

Cordelia looked relieved. Aggravation wound through him. She should want to be near him, need him, as he needed her. Now she looked so happy he was leaving.

He stood and walked to her chair. He took her hand and raised it to his mouth. He did not kiss above her hand as was society's way. He pressed his lips on her flesh. The scent of her blood had his body reacting. His own blood quickened, and his fangs started to descend again. He pulled himself back, figuratively and physically.

Cordelia rose, and he shook his head. "Stay with your sister. I can find my own way out."

By the time he reached the street, he was feeling somewhat normal again. He drew in a deep breath of London air and immediately regretted it. He hated the city. Too many people, too much dirt…and a man to hunt. Once he had everything secured with Cordelia, he could focus his entire attention on the mystery.

All would be easy once he could settle Cordelia. Once she was officially his, life would be easier for him.

* * * *

As the door shut behind Nico, Cordelia waited for her sister to say something. Diana always had an opinion, and she rather liked letting Cordelia know what it was. It did not take her long.

"Really, Cordelia, do you not have a thought for your future? You are marrying a commoner."

She frowned at her sister. "What is so wrong with that? You did."

"There is a difference between someone like Michael and that man."

Yes, there was in Cordelia's mind. Michael had never been much of a man, and he definitely could not compete with Nico. On any level. There was something so good…so right with Nico. She could not understand what it was about him, but something told her he was someone who always honored his promises. It went beyond his proposal of marriage.

"I would think you would be happy for me. At least now the poor relation will be taken care of."

Diana pursed her lips, a sure sign that she was angry. Diana controlled so much, from her own household to her emotions. It had not always been that way. There had been a time when she was Cordelia's entire world, but marriage had changed her—and not for the better. Now Cordelia always felt stifled in her presence.

Everyone could tell they were sisters. As their father had told them in many of his drunken tirades, they both had the look of their mother. Diana, though, just as their mother apparently had, knew how to make the most of her attributes.

The outfit she wore was perfectly suited to her petite, rounded frame. The color of gray would make a lot of women appear worn out, but of course it was perfect for Diana. She had been outside on a windy day, and she did not have a hair out of place. She had her long blonde locks trapped behind her head. It looked painful to Cordelia.

"I do not think that way about you. I even asked you to come live with me once you reached your majority."

She had but Cordelia had felt intrusive. One week and she had wanted to leave. Michael had not been a nice man.

"Yes, but that was not to be."

Diana set her teacup down on the service tray and studied Cordelia. "And, you are fine wedding a man you barely know?"

"Is this any different than your marriage, or the hundreds of marriages that take place within the *ton* each year? I do not know one woman who can truly say they know their husband. Most of them believe the fairytale that they will marry for love. Within a month, most women wake up to the painful reality. I do not have that problem. At least I know he has the ability to take care of me."

"Yes, he is rich."

Cordelia sighed. "Yes, there is that. But the incident last night came upon us because I was attacked. Mr. Blackburn protected me."

"Are you telling me you were not truly compromised?"

"I have been in London, on my own, and lived with a father and brother who had the most debauched parties in recent memory. Amazingly, I kept my virginity intact. I do not think a few minutes with a man in a darkened library would have made me lose my head."

She didn't think she was telling that big of a fib. She had lost her head there for a moment. The truth of the matter was there was a good chance he could have very well taken her virginity, and she would have been happy to give it to him. Even the memory of his hands on her, his breath feathering over her flesh, had her fighting the shiver that slipped through her.

"Indeed."

She glanced at her sister. Diana's expression had grown even more impenetrable. They had not always been like this. With her mother dead the day after her birth, Cordelia had spent a huge amount of time with her sister. She had been her primary caregiver...until she abandoned her to get married.

She pushed that thought aside. It did no good for either of them to dwell on the past.

"Yes. I have been independent since my majority, and since I did not want to live with our brother, I chose to come to London." Although she loathed every minute of it, actually. London was dirty, the air sometimes foggy with the waste from the march of industry. Still, she could not admit that to her sister.

"That was not what should have happened."

She studied her sister, trying to discern the emotion behind the statement. As usual, Diana kept it hidden.

"Well, you have your father to thank for that. According to his will, I am truly not part of the family. The way it is written, the family has no say in what I do."

That was the truth, and they all knew it. The will had effectively cut her off from the family. It had not hurt so much...they had been lost to her years ago. But the financial blow had been hard to accept. Until she had found writing.

Her sister looked away, and for the first time, she looked vulnerable. Then her jaw tightened. "You are right, and I guess there is no reason for us to go over old problems."

She wanted to fight it out, yell, but the truth was it would do no good. "I am assuming there are places I need to go shopping for a dress...I guess." She shrugged, almost overwhelmed by what all needed to be done. Cordelia did not know if she would ever be able to accept her fate.

"Yes. I guess I can take you around to the shops today."

Cordelia sighed in relief. "I would like to wait one day if

possible."

She would never admit it to her sister, but Cordelia was exhausted. She had little to no energy now. Once Nico had walked out the door, it was as if he took all of her will to actually work for the day. It was not like her, but she was assuming that it had been the stress of the night before and now this morning that did her in.

"I think that can be arranged." Diana glanced around. "You should come to stay with me."

For a moment, Cordelia did not know what to say. Her sister did not come to town often, and she did not offer Cordelia assistance. Ever.

"I am not sure that is necessary."

The look of disdain Diana sent her way would have shriveled most people. Cordelia was accustomed to it, though.

"No, you do not understand what you are about to deal with. You will become an interest for people, and they will watch your every move."

Cordelia did not like the sound of that.

"From your frown, I can tell you did not think of it. Blackburn might not be one of the *ton*, but as he said, he has links to some of the most powerful people in England. If he can get the young Duke to do something like this for him, that is big. *Very big.* You will be the subject of much gossip, and your life is now not your own."

The panic she had been fighting earlier returned. It was now churning her stomach. "I can ignore it."

"Yes, but if there is one thing I know about the Blackburns, they will not. They might be mysterious and they may shun the London society, but they do take any slight against their family seriously. They have ruined others for less."

She knew they had a lot of power. That is why she had assumed the Blackburns had something to do with moneylending—or smuggling. If you have the money, you could control so much. Still, she was just the woman their son was marrying…and not by choice. She doubted that they would consider it a slight if it was done to her.

"I think you are exaggerating."

Diana shook her head. "No. I heard that they left the Earl of Eddington to rot after he made a disparaging remark about a second cousin of theirs."

"They were the ones who ruined him?"

"The only thing they would help with was the care of his family members. If I remember correctly, Adelaide Blackburn said she could not let his children suffer because they had a man of loose morals and a small mind as a father. That is your mother-in-law to be."

"Good God."

"Really, Cordelia, do you have to be so vulgar?"

Cordelia smiled. "No, but sometimes I like to do it."

Her sister rolled her eyes, and for a moment, Cordelia was thrown back into her childhood. Diana had been a willing caregiver and very indulgent with her. It was because of those memories she could never truly blame her for abandoning her to marriage.

"All right, it is decided. I rented a very nice townhouse over in St Andrew's Square. There is more than enough room for you until you get married. Knowing that Blackburn's family lives near Scotland, it will take a few days to get them assembled for the wedding."

She opened her mouth, but Diana stopped her by holding up her hand. "You might not care what others think, but you can be sure the Blackburns and our brother will. You do not want to give Alex a reason to appear in town and cause any problems. You know from experience that he is a man who excels at little else than that."

What her sister said was correct. Alex had always been a problem. He did not fall far from the paternal tree in that regard.

"Believe me, you will be much more comfortable with

me."

She wanted to say no. She did not know what it was about Diana now, but there was something so…uncomfortable to Cordelia when she was in her presence. But she was offering to help, and if she didn't do it for herself, she would do it for Nico.

"All right, I will come."

For the first time since the debacle in the library, she looked forward to her wedding day. She prayed his family would make the trip quickly because Cordelia was unsure just how much of society—and her sister—she could take.

* * * *

"So, I take it you arranged everything today with your bride," Malik asked as he buttered his toast. It was midafternoon, and as with many of their kind, Malik had just risen. Nico had been surprised to find his friend awake when he returned. The night before could not have been easy on him. Dealing with Mades always brought back bad memories of Malik's turning. He never spoke of it, but Nico knew it had been painful and degrading.

"Yes. It was a close thing, but I convinced her. It did not help that her sister appeared almost as if out of air."

Malik stopped his actions and looked at him. "This is the one who lives up north? She just showed up?"

"Yes."

Malik frowned.

"What?" Nico asked. In the several centuries they had known each other, Nico had learned to respect Malik's intuition.

"From what I gather, she never comes to London."

"From what you gather?" Nico asked.

His friend took a bite of toast and shrugged. After he swallowed, he said, "I asked around. I did not want you going into this blindly following your lust."

Even the idea had Nico irritated. It might be the fact that he was doing that, but that did not mean he would accept it.

"And you can get mad at me, but I wanted to protect you, Nico. I have never seen you act this way with another woman."

He shrugged, trying to dispel the worry now settled on his shoulders. "She's a Carrier."

"No. That is not the reason. You have been around many other Carriers without this visceral of a reaction."

"It does make me wonder who her birth father was. I had no reaction to Diana this morning."

"Yes, the sister. What don't you like about her?" He looked at Malik, and he shrugged again. "I can tell by the way you talk about her you do not like her at all, do you?"

Nico rose and started to pace. It was the only way he could work through his thoughts at times. "She's...not a nice woman."

Malik chuckled. "That has never made you not like a woman before."

"That is true enough. But this woman...I felt a reaction to well...protect Cordelia."

"Of course."

"What do you mean by that?"

"You might not have mated, but you have chosen to be her mate. From what I can tell, her sister abandoned her to run off and get married. And you know what the earl was like, and now his son. No woman in her right mind would leave a young girl in that house. There was no come-out for your bride-to-be, either, and her sister could have easily afforded it, but she did not. It makes sense that you would not like her."

"But I didn't know all of this."

Malik opened his mouth, then snapped it closed.

"What?"

"I think you might have an issue with that now."

"Do tell me your thoughts, Malik."

His friend rarely held anything back, but he could tell that he was choosing his words wisely.

"We have never been truly mated, either of us. We definitely have not bound ourselves to anyone. But I do know others who have, and they tend to be connected even before the binding."

"What do you mean?"

"You felt threatened by Diana because of what she had done to Cordelia, although you did not know the entire story."

"I still don't."

And that had to be what was bothering him. He could not understand how a woman of Cordelia's means had set out to London with little to no support from her family. Not many women could do it, and he would wager those who could were not of her class.

"No, but you sensed it in Cordelia. She felt threatened in some way by her sister, and thus, you did."

He did not like that one bit, especially when he was even wondering now if it were true. Feelings like that could trap him into binding with her, and after watching what happened to his brother, he would not do that. Could not.

"Either way, her sister is a cold-hearted bitch."

Malik gave him a knowing look but said nothing. "Yes, I am sure she is. Not much warmth in that house after their mother died. But there is one thing you need to worry about."

"You mean other than a rogue Born running the streets of London and making vamps?"

"Yes. Your fiancée is a Carrier and so is her sister. Her widowed sister. Who just happened to appear the night you compromised Cordelia."

"I did not compromise Cordelia."

Malik let one eyebrow rise.

"Well, not entirely."

"That might explain why you are being such an ass. But if Diana is telepathic, or at least empathic to her sister, which we know Carriers often are, you are going to have to win her over or she will cause you problems for years to come."

"She has no power. She is but a widow."

"A woman, yes, and a man who is not leery of a woman's power is a man about to have the rug pulled out from beneath him."

He opened his mouth to tell Malik to bugger off, but the door burst open. He recognized the boy from Gray's house.

"You have information for me?"

"Yes," he said, holding out a note.

Quickly he read it, then nodded. He looked at Malik.

"Let's go. It seems our viscount has awakened."

Chapter Five

Nico and Malik were shown into an upstairs parlor room where Gray greeted them. Their usually well-dressed friend was now a mess. His hair stuck up on top of his head. His shirt was torn, and the tails were hanging out of his trousers. He had not slept, and Nico was positive he probably had not fed. The ashen cast to his flesh was testament to the long night.

"You look like hell," Nico said.

Gray made a face. "I feel like it. It was one long, hellacious night and day. I don't think I ever want to go through that again."

Malik was frowning and had been since they received the summons. "It usually takes longer than this."

"Yes, I know. I consulted Bingam about it."

The physician was a highly sought-after Born. "And?"

"He said it depended on the individual and the fact that he had our blood, a mixture of it at least, seems to have helped. You know there is some kind of dependency at times with the Born who offers his blood."

"I thought it made him more dependent on the Born who turned him," Nico said.

"Bingam said that if he was fed that same person's blood, he assumed he would be beholden to him. But, being fed a mixture of Born blood made it easier for him to break the bond. Of course we don't know for sure. These are all just theories."

"It is because the Borns are afraid of researching," Malik said.

"What do you mean?" Nico asked.

"Borns fear anything that would allow the underclass of Mades to gain ground. If it is known just how to battle it, they would lose their caste system."

"Bingam also said we might have caught him earlier than others who have been turned. He had not had a kill, or at least I hope he has not." Gray sighed. "What a bloody mess."

"He is in the room?" Malik asked, nodding his head toward the doors.

"Yes. He finally came out of the trance he was under. He remembers nothing."

"He does not know who turned him?"

"No. What is worse, he is wondering why he is here. He knows something is not right."

"If he woke up naked in that cage, I am sure he has more than just a few questions," Nico said.

"No, he did not wake up there. He collapsed and we moved him up here."

Nico nodded.

"He truly cannot remember?" Malik asked. "I find that odd."

"I did too, but Bingam told me there are things you can do to alter that. If the Born who made him wants to keep his identity a secret, he said there are new serums that work very well for that."

"Well, bloody hell. I was hoping for him to tell us who bit him."

"Everyone is. There was another killing last night in White Chapel," Gray said. "Borns are already starting to get restless."

"Being restless does not help if they are not ready to take action," Malik said. "The Borns are going to ignore it until they have no choice. And then, it will be too late."

Nico tried to ignore what Malik said, but he knew it to be true. So many of the Borns were lazy, content with the way things were. They expected this to just disappear because they were the chosen ones.

"Do we have the killer?"

Gray shook his head. "He left a woman on the street,

completely drained of her blood. It is not like the others."

"How so?"

"From reports, she was not raped. She was just drained."

"Not a Made then," Nico said, nodding. "Possibly the Born who is making them."

"That will not matter when the hysteria sets in. They will be out for Made blood," Malik said.

Nico wanted to argue, but he knew his friend was right. The fear of another Vlad always simmered in the back of everyone's minds. It had almost torn their world apart and exposed them to more than the occasional tale of bloodsuckers. It had threatened to bring their entire world crumbling. And from that, the Vampire Alliance had formed. They had no major problems until now.

Knowing it would not do him any good to dwell on the past, Nico put it out of his mind. "Let's go see the patient."

Gray nodded. "He has not really spoken. He did wake once, took some water in, but that was all."

He opened the room, which was decidedly darker. It was a large cavernous room, and from the look of it, it was not one for the family but for guests. "Who is there?" a weak voice asked from the bed.

"He cannot see?" Nico asked.

"It is hard to see when you first turn."

Nico had not asked Malik of his turning, but he did know that there was much of it that he hid from everyone. Too much. He hated that he might have to push Malik to tell him more. Truly, Nico did not want to know, but with things progressing this rapidly, he might have to ask. And worse—he would have to listen.

"You are adjusting to the new genes in your system. Your body can take up to a few weeks to grow accustomed to it."

He nodded in understanding.

"He is safe now?"

"I would not take him out in society for a few weeks.

That is if he survives being told that everything he once knew is altered."

Gray led them to Hurst's bedside. The man once known as Viscount Hurst looked as if he had been sick for months. He had lost weight, his facial bones more pronounced now. It was hard to believe that the man who had attacked him the night before was the wasted Made now resting in the bed.

"Do you remember anything yet?" Gray asked.

"No. Just as I told you earlier. I cannot remember a thing." He swallowed as if trying to pull himself together. Nico imagined that he was. It was hard enough waking up in the unknown, but he was sure being in Gray's possession truly confused him.

"Does someone want to tell me what I am doing here?" he asked.

"You remember nothing of what happened in the library or before that?" Gray asked.

"I remember going to a bawdy house a few nights ago...or was it weeks? Then nothing. It is foggy. Did that just happen last night?"

Nico shared a glance with Malik.

"Do you know the date that you went to the whorehouse?"

Slowly, he lifted his hand to rub his eyes. His actions spoke of a man who had been to battle and lost. If Gray looked ashen, their newly Made looked like death warmed over. Nico assumed that every bit of his strength was being used just to lift his hand.

"I believe it was the fifth...why?"

It was ten days later. "That was over a week ago," Nico said.

Hurst's eyes widened. Their color had lightened, and the pale green almost matched Malik's.

"That can't be. Do you mean to say that I have been sleeping for days?"

"No, you were awake," Gray said.

He frowned. "I do not remember."

"No, I don't believe you will," Nico said.

"It will be best that you do not," Malik said as he walked forward. "Remembering what you have been through will do no good for you, so it is best not to worry."

Nico knew then that Malik remembered ever second of his change, and knowing the person he was, he would relive it every night.

"Remember what?" Hurst tried to sit up but ended up collapsing against the pillows. His eyes narrowed as he raked his gaze over them. "Just tell me what the bloody hell is going on?"

Nico looked at Malik. "I think you would be the best to explain everything."

Malik studied Nico for a moment, then nodded. "Hurst, what you know of your life is over."

* * * *

By the time Nico returned to his own house, he was exhausted. Most of the night before he had been working with Gray, then the early day visit with Cordelia, and then back to Gray's. He needed a healthy night's rest, or maybe two.

Worse, watching Hurst discover that his life was completely changed, that everything he had known was now gone, had been draining. Sure, he could live as someone in the *ton*, but he would spend his life watching his friends and family die. Nico himself had been through that, and it had been horrifying. It was something he did not wish on anyone, Born, Made, or human.

"You should probably stay in tonight, old man," said Malik. "Not sure if you are up to a soiree."

He shot his friend a nasty look as his butler opened the door. "Bugger off."

"That is no way for a gentleman to talk, Nicodemus."

He glanced down the hallway and found his parents standing in the foyer. Bloody, bloody hell.

"When did you arrive?" he asked as he strode forward to hug his mother. The smell of lavender immediately surrounded him. He could never smell the blossom and not think of his mother.

"Just in time," she said, then gave him a kiss and drew back. "Are you going to tell me what all the gossip is about?"

"Always cutting to the chase, mother?" Nico asked.

She gave him a knowing look. In all his five hundred years he could never fool his mother. The woman was one of the strongest Carriers he knew. She didn't suffer fools, and she always knew what he was up to. It was a bit disconcerting that his mother was so tapped into his life.

"Adelaide, do you think we could possibly let the boys join us in the parlor? Nicodemus looks like death incarnate at the moment," his father said.

She sighed and nodded. Then she looked over his shoulder. "Do not think you will be getting away tonight, Malik. Come, join us."

He glanced at his friend and smiled. The irritated look on Malik's face told Nico that he still was not comfortable with his mother's insistence that he was part of the family. She did not wait, though. As usual, she turned and started to walk into the parlor. His father gave him an amused look and followed.

"Come on, Malik, there is no way out of it now."

He said nothing but he did follow Nico. His mother took a seat on the couch and was joined by his father. He studied them for a moment. His father did not look a day over fifty and his mother the same. No one would expect that they were both over six hundred years old. For their kind, being surrounded by family usually gave them a sense of peace. It had been even more so after his brother had died. For some reason, he felt as if he itched from the inside out.

"I want to know what is going on."

"Yes, mother I do believe you did mention that earlier. I sent you a message, but that was only a few hours ago. What I am trying to understand is why you are here?"

She was stoic, her expression telling him nothing. Still, he could feel something simmering beneath the surface. She was barely holding on to her temper.

"Your mother had a feeling," his father said. The low tone told him the trip had not been easy on either of them. For bonded mates, especially those with a long relationship like his parents, the empathic connection was strong.

He shared a look with Malik. No one inside the family, or even close friends, ever doubted her intuition. She was the one person who did not like Neal Pearson when he had befriended Nico. Their family would have been better off if Nico had listened to her at the time.

She looked between the two of them. Nico had a feeling that his mother was taking the time to choose her words carefully. "I insisted that we leave. You down here doing your investigations…I was worried."

"You thought I was in trouble, and of course you rushed down. Do you not think that you could put yourself at risk by coming here?"

The look his mother gave him would shrivel a lesser man's manhood. He had centuries to learn to be immune but it still made him twitch. "Do not speak to me in that tone, Nicodemus Alexander Blackburn."

He heard a snort from Malik. Every Blackburn knew he was in trouble when Adelaide Blackburn used all of your given names.

"I just wish you had sent a messenger, but it is moot now. You need to be here for the wedding."

His father laid a hand on his mother's fist. "Yes, son, tell us about this woman you are marrying."

He should not be embarrassed. Their kind was well known for their sexual needs, and it was never a taboo subject in his house. It was respected as part of their makeup.

But…this was somehow different. There was a part of him that was still appalled by the way he had acted the night before.

"Your son lost his head over a Carrier, a Made tried to interrupt him, and the Carrier was compromised," Malik said with relish. Nico could tell from the expression on his face Malik was enjoying this way too much. "Now your son must marry."

"Thank you for your description," he said from behind clenched teeth.

Malik's grin widened. "No problem."

"Who is this Carrier? Do we know her family?" his father asked.

"No. Well, we do know them, or know of them. The Earl of Collingsworth's daughter."

His father frowned. "I did not know they were Borns."

"I am not sure they know either. Truth of the matter, the rumor is that my soon-to-be wife is…a bastard."

His mother nodded in understanding. "Of course. That would explain why she did not know. Her mother died in childbirth, if I remember. I really did not like her father, so it is a good thing she is not blood related to the man."

"Rightly so," his father commented.

Once again, Nico was happy that his family was not considered aristocracy in the human world. They did not care that Cordelia did not know who her father was. In fact, for the most part, his family shunned most aristocracy. They dealt with them in their world, but other than Gray's family, they avoided any personal entanglements.

"When do we get to meet her?" his mother asked.

Of course she would not ask him "if" she could meet her, but "when." Yes, she was going to be his wife, but most mothers would not be so forceful. They were not Adelaide Blackburn.

"I am sure I can arrange a meeting tomorrow."

"You are not going out tonight?" his mother asked.

"No. We spent the day with a Made."

That brought silence in the room. Again most people would not include their mother in dealings such at this, but it was different in his family. They were ruled by democracy, and his mother had amazing insight. Most Carriers did, but unfortunately, the majority of their male Borns ignored it.

"He survived?" she asked.

"Yes. Thanks to Malik and Gray."

His father glanced at Malik. "We are again in your debt."

Malik said nothing, but nodded his head in his father's direction.

"Do you think he will survive?" his mother asked.

"He has a good chance. He seemed recovered from the Blood Lust, although he was very weak, as if he'd been sick."

"At least there is that." She patted her hair. "Now, on to your Cordelia. You are sure she is a Carrier?"

"Of course."

"I am not happy with the situation because we do not know a thing of her bloodlines," his father said.

"That has never been important to you before this."

His father shook his head. "Her background is usually not all that important. The situation now is very serious, though. With the new wave of attacks, we need to make sure she is not being thrown in your path."

"I assure you that is not the case, and even if it is, anyone concocting such an idiotic plot should know it would not work. I have better control than to fall for a woman trying to infiltrate our investigation."

He heard a snort from Malik, but he ignored it.

"True, but tell me, is she your kind of woman?" his father asked.

"I have one?"

"Don't be cheeky. What your father is trying to discern is if they know we are investigating."

He nodded. "I understand. I assure you that is not the case. I have a feeling she has no idea she is a Carrier. Which will cause other problems, but I will worry about those later."

"Later? When?"

"At the moment, I am trying my best to get the wedding set up. It is good that you are here. We do not need to wait for your arrival now, so we can marry soon to save Cordelia any more embarrassment."

"If you wanted to do that, you shouldn't have gone into a darkened library with her," Malik commented.

"I didn't go into the library with her. I was there, and she came in trying to avoid Hurst."

"And tied you down to the couch?" Malik asked.

"Shut up."

His mother was studying them as they bantered back and forth, her expression blank. "So, when will I meet her?"

"Tonight is too late. I am assuming that she is not going out."

"Why would you assume that?"

"She is now engaged."

His mother rolled her eyes. "Of course. Because once a woman nabs a man, it is her duty to sit at home and wait."

He opened his mouth to respond, but his father saved him. "Take my advice, son, do not argue with a woman—especially a Carrier."

His mother gave his father a warning glance and then faced Nico. "'Tis not too late for us to go out. Send a boy around to find out where your intended is going to be tonight. If she is not going out, then we shall set up a meeting tomorrow."

That sounded ominous. Cordelia did have a spine, but he was not too sure she could handle his mother. Not many people could—including himself at times. From the determined expression on her face, this was one of those times.

"Of course."

"And the announcement has been sent of the marriage."

It was not a question. His mother and father hated society slightly less than he did, but they understood how the game was played.

"It will be in the morning editions."

"Good. Get that message done. I am going to get settled in my room."

She gave him a kiss on the cheek and then turned to walk out the door. "Oh, and Malik, I expect you to be there."

The beat of silence that followed her departure was almost deafening.

"Your mother was a bit worried on the trip down."

He glanced at his father.

"I understand."

"Do you?" he asked as he rose from the couch. "I don't think you do, not yet. Maybe your Cordelia will teach you all about it."

As the door shut behind them, Malik sighed. "You had to expect that they knew something was going on. Your mother's intuition has been the bane of our existence for years."

Nico sighed and walked to the cabinet where he kept his whiskey. After pouring himself a good bit, he tossed it down. He poured another glass and faced Malik.

"Yes, she has been. But it does not matter. Having her here will actually make it easier. If Adelaide Blackburn accepts her new daughter-in-law, our society will follow suit."

Malik nodded. "Let's just hope your mother does not scare her off."

"I have a feeling Cordelia will be able to deal with her after a fashion."

"And if not? Would you be willing to walk away?"

He wanted to say yes. Nico had done his best not to become too attached to any of his paramours, favoring women who knew the score. But when he opened his mouth to say so, every fiber of his being revolted at the idea of letting her go. He snapped his mouth shut.

Malik smirked at him. "I thought not. Well, old man, let's just hope once you get her in your bed, you will be able to think straight again."

Nico hoped so because he did not relish being so smitten with Cordelia that he couldn't think straight.

Once he had her in his house, in his bed, under his control, all would be right in his world again.

Chapter Six

The swell of music filled the ballroom as Cordelia tried to keep her eyes open. She wasn't one who liked late nights. When she had been hired to write her column, it had become a necessary evil. After a night of no sleep, getting engaged, and moving to her sister's rented townhouse, she wanted to curl up in bed for three days.

Cordelia had not wanted to come to the ball tonight. Diana had insisted. When her sister decided on a matter, there was no way to avoid doing what she wanted. In fact, her father had said both of them had been cursed with their mother's pride. Diana apparently inherited more than she had because Cordelia was standing in a hot ballroom watching people dance.

"Do stop moving around, Cordelia."

Cordelia drew in a deep breath and almost coughed. "This dress is just a bit tight. I cannot seem to get comfortable."

Diana glanced at her. "I did not know you had filled out so much or I would have made sure to have it let out."

"Why did I need to make an appearance? I do not understand what it will help."

"You know why. What I cannot understand is why you did not tell Mr. Blackburn where you would be tonight."

She shrugged. "I did not even contemplate that."

"Why not? Soon you will have to answer to him."

Her stomach muscles clutched at the thought. "Mr. Blackburn does not like society that much."

At that moment, it felt as if something brushed the back of her neck. Her heart quickened as she shivered.

Nico.

She did not know how she knew he was there, but she

did. It was as if her blood had warmed ten degrees. Her body tingled with excitement.

Cordelia looked around the room and saw the tall Egyptian-looking man who had been with Blackburn the night before. He was so tall that he was easy to see. Her gaze shifted, and she saw that Blackburn was with him.

"It seems that he tracked me down."

Diana looked at her. "Whatever do you mean?"

"He is walking toward us."

Diana followed her line of vision. "Oh, he does not look too happy."

"He rarely does."

Her sister glanced at her then back to Nico and Malik. "Who is that man with him?"

"Blackburn called him Malik last night. I am unsure of his full name."

As if he had some kind of special powers, the crowd parted, allowing the men to walk through it with ease. He stopped just inches in front of her. He stared at her for a moment as if he expected her to do something. She could not. Her heart was beating hard against her breast, and it seemed that the heat of the ballroom was finally getting to her because she was lightheaded.

"Lady Cordelia." He took her gloved hand and even through the material, she could feel the heat of him warm her hand. Again, he ignored etiquette and pressed his mouth against her glove. It was blatantly sensual and completely against the rules. There was one thing she had learned about her soon-to-be husband and that was he had never really worried about society's decrees of proper behavior.

Instead of letting go of her hand, he stepped beside her and set her hand on his arm. "You met my friend Malik last night, of course. Malik, this is Lady Diana, Lady Cordelia's sister."

He nodded in the direction of her sister but said nothing. He looked a little too stunned to speak. When she looked at her sister, Cordelia was surprised to see Diana's cheeks pink, and for once she seemed speechless.

"I did not know you had moved to your sister's home."

She heard the reprimand in his voice, and she did not like it. "I apologize."

The look he sent her said he knew she was not truly sorry. His lips twitched. "I was worried. My mother arrived and wanted to meet you."

"Your mother?" she asked loud enough for a few people around them to look at her strangely. She cleared her throat. "I apologize. I was just taken aback by the announcement."

"She is here, as is my father. They would like to meet you."

Her heart was already beating out of control and now he wanted her to meet his parents? She was not good at socializing. Her father had never thought it important to have her trained, and she had been happy not to worry about those things. She had spent her days reading and riding horses. When she had found herself in need of money, she had learned the rules. She only put on airs to gain access to the *ton* so that she could investigate them. Nico wasn't truly part of the *ton*, but he moved in their circles. Which meant she was marrying into it.

Her panic exploded but she fought the need to run from the ballroom screaming. She only knew of society mothers…and that did not make her feel any better. Her own sister's mother-in-law had been horrid from memory.

"Here? In the ballroom?"

He gave her a glance. "No. They are waiting in the study to meet you. Mother could not put it off any longer."

That sounded very ominous. "Indeed?"

He leaned down so that only she could hear him. When he spoke, his breath caressed her ear, and she shivered. "She does not bite unless you threaten her offspring."

Her sister shifted beside her, and Cordelia pulled her attention away from Blackburn to look at Diana.

"I think you should go with him to meet his parents, but I will go with you."

She looked at Diana and realized that her sister was worried about her. It had been too many years to count since someone had actually sought to protect her. Now she had a husband-to-be who was marrying her to protect her, and a sister who had ignored her for years stepping in to ensure she was safe. Her world had certainly become strange.

"Of course. They would like to meet more of your family," Blackburn said.

"I am sure they would," she said, unable to keep the sarcasm out of her tone. No one really wanted to meet her brother.

"Come."

She did not like to be ordered. By anyone. She hesitated for that reason. He sensed it because she saw his jaw flex. One thing she wanted to avoid was another scene. They were already the objects of fascination of most of the ballroom.

With a sigh, she went with him. Out of the corner of her eye, she saw Malik offer his arm to her sister. Cordelia was surprised when Diana didn't hesitate as she had. It seemed to take so long to get to the library. The spectacle of their departure was definitely noted by everyone as they made their way through the milling crowd. More than one or two people tried to catch Nico's attention, but he ignored them.

"People are going to think you are rude," she said.

"I am," he said.

Cordelia glanced at him out of the corner of her eye and noted the stoic expression. She sensed that he was trying to warn her not to expect him not to be.

By the time they reached the oak doors of the study, she wanted to scream. Her nerves were already on edge and having to meet his parents...it was a little too much. She had never thought to marry, and now she had to deal with in-laws.

Nico opened the door and led her into the room.

Cordelia did not know what she had been expecting, but the diminutive woman was not it. Even with her sitting beside her husband on the couch, it was easy to see she was probably a few inches shorter than Cordelia—and she was considered short. It wasn't until she saw the power in her dark blue eyes that she knew this was a woman to be careful of. The lavender dress was the perfect shade for her peaches and cream skin. Her hair was as dark as Nico's, but there were threads of silver throughout it.

Her attention shifted to the man beside her. For a moment, she was transfixed. Nico's father was an older version of her fiancé, his hair heavily layered with gray. She realized this was Nico in thirty years, although his father's smile was much more pleasant than Nico's constant frown.

"Cordelia, Lady Diana, these are my parents, Adelaide and Samuel Blackburn. Mother, Father, this is my intended and her sister."

Adelaide's gaze raked over Diana, then she met Cordelia's. Her inscrutable expression dissolved into a welcoming smile.

"Cordelia," she stood, as did her husband. "I am so very happy to meet you."

Relief swept through her along with another feeling she could not discern. It was as if she felt a kinship with the woman, as if she was meeting an old family friend. It made no sense at all.

"Thank you."

Then his mother looked past her to her sister and Malik. Something stirred behind those blue eyes, but she said nothing. Her smile widened.

"Please, have a seat, Cordelia," his father offered. Adelaide sat back down and patted the couch next to her.

"Yes, do. We need time to get acquainted."

She nodded but Nico held her hand against his arm. His mother shifted her attention to him. For a moment, she thought Nico would not allow her to walk forward, but the struggle was won by his mother. That was something to note. Her very powerful fiancé apparently acquiesced to his mother. She did not know if that was good or not.

She settled beside Adelaide, and her sister sat in the chair beside her.

"Now, you can leave," Adelaide said to the men.

All three men frowned. Cordelia had to bite her lower lip to keep from smiling. The men in the Blackburn family might be powerful, but after this meeting, Cordelia was sure who really held the power.

His father sighed. He bent down and brushed his lips against his wife's cheek. He whispered something to her. She looked up at him, and for a moment, Cordelia could not look away. The love and admiration between them almost overwhelmed her. She knew it was a private moment, but she could not seem to tear her gaze away from the couple. Then he straightened and looked at Cordelia.

"It was very nice to meet you, Cordelia. And you, Lady Diana."

She glanced at her sister and noticed she was blushing again. Lord, her night was descending into something definitely odd.

Samuel walked out, and after a quick glance and nod in Diana's direction, Malik followed him out. Nico hesitated.

"You can leave, dear boy. I have refrained from cannibalism lately. I will not harm your Cordelia."

He gave his mother a warning glance as he stepped forward. He bent down in much the same fashion that his father did, but he did not kiss her. Her breath was hot against her ear as he spoke.

"Do not allow her to push you around."

She smiled at him and turned to meet his gaze as he was pulling back. Something hot and scary filled his eyes as he stared at her. Everything in her body heated, her nerve endings dancing, and she felt herself moving toward him without thinking.

"Really, Nico," his mother admonished. "Control yourself for one night."

Cordelia dropped her gaze to her lap, a blush heating her face.

Nico straightened. "Has anyone told you that you are too blunt, Mother?"

Mortified, Cordelia looked at Adelaide, expecting her to be mad. She was surprised to find her smiling.

"Your father just told me that very thing earlier today. I find it is one of my most endearing qualities."

He chuckled. "I fear you are correct."

He bowed his head to her and Diana one more time, then walked out of the room, closing the door behind him.

Adelaide sighed. "Thank goodness they are finally gone. I love my men, but sometimes they can be too much when you have them all in one room together." She smiled at Cordelia. "Now, tell me about yourself, Cordelia."

She panicked for a moment. What did she tell the woman? That she was a bastard, one whose own father and brother left out in the cold to survive?

"Cordelia is a lover of words," Diana said. She threw her sister a grateful glance and was surprised to see the determined look in her eyes. It struck Cordelia that her sister was ready to do battle with Adelaide.

"I would assume so. I knew when my Nico fell for a woman she would not be an idiot. Normally, I would not like you speaking for your sister. I believe I asked her the question, not you." She settled back against the pillows. "But I can see that you think you are protecting her from me. There is no need, Diana."

The silence that followed was strained. Cordelia could not take it. Growing up in a household where long silences were usually followed by screams and a smack or two, she always tried to keep things happy.

"I am sure Diana meant nothing by it."

Adelaide leaned forward and patted her leg. The

familiarity was one of a mother or aunt. Any other time, Cordelia would be disconcerted by it. She was not accustomed to physical affection, especial from a matron. But tonight, she was comforted.

"Oh, I think she did, and I applaud her. I was an orphan by the time I married my husband, and calling his mother a harridan would be kind. I have more respect for your sister for trying to protect you. I would say she is a little late to the job, but she is making up for it, I am sure."

Cordelia did not know what to say to her. She glanced at her sister, whose face had no expression whatsoever.

"Oh, dear, I was too blunt again. It is something I have never been able to free myself of. I would rather have plain speaking than pretty words. And I think you are the same way."

Cordelia couldn't help but return the smile. "Yes."

"Wonderful. Now, why not a good spot of whiskey?"

She stood and walked over to the table with the liquor and glasses.

"Mrs. Blackburn, I am sure you understand society's rules," Diana said in admonition. They both knew women did not hide in libraries drinking.

Adelaide said nothing for a moment as she poured two glasses. She handed one to Cordelia as she studied Diana.

"If you know anything about the Blackburns, dear girl, you would know that we don't like rules."

And with that, she tossed the entire glass of whiskey down. Then she sat next to Cordelia again and said, "Why don't we become better acquainted."

* * * *

Nico glanced down the hallway for what seemed like the fifth time in as many minutes. He could not get past that feeling that he needed to check on Cordelia.

"Your intended is not in any danger from your mother,"

said his father, humor lacing his voice.

He glanced at the man who taught him everything he knew. "I would not be so sure of that. You know mother can be slightly scary to new people."

"She likes Cordelia."

"How do you know that?"

"After the years we have been married, you know I can sense her feelings. I believe you are starting to understand this more now. You definitely will after the mating."

Nico sighed and fought the urge to pace the ballroom. He wanted nothing more than to leave the house with Cordelia, take her home, and strip her naked. He was sure the primitive feeling to protect her would stop once he did.

"And you believe me now?" he asked his father.

"You were right. She is definitely a strong Carrier. What I cannot understand is how they went undetected for so long? Diana is strong also, but not as strong as Cordelia. She must have had a Born as a sire."

He nodded as he noted there was no one nearby. "It is rumored they all had different fathers."

"I am sure that is why Malik reacted so strongly to the woman," his father remarked. Malik had not stayed. In fact, he had made excuses that he needed to check on Hurst. They both knew he was just trying his best to run away.

"You think he's attracted to Lady Diana?"

His father nodded. "It would be hard for him not to be, but we both know his feelings on mating. Of course, fate is fickle. Look at yourself."

"What does that mean?"

His father shook his head. "No, I will not reveal all. I believe you need to accept your fate, and this old man is going to enjoy watching."

He hated when his father talked in riddles, so he decided to change the subject. "I hope to have the wedding tomorrow."

"I would wait for a few days, son. Women do not like to

be rushed."

He frowned. "I need to be working on the investigation."

His father nodded. "You can do that while waiting for the arrangements to be set in place."

He did not like that. Waiting days until he had her in his bed...it would not work for him. He did not know how he would be able to go days without touching her, feeding from her. Nico never had a problem controlling his need to feed. Since he reached his majority, he had a firm hand on his baser needs—sex and feeding. But now, he felt as if he had no control. Even now he wanted her, wanted to taste the sweet blood he had scented. His feeding teeth descended, and not for the first time that night, he had to grind them back up.

"It will just get worse, you know."

He glanced at his father. "What are you talking about now?"

"The need you have for her. It is going to be worse after mating."

Nico did not know how that was possible. Right now, he felt sick from the demands of his body. Worse, every other woman he saw made him almost physically ill. His hands were shaking. It was as if overnight he had lost his desire for any other woman than Cordelia.

"You will have to let go, Nico. Let go of the past, and allow yourself to enjoy having a mate."

They both knew he had reservations about mating and bonding. He had been with his brother near the end. His father had not. He did not want to suffer the same fate. Losing a bonded mate, then slowly dying—there was no way he could endure.

The scent of her blood reached him before he knew she was in the room. He could not see her at first, and he felt the first stirrings of panic. He needed to see her, know she was all right. Then he did, and his body responded.

He had been irritated when he first saw her. The embarrassment that she had not told him of her move had been enough, but seeing her body so exposed almost sent him over the edge. In all the time he had known her, Cordelia had dressed modestly. Her clothes had been a season or two out of fashion, and he liked it that way. The red dress draped over her generous curves brought out a golden hue to her flesh. Her breasts were a little too much on display for his liking. He licked his lips, thinking of tasting the blood that was now calling to him.

His father gave him a nudge. It took every bit of his power to pull his gaze away from Cordelia. He looked at his father, who wore a knowing smile.

"There will be no wedding tomorrow, but from your reaction tonight, I will try to convince your mother it should be sooner. If not, you will make yourself sick."

"Sick?"

"I will talk to you about it later. It seems our women are ready to be entertained by us."

He wanted to push for an explanation, but he decided against it. They were already under the scrutiny of the crowd.

As Cordelia neared him, some of his inner beast seemed to calm. He still wanted her, but the moment she took her place beside him, he felt as if everything settled.

"Do you feel all right, Diana?" Cordelia asked.

It was then he noticed that her sister did not look well at all. She was perspiring, her eyes filled with pain, and her flesh was white.

"I have one of my headaches. I think I need to go home." Instead of the commanding woman he had met earlier, her voice had diminished. Every word she said looked as if it pained her to utter.

"Do you have a carriage?" his father asked.

"Yes. I…" she swallowed. "I guess I am a little more tired than I thought."

"Well, we can go home. You need your rest," Cordelia said.

"No."

Diana paid him no mind, but his parents smiled. Cordelia frowned at him. "She needs someone to take care of her."

"I can get home on my own."

"I will accompany you home, as will Samuel. Nico can use our carriage to accompany Cordelia home," Adelaide said.

Cordelia opened her mouth but he stopped her.

"It is perfectly acceptable for me to do so being your fiancé."

She wanted to argue, he could tell. It was skirting the edge of propriety, but before she could disagree, Lady Diana almost fainted. His father caught her in time to keep her from embarrassment.

"Let me take her home," his mother insisted. "I had the same issue when I was younger, and I know just what kind of medication to give her."

His fiancée looked torn. It amazed him that she would worry so much about a sister who had abandoned her when she was younger, but apparently she did.

"I will take good care of your sister," his mother assured her.

She nodded. "Are you comfortable with leaving me here, Diana? Mrs. Blackburn will take care of you."

Diana must have been in pain because she nodded and accepted his father's arm. He led her out as his mother took Cordelia's hand and squeezed it. "I will take good care of Diana."

With that they left. "I assume you would like to get something to eat."

Cordelia looked at him. "I am not all that hungry."

Before he could insist, a gaggle of matrons arrived. He was sure they were there to find out what was going on between them and what happened to Lady Diana.

He did not move. He stayed, ignoring the pointed glances from the matrons. They wanted him to leave, but it went against everything stirring in his body at that moment.

He had to stay, for his own sanity. Walking away and leaving her would never be an option. When one of the old biddies made a nasty comment, he felt the first stirrings of irritation. As if she sensed it, Cordelia gave him a censoring look. He ground his teeth and fought the need to drag her out of there. He would endure it until they left because then he would have her alone in a carriage.

At the moment, he would do anything for a small taste of her, even if it meant ignoring pointed stares and recrimination from the matrons.

* * * *

Cordelia allowed Nico to hand her into the carriage. She sat as he took the seat opposite of her.

"I would have never believed you would have stayed so long tonight."

He glanced at her. "You were there."

She waited for him to explain more, but he did not. He continued to watch her. For some reason, she had the feeling he was a predator…and she the prey. It was a bit disconcerting, especially since she was trapped inside the carriage with him.

"I have been able to handle myself in ballrooms for years."

His frown turned darker. "Not dressed like that."

"Whatever do you mean?"

He gave a pointed glance at her bosom. "I have never seen you so ready to put yourself on display."

She did not like the dress especially. As she had said earlier, it was too tight, and she did not like having men stare at her chest. Well, most men. When Nico looked at her, something inside her stirred, hot and needy.

"Diana insisted, but she did not realize that well…I have a little more on top."

"Anyone can see that by looking at you."

"Nico!"

"It's the truth, Cordelia. You should have never left the house looking like that. What will people think?"

For a moment, she couldn't think. The rage in his voice should have upset her. She did not like arguing, but for some reason, she felt invigorated by it.

"What will people think?" she asked, allowing the sarcasm to drip from her voice. His eyebrows raised in surprise. "Are you Nicodemus Blackburn? Because the Nico I know doesn't give two wits about what society thinks."

For a second or two, she thought he would yell back at her. Instead, he reached across, grabbed her and pulled her onto his lap.

Chapter Seven

Nico nuzzled Cordelia's neck, his fangs already descended. He wanted to bite, to feed, but he knew he could not do that. For a Carrier, being fed from the first time would be draining in more ways than one. After that, it would be easier, but that first one it was much like losing your virginity.

"Nico," she said again, this time her voice deepening over the syllables. Need threaded every word.

He thought she would push at him at least a little. Instead, she tilted her head to one side to give him better access. He could smell her blood, that sweet liquid calling to him. He grazed her neck, enjoying the moan of pleasure that slipped from her mouth. She was made for this. Centuries of breeding would take control, and he knew he could have her then. Nico knew she did not understand what she was going through, not a virgin. And she could not even recognize her desire to offer nourishment to him.

He pulled back from her neck, then drew her face closer. He kissed her, knowing it would not satisfy either of them. If anything, it would make their dawning need worse. He understood this. She did not. He slanted his mouth over hers, sliding his tongue between her lips. He could taste her then, or at least a bit of her essence, but it was not enough. Pleasure crawled through him as he continued to kiss her. He molded his hand to her breast, enjoying the gasp of surprise mixed with delight. Her nipple was already tight. He moved his thumb over it slowly as he nibbled at her bottom lip. Unable to help himself, he grazed it.

"Oh," she said as he sucked the small drop of blood from it.

Lord, that was a mistake. He had been right. Her blood

was sweet and savory. It danced over his taste buds, and his head started to spin. He had never tasted something so delectable in his life. The tang of her called to him. His craving for her increased. He wanted her beneath him as he plunged into her and drank from her. His cock hardened, beckoning a need for release that he had never had before. It was as if his body already knew this was his mate.

He knew he was losing control of the situation, but for one long moment, he did not care. He wanted her then, needed her. Waiting was not an option.

He tugged on the material of her bodice and freed her breasts. He kissed his way down her neck, grazing but not breaking her skin. He did have enough sense to know that if he sunk his fangs into her, that he would never be able to pull himself back.

He took one of her nipples into his mouth as he pinched the other. She moaned then, his name, and he felt a stirring in his soul that shocked him. The tight reigns of control he held on his baser needs started to sleep. His own blood pounded. His fangs ached to feed.

Then the carriage came to a shuddering stop. It took him a moment to realize they were outside her house, and soon his driver would be knocking on the door.

He gave her nipple one last lick before pulling himself back from her.

Good God, she was a sight. Her hair was slightly mussy, her nipples were still hard with need, and a part of him yearned to damn everyone to hell and take her then.

But that would not do.

He ground his teeth together then pulled up her bodice. "Cordelia, love."

Her eyelids fluttered then she opened them. Deep within her blue eyes, he saw the desire he felt.

"We are at your sister's townhouse."

For a moment she did not react. Then her eyes widened, the passion dissolving into embarrassment.

"Oh, my goodness," she said, her tone still filled with unfulfilled passion. "I-I cannot understand what came over me."

"I do, but we will not worry about that at the moment."

He gave her a sweet kiss, barely brushing his mouth over hers. Even that had his need for her rising. It took all his control to pick her up and move her to the opposite seat. He ground his teeth together, although his fangs did not ascend completely. He wasn't sure that they would until he truly mated with her.

She was busy righting herself as much as possible.

"Just pull your cape over you, and no one will see."

She sighed and did as he instructed.

"Nico...I..."

She seemed to be at a loss for words. When he really looked at her expression, he could read the mortification. For Cordelia, healthy sexual needs would have been seen as something to ignore. Not only did she live in the stifling society of London, she had grown up the daughter of a woman who was notorious for her affairs. He knew it could not be easy for someone like her to deal with the need she had for him.

There was a knock at the door.

"Just a moment, please," he said. He took Cordelia's hands. "What is it?"

"I just want you to know that I have never done anything like that. Well, except for last night. I don't know…"

She raised her hands to her face and covered it. He knew her feelings for him were normal. Their kind would always need sexual satisfaction. But she was not ready to hear it now.

He gently pulled her hands from her face. The unshed tears in her eyes almost unmanned him. She was confused, especially because she did not understand.

"There is nothing wrong with your behavior, Cordelia. It is natural."

She sniffed then looked away. "I really fear that I have turned into my mother."

She said it with such disgust that he felt the need to ease her worries. Nico knew he could not tell her everything. If he were to reveal all to Cordelia, she would panic and run. He would follow, that much he was sure of.

He tightened his grip on her hands. "Look at me." He waited until she lifted her gaze to his. "There is nothing wrong with you for wanting me. Do not ever think less of yourself."

She did not look convinced.

"Tell me this. When you see Malik, do you want him to touch you?"

She actually looked repulsed by the idea. Then she smoothed her expression. "Oh, it is not because he is…from somewhere else."

"I know. What I was alluding to is that you have these feelings for me. You have been in society for a long time, Cordelia."

She frowned. "Not that long."

He smiled at the indignation in her voice. He knew he had hit a nerve. "Tell me, have you ever had a chance to be compromised?"

She sighed. "No."

"Do not doubt the attraction we have for one another. It is good to be this way with your chosen mate."

She studied him for a moment then nodded. "I think I better step out now or we will cause another scandal."

A sense of satisfaction filled him. He might not have wanted a mate, but he had chosen well. He lifted her hands and kissed them.

"But of course."

* * * *

Cordelia looked out over the street from her sister's

bedroom window. She had not slept. She could not. She had felt relieved when she first returned home. After checking on her sister, who was sleeping peacefully, she had changed into her nightdress, slipped into bed exhausted, but found herself unable to sleep.

She had thought she would be too tired to even dream, but she found herself staring at the canopy of her bed. After several wasted hours, she decided to go to Diana's room to watch over her.

Cordelia glanced at her sister's still form. It had been years since she had seen Diana suffer from the headaches. She had assumed she had grown out of them, but now she wondered if Diana had just kept herself in the country because of them.

With a sigh, she looked out over the street again. The sun was just starting to peek over the tops of the houses. The only people she saw were workers hurrying to their jobs for the morning. She was a person happy with her own counsel. Groups of people had always made her nervous. Once Diana had left home, she had spent most of her days by herself. Occasionally, one of the staff would take pity on her and entertain her, but that was not so often. The only reason she had gone out in society was necessity. To eat she had to learn to overcome her misgivings. Truthfully, she would not have a problem abandoning it if she didn't need the money. She always felt hemmed in when she dealt with society. The rules had always been something she never agreed with. Why was it acceptable for her father to have dozens of paramours, but not her mother? But that had not been what had bothered her as much as the feeling of restlessness that moved through her every time she stepped into a ballroom.

And now she had the embarrassing situation of needing Nico. It had taken her a good hour of thinking to realize the reason she was feeling out of sorts was because Nico was not there. He drove her insane with his attitude and his kisses, but there was something in her that resonated with him when he was near. It was as if he soothed her in a way no one else could.

And that thought had scared her. Needing a man was not a position she ever wanted to be in. She had seen what it had done to her sisters.

"Cordelia?" her sister asked weakly.

She rushed to her side and was happy to see that while her sister looked confused, she no longer looked to be in pain.

She hesitated when she reached the bedside then threw caution to the wind and sat on the mattress.

"How are you feeling?"

She sighed and leaned back against the pillows. "Better, though I feel as if I am walking through a fog."

Cordelia nodded, remembering that after an attack, her sister usually spent the day that followed in bed.

"You needed rest from your trip."

Diana glanced at the window.

"Do you mind pulling the curtains shut? My eyes are still sensitive to light."

Cordelia nodded and did as she was bid.

"Did you wait all night here?"

Cordelia shrugged. "I could not sleep."

"Thank you."

She glanced back over her shoulder at her sister. "I thought you did not have spells anymore?"

"Not often. I fear you are correct about the traveling, though."

"You never did learn to slow down when you started feeling bad."

They looked at each other, the room filled with unspoken memories. It was hard to be so formal with her sister now. When she had been growing up, Diana was the one person she shared everything with. Until she left.

"Yes, but you need your sleep. Whatever Mrs. Blackburn gave me last night worked apparently. I do not remember anything after she gave me the concoction to drink. You did not need to watch over me."

The admonition had Cordelia straightening her back. "I apologize. I will leave you alone."

She was almost to the door when Diana stopped her. "Cordelia."

She turned and faced her sister.

Diana gave her a weak smile. "Thank you."

Cordelia nodded and slipped out the door. One of the maids was waiting in the hallway. "I think you need to get my sister some tea and just a bit of bread this morning."

She curtseyed and ran to do Cordelia's bidding. Cordelia made her way to her room. If she had hoped that Diana and she would forge a new relationship, she would have been disappointed. But for the most part, she had not expected it. If anything, she had expected her sister to notify her brother of her situation. She shut the door behind her and leaned against it for a moment.

Cordelia stood there trying to understand her problem with sleeping. She had not had a good night's rest in two nights. First, the worry of being compromised. Then, last night. It could have been the surroundings that kept her awake. Cordelia did not do well in new surroundings. Before leaving her family's estate to come to London, she'd only left there on occasion during her childhood. She was truly a country mouse, one who could care less about the city. But it had been a necessity. Her brother's drinking was getting out of hand. Not to mention the parties he was throwing. The earl had been bad, but nothing like the debauchery her brother was now hosting on the estate. There was a time or two she had worried not only about her virtue, but sometimes her life.

She brushed the unpleasant memories away and walked to her bed. She would try to sleep, but she was not sure it would come. The moment she slipped into bed, her muscles relaxed, her mind easing. She was almost asleep when she thought she felt arms wrap around her. The warmth surrounded her, and her body drifted off to sleep...but not before she registered the scent of bay rum.

* * * *

Nico settled on the bed next to Cordelia. He knew he was breaking rules. As usual, he didn't care. Truthfully, he wasn't quite sure what he thought he was going to do when he snuck into the house. It had been embarrassingly easy, but it usually was for him. Humans saw only what they wanted.

All he knew is he needed to be there. Even as his body yearned for release he knew would not come, he felt a strange comfort move through him.

He had spent the night talking to Malik, then pacing his own room. Then, at dawn, he had given up. He'd walked to her sister's townhouse.

"Nico?" she asked sleepily.

He froze. "Yes, love."

"Oh, good."

Then she relaxed completely into sleep with a small smile on her face. He glanced at the door, noting that she had locked it when she came in. Something most women of her station would never do, but he had a feeling he knew why.

He wanted to beat the bloody hell out of everyone in her family, but he let it go. Instead he settled his head back down on the pillow, sighed with contentment, and drifted into sleep with her.

* * * *

Cordelia came awake slowly. She stretched her arms over her head. She could not believe how fast she had fallen asleep after going to bed. Two sleepless nights had apparently caught up to her. She shifted her leg and hit something...another leg. A scream vibrated in her throat when a hand slipped over her mouth. She noted the scent of bay rum, and she knew then it was Nico in her bed.

"I would suggest you do not alert the entire household," he said, his mouth pressing against her ear. "Our announcement just hit the papers. More gossip would be very trying."

She nodded, and he released her. She slipped out of bed and frowned at him. His hair was a mess, and he had a day's growth of beard.

"What in heaven's name are you doing here?"

His gaze slid over her, slowly working its way down her body then back again. She realized she was wearing her plain nightdress, but it was definitely easy to see through. Heat filled her face as she grabbed her robe. After slipping it on, she felt better. The smirk he gave her told her it didn't matter.

"Are you going to answer me?"

He sat up, and she realized then he was bare chested. She was mesmerized. She had never seen a man up close and almost naked. His chest was broad and muscled, with a spattering of hair over his golden flesh. The hair trailed down his stomach. When she found herself wondering just how far the trail went, she blushed and glanced up at his face. He was smiling.

"If you are going to look at me like that, you better get back in the bed."

Her face got even hotter.

"I will repeat. What are you doing here?"

He sighed then mumbled something.

"What?"

"I couldn't sleep."

She blinked at the anger she heard simmering in his voice.

"You couldn't sleep, so you broke into my sister's townhouse? You are not making any sense."

He looked as if he wanted her to shut up. When he stood, she covered her eyes.

He chuckled. "I'm wearing trousers."

She peeked through her fingers and dropped her hands as soon as she realized he was telling the truth.

"So, you broke in here to sleep with me? Wearing your trousers?"

He said nothing as he slipped on his shirt.

"Nico."

He glanced at her. "First, I told you. I could not sleep. I went out for a walk and found myself at your sister's door. Secondly, I was wearing my trousers because if I had been naked, you would not be standing there complaining to me."

Irritation slapped her hard. He was in her room, without invitation, and he had the nerve to sound aggravated with the conversation?

She settled her hands on her waist. "And just what do you think would happen?"

"You would be beneath me moaning my name," he said in a near shout.

For a moment, she could not think. His shirt was still gaping open, and he had started to stalk her. She felt her eyes widen as she stepped back.

"I-I think you should leave now." Even as she said it, her stomach threatened to revolt.

"Do you?" he asked as she came up against the wall.

"Y-yes."

He slapped his palms against the wall on either side of her head.

"I think you don't. In fact, I can hear your heart beat. I know that right now, heat is rushing through your blood."

He nuzzled her neck much as he had the night before in the carriage. She thought she felt a scrape of his teeth, and she shuddered.

"Good God, woman, you have no idea what you are doing to me. I cannot sleep, I cannot feed…I need you so badly."

She barely heard the words. His voice had dipped lower, and his breath heated her flesh. Never in her life had she felt this from anyone. A completely delectable man wanted her, needed her, he said. Something unfurled in her belly as heat shot through her blood just as he said.

She turned her head and met his lips. It was so delicious, kissing, feeling the way his tongue darted into her mouth. He kissed her as if she were the only nourishment he needed. Slowly, she lifted her hands to his shoulders. She slipped her fingers beneath his shirt and laid her palms on his skin. He was hot, as if he were burning with fever.

He muttered against her mouth and deepened the kiss. Over and over he thrust his tongue into her mouth. She wanted this, needed to feel his skin next to hers. Something in her seemed to rejoice the moment she felt the bit of teeth against her tongue. Her mouth still hurt from where he had bit it the night before, but she didn't care.

It was primal, she knew that. Any other time she would be embarrassed or ashamed, but with Nico, she seemed not to care. Instead, she felt her body urging her to take, to be taken. She pressed against him.

Then, just as she was about to demand satisfaction—although she had no idea what that meant—there was a knock at her door.

"Lady Cordelia?"

She recognized the butler's voice.

Nico growled as he pulled himself back from her.

"Yes?"

"There is a Mrs. Blackburn downstairs. She said she is your intended's mother and that she wants to talk with you."

Nico had rested his forehead against her shoulder, and he cursed under his breath but she could make out the words.

"Tell her I will be down shortly."

"I think you should tell her to go away," Nico whispered, his mouth against her ear.

"Lady Cordelia?" the butler said.

"I will be ready in a few moments."

She could sense he hesitated, but he finally left. When

she heard his retreating footsteps, she let out a sigh.

"Why did you say you would be downstairs?"

She looked at Nico, who was now staring at her. His gaze was hot. Her body responded to what she saw there. She wanted him, needed him, just as he apparently needed her.

"I cannot tell your mother to go away."

"Then I will," he said and spun away from her.

"Nico!" she grabbed his shirttails. "You cannot go down there and tell your mother to leave. This isn't your house."

He leaned his head against the door and took two long breaths.

"All right. I will accept that." He turned to face her. "I will wait one more day. That is it, Cordelia."

He stuffed his shirt into his trousers, slipped his boots on, then his jacket.

"How do you plan on escaping unnoticed?"

He said nothing for a moment, then he stepped forward and kissed her. It was long, wet, and she sagged against him when he was done. Then he stepped back and grabbed his walking stick.

"One more night." He opened the French doors to her terrace.

"What are you doing?"

"I am going out the way I came in." He climbed up onto the stone railing. "Tonight is the last night I sleep alone. You make the choice. You can do it as my fiancée or my wife."

Then he stepped back off the railing. A scream strangled her as she rushed forward. When she reached the edge, she saw him below in her sister's garden. He gave her a cocky salute, and then turned to walk away.

Her heart was still beating hard against her breast, and she felt a little lightheaded. Cordelia watched him until he turned the corner, then she sagged against the railing.

"Bloody hell," she whispered as she closed her eyes. "What have I gotten myself into?"

Chapter Eight

Nico stepped into the foyer of his townhouse, somewhat energized from his walk and the time spent with Cordelia. Even though they had not mated, their bodies were already in tune with each other. It was normal since he had chosen her to be his mate, but he didn't think it would happen so quickly. He was thinking about his wedding night as he turned the corner. He came to an abrupt halt. His father and Malik stood as if waiting for him. The expressions on their faces told him they knew where he had been.

"Nico, I believe your mother told you to stay away from your bride."

Malik chuckled. "Your son has had a problem with her from the first."

"Just what do you mean by that?" Nico asked.

"I have a feeling our friend means that if you could have controlled yourself to begin with, you would not be planning a wedding," his father said.

"And I thought both you and mother were happy with that particular development."

"Yes, but you have usually had better control of your needs than you have with your bride-to-be. It might be a good sign. I hope that your mother was able to take her out shopping today. The first feeding with a Carrier can be quiet tiring."

"Nothing happened."

His father's eyebrows rose. "Indeed? I don't think I asked."

"You did not. Now, he is sounding rather defensive about his actions, which makes me think he is lying," Malik said.

He looked from one man to the other, not even trying to

hide his exasperation. "Do you truly think I would be here now if I had actually taken her? Give me at least the respect to know we would still be in bed."

He brushed past them and into his study. It was midafternoon, too early for a drink. Well, if his mother had not been in residence it wouldn't be, but Adelaide Blackburn had rules. One of them was no liquor before five in the evening. So, he would not drink. Although he desperately needed one. For the first time in his life, he suppressed the urge to ignore his mother's rules. When he heard their footsteps following him, he fought the need to curse.

"Gray sent around a note saying that Hurst's family was looking for him," Malik said.

Needing to concentrate on anything other than the woman who was driving him insane at the moment, he turned his attention to that.

"Did they show up at his house?"

Malik shook his head. "He heard it through Alistair."

"Saint is in town?" Nico asked, a bit alarmed. Nico's distant cousin avoided all of society, even in the little village he lived in.

"I asked him to come," his father said. "We might need him. He agrees with us that there is something going on."

"But…it's Saint," he said, shaking his head.

"We won't let him out in society," his father said with amusement. "He has always tried to avoid it, as you know, and since he has come into the title, he truly avoids it. We need him for his underworld contacts. He will be able to get more information than you can. It's going to be worse once you get married."

Nico frowned. "I do not see that as a disruption."

His father shared a look with Malik. His friend turned to him. "I am going to go over to Gray's and check on the patient."

"Wait, what did he do about Hurst's family?"

"He sent around a note and told them that he fell ill and

was making a speedy recovery."

Malik nodded to Nico's father and left them alone.

"Dammit. I should have taken care of sending a note around to his family."

"You have been preoccupied, and it was better coming from Gray. People will question you. They will not question a duke."

Nico nodded.

"And there is nothing wrong with being preoccupied by a woman." His father's tone was light, but Nico sensed something serious beneath it.

"Not now. Not when there is so much at stake. I need to focus on the hunt. I have been here almost a fortnight and have gotten nowhere."

"Yes, you have. You know now that this person is moving within the *ton* in some way. I talked to Malik about it. Saint is going to search in some of the places you cannot go."

"Is that an order?"

His father chuckled. "Son, I know now that you will not be able to go to a whorehouse any more than I can. First, you don't want to. Secondly, I have a feeling once you mate with Cordelia, she will become a walking terror like your mother." He studied Nico for a few moments. "It has been a few hundred years since we have had something like this. We will prevail."

"How do you know?"

"In all our history, we have never lost. We might have lost a few of our people. We all must move to our afterlife at some point. Good will always prevail. Do not worry. And it is important to have more of your generation building families. Too many of you have waited too long."

He heard the admonition in his father's voice. He knew he deserved it, and until now, he had not had the urge. "Now you have a mate."

He nodded.

"You could not sleep without her by your side, correct?"

He glanced at his father then settled in the chair behind his desk. "It is insane. I have never slept with her until this morning."

"This morning?"

"She spent the night by her sister's side."

"Ah," his father said, nodding. "She is a good woman. I am confused as to why she is not married. But English society only sees what they want to see."

"Yes," he said. "Wait, what do you mean by that?"

His father shrugged as he pulled out a cheroot. "Do you mind? Your mother hates them, and since she is out shopping with Cordelia, I think this might be the only time I have a chance to do this."

He nodded. "What were you saying about English society?"

His father lit the cheroot and then puffed a few times. "Well, human society truthfully. They only look at the surface. This generation is worse than any other I have known. Although, my generation was quite obtuse. Your mother was considered a wallflower."

"Mother?" he shook his head. His mother was not a flashy woman, but she demanded the attention of most men when she walked into a room. Even humans were drawn to her, but that was usual of such a powerful Carrier.

His father smiled. "She was a bit. Orphaned, no family to look out for her, much like Cordelia. She has family, but they did not do her any good. I am not sure what would have happened if we had not found each other. But, your mother came alive when I made her my mate."

"Came alive?"

"Carriers can be flamboyant but many of them can hide it well. Their true beauty will shine easily as they move into our society, but they make sure that most humans do not sense it. And those are the ones to beware of, Nicodemus. Cordelia is a wonderful young woman from what I can tell.

Be careful of her."

"You think that she would hurt me or do something wrong?"

"No. But if you ignore her for what she is, what she makes you, you will regret it. Believe me, there was a point in my life I almost lost your mother. Value Cordelia. Know that she is all that is important in your world."

"I do not think that a woman should control my every thought."

"Oh, my son, you are in for such a challenge with Cordelia, but I will enjoy it. And you will be a stronger man for it. Now, I am going to have a little nap before your mother returns. I understand the wedding will be tomorrow."

Nico nodded.

His father smiled, "Good. I would probably join Malik over at Gray's if I were you. There is much to discuss, and I would go but the young duke is intimidated by my presence for some reason."

He looked at his father and smiled. Of course, his father did not understand why someone like Gray would be in awe of him. Seven hundred fifty years old, a leader in the Alliance, and if anything, the stories of his role in their history had been downplayed.

"I am going to go wash up and go over there and talk to Malik and Gray, see if we can gain any more information from Hurst."

"Are you positive the Made was yelling *Suprema*?"

Just having the question put to him brought the memory back of killing the Made. Even now he felt ill. "Positive. There was no mistaking."

"You know the history of that, of the idea there would be one *Suprema*?"

Nico nodded. It was not truly talked about on the council. The Alliance would like to pretend that nothing was wrong. The majority of them. It made it worse that his father and Gray's remembered the last time it happened. One vampire, one army, total control. *Suprema*. The Alliance had been born out of that experience, but all of them seemed to think that they were above it.

"I understand the problem father. Just as you said, we will prevail."

His father nodded and left him alone.

* * * *

By the time Nico arrived at Gray's he was feeling sluggish again. He had several hours sleep, but for some reason, he was now tired again. He knew he needed to feed, but of course, he would have to wait until tomorrow for that. It was an overcast day in London, so at least the sun wasn't draining his energy. He followed the footman up the stairs to the room where they were keeping Hurst. When he walked into the room, he was surprised to see the man sitting up and eating. He still looked ill, but he no longer looked as if he were going to die.

"Good morning, Blackburn," Gray said. "I have your license."

"Good."

"Yes, very important as his bride might have second thoughts," Malik said, smiling.

"Sod off," Nico said with little heat. He looked at the viscount. "How are you doing this morning?"

"Somewhat better, considering that my life was completely transformed in one night."

Nico nodded as he sat in the chair opposite of Hurst. "You are lucky, though."

Hust's eyes narrowed. "Please enlighten me, Blackburn. I am lucky? I have to live a life I never wanted."

He could sympathize with the man. Having your entire world turned upside down with no hope of returning to your former life had to be hell. The defiant look on his face stopped Nico from saying just that. Hurst might still appear half dead, but he did not want sympathy.

"And don't patronize me as the duke has tried. I had my life set up for me just the way I wanted it. Now, I have to skulk around and look for women to feed off of or I will die. What kind of life is that?"

Nico opened his mouth to explain that they had dispensaries where women were paid for their blood, but Malik interrupted him.

"Well, isn't that just so sad for the viscount?" Sarcasm dripped from his voice, his anger easy to see. Malik always had a bad temper, but he usually controlled it. Malik knew how Borns viewed him so he did everything he could not to show it. But Nico knew better than most that Hurst had struck a chord. "Poor man has to adjust the way he lives his life. Such a pity."

Hurst gave Malik a malicious look, but Nico knew nothing would happen. On a good day, when the viscount was fully well, he could not beat Malik in a fight. Now, though, the viscount could barely walk by himself.

"And don't whine to me about it. I'm Made like you. Want to know how many years? Hundreds. I had no choice just like you. You want to know what happens to Mades who are not saved? They become animals."

Hurst swallowed. "Is that so different from what I am now?"

"You think it can't get worse? Well, ask Blackburn about the one he had to kill recently. He became a beast, unable to control his urges, both sexual and appetite. They became one in his mind. The Made that Nico killed was in the process of raping an eighteen-year-old virgin, who then died from the attack. You think that would be better?"

Hurst said nothing, but Nico could tell from his expression he was horrified. They had told him a bit of their world, but they had not disclosed what could have happened if they had not saved him.

"If it wasn't for us, you would be hunting right now,

unable to control what you do," Malik said. "Worse, you would be damned to hell so once you died, which would happen in the next few weeks, you would spend eternity paying for your sins. You were the one who went to the whorehouse, the one who put himself in the situation. So, please, spare us your whining."

With that, Malik shot up out of the chair and stomped out of the room. Nico followed him out, knowing that when Malik was in one of these moods, he could be deadly to anyone who got in his path. He caught up with him in the hallway and grabbed him by the sleeve.

"Settle it down, old man."

He gave Nico a nasty look.

"Remember, you already scare most of the Borns and society. If you go around looking like that, you will definitely allow their fear of the Mades to grow. Whether you like it or not, you are considered one of the elite of the Mades. If you lose it, they will definitely turn on your kind."

Malik pulled his arm free of Nico's grip, but he did not leave. Instead, as Nico had seen hundreds of times before, his friend closed his eyes and took a few calming breaths. When he opened his eyes, he was still mad, but Nico knew he had a firm grip on his temper.

"I could not help it. Sitting there complaining like a little boy who has had his favorite toy taken away."

Disgust dripped from every word. "I don't disagree with you or what you said. I think he needed it."

Malik's lips twitched. "Is that right? You would not have been so blunt."

"No, but he needed it. He was acting like a boy in short pants. He is the only boy in the family, and his father is ill and will not last long. He has been treated like a prince most of his life. So, I agree, this was good for him."

Malik nodded.

"You seem out of sorts. I thought you went to bed early since you disappeared from the ball so fast."

"You know I can never take those gatherings." He made a sound of disgust. "I hate the upper classes and their idiocy."

Nico almost smiled, but from the look on his friend's face, it would have not been prudent.

"So, it had nothing to do with Lady Diana?"

Malik shook his head.

"Well, it is just as well. She seems a little...delicate."

"She's as delicate as a fishwife."

Nico cocked his head to one side and studied his friend. "I just assumed she was because she became so ill last night."

"What do you mean?" Malik asked, his words whipping out. His friend was truly interested in the woman.

"The heat of the ball apparently was too much to take. She took to her bed."

"Has she seen a doctor?"

"Mother took care of her."

Malik's eyes narrowed. "I do not have time for this. I am off to my bed. Tomorrow is going to be a very trying day."

Nico smiled as he watched Malik retreat down the hallway until he disappeared from his sight.

Nico made his way back to the room. They were going to have to work with Hurst on his memory. He did not want him to remember what he went through. The turning of a Made was not pleasant. Nico had never seen it, but he had heard the description from others. It wasn't easy for the human to change his biological makeup into one of their kind. Being almost drained completely of blood, then slowly coming back to life...it wasn't something he wanted to contemplate.

The door to the room opened before he reached it. Gray stuck his head out. "He's back in bed again."

He slipped into the hall and motioned with his head for Nico to follow him. He couldn't help but smile at Gray's behavior. Nico might be the top of the pecking line within the Alliance, but his friend was a duke in society. Some things one could not shake off.

He showed him into a parlor and shut the doors behind them.

"He still remembers nothing of the change."

Nico nodded. "And hopefully, he never will."

"But, he did remember what gaming hell he was in that night."

"Hell? I thought he was at a whorehouse."

"He remembers playing cards with a strange man. Said he had dark black hair, average height, and blue eyes."

Nico snorted. "That describes half of London."

"No. He said his eyes were a strange color...like ours."

Nico's blood quickened. "Ah, he met up with one of us, maybe the one who turned him or the one who is collecting them for someone else. What else did he remember?"

"He played hazard for a while, then everything becomes foggy."

"That is very good. What hell was it?"

"Devil's Temptation."

Nico rolled his eyes. "Humans."

"I am not so sure that it is a human who owns it. There are a lot of rumors about the true owner."

"What kind of rumors?"

"Just the usual, about where the man obtained his money, and no one knows his name. He calls himself 'Devil.'"

"As I said before, humans." He shook his head. "I guess we need to make a trip there tonight."

"No, you can't."

"What do you mean?"

"First, you are too conspicuous. Everyone in our world will recognize you and know that your father is more than likely hunting the killer." He crossed his arms over his chest. "Besides that, you are getting married tomorrow, Blackburn. I have a feeling your fiancé will not take kindly to rumors of you at a hell the night before you marry."

Nico rolled his shoulders, trying to ease his irritation.

"Bloody hell. Okay, so who should we send?"

"Malik said your cousin is in town. Everyone knows his name, but they do not know him by sight. He would probably be very good to send in."

He nodded. "I will have father discuss it with him."

And at the moment, he felt so very tired. He had never been one for daytime hours, but he could not remember getting this tired.

"I should return home to see if there are any more sightings."

He turned to leave, but Gray stopped him.

"Are you forgetting something, Blackburn?"

He stopped with his hand on the knob. "I cannot think what it is. We have someone looking out for attacks in most areas, even in Scotland."

Gray shook his head and picked up a piece of paper. "Your license for tomorrow. Oh, and I arranged to have the Bishop of Canterbury do the ceremony."

He took the paper. "Of course. Thank you."

It wasn't until he made it to the street that the enormity of how his life had changed hit him. He strode down the cobblestones, wanting a good walk to clear his head. He had never thought to mate. For his kind, sex and feeding were normal, and in their classes, it was not looked down upon for a woman not to be a virgin. They understood the needs of everyone, including Carriers.

He was amazed that Cordelia had made it this long without losing hers. Her Carrier status must have been recognized by others. And she had spent many years within the *ton*, but apparently, she had been able to hide from them.

He'd been walking several blocks, thinking of their next moves with the investigation, when he noticed a figure following him. The sun was beginning to sink behind the buildings. The ominous feeling was one he knew well. He increased his pace a bit and turned a corner. Then he flattened himself against the wall of the building, waiting for whoever was following him. He saw the faint shadow appear and readied himself for a fight. He pulled his knife from his boot and stepped out. In the next instant, he felt the slam of a fist and he fell back, landing against the cobblestones hard. His vision wavered then slowly faded to black.

Chapter Nine

"Come on, Blackburn, open up those pretty blue eyes of yours," said someone with a thick Scottish brogue. His head was aching, his body throbbing from what would surely be bruises up and down his back. Slowly, he lifted his eyes. At first, everything looked blurry, as if he needed spectacles, then his vision focused and he found his cousin leaning over him.

"Ah, there you go, sleeping beauty."

"You bastard," Nico said and smacked him upside the head.

"Dammit, Nico." He lifted his massive hand to his ear and winced, but he did back off so Nico could lift himself off the ground. "I can't believe you boxed my ear like when we were kids. Don't you know how to fight like a man?"

He ignored Saint's diatribe because Nico refused to be drawn into an argument with him. There was nothing he liked to do more than argue. Well, other than shun most living beings. He was a big man, bigger than even Nico, and a head taller than Malik. As with most Highlanders, he did a lot of work outside, even if he was Laird of his clan. His bushy beard hid his face, and the dark auburn hair was several inches beyond what was fashionable and definitely in need of a comb. Nico understood why most people thought he was a beast.

"What are you doing hitting me for no reason?" Nico asked.

"You had a knife."

Nico rolled his eyes and felt the back of his head. It was damp with a little blood, and he could already fill the beginning of a lump. "Why were you following me?"

"I wasn't following you. I was catching up to you. I went

by that duke's house and you had already left. So I followed the path I assumed you would take home. The fact that you were walking down the street daydreaming about your wedding night is not my fault." His frown turned blacker. "You should be more careful, Nico."

The fact that his cousin was correct did not mean he had to agree with him.

"What did you need?" he asked as he started on his way and his cousin fell into step.

"Your viscount was in a hell a few nights ago."

"We know."

"Well, why the bloody hell am I skulking around looking up information? I told your father I didn't want to come down here, and now you have me running around for no good reason."

Nico glanced at him. "We just found out. He remembered playing cards with the owner."

"He knows his name? No one seems to know."

"No. He assumed he was the owner. He remembered calling him Devil."

His cousin snorted. "Humans." He spat the word out as if it were poison. Saint hated all of man and vampkind, but he definitely hated humans more.

He nodded and then winced immediately. Pain filtered throughout his head, and he felt the beginnings of a headache. "Indeed, but I am wondering if this one is a Born. He mentioned he remembered his eyes being our shade of blue. Not that humans don't have them, but a little bit of a coincidence, yes?"

"I agree. I am going to go back around tonight. The owner was not out in the hell last night, but I think he was there."

"Do you need backup?"

He snorted. "Really, Nico, you ask the silliest questions."

They reached his townhouse, and he stopped to look at

his cousin. Just because he was big did not mean he could handle the Born who was turning humans.

"You need to be careful, Saint. The Born we are dealing with doesn't give a wit about what he is doing. I cannot for the life of me understand his actions. But, know this, the Born doing this is at a level of depravity that neither of us will ever truly understand."

Saint studied him for a moment. "I understand depravity."

"Not this kind. Think of the kind of Born this has to be. He thinks nothing of turning the men…he does not even try to help them. He unleashes them on society, and I have a feeling he gets some kind of enjoyment out of watching them fall into their Blood Lust. He is not to be taken lightly."

Saint nodded.

Nico drew in a deep breath then let it out. He could not let this Born get to him. That is when he would make a mistake. "Why don't you come in for a bite to eat?"

He shook his head. "I need to feed before going back out tonight."

Nico smiled. "Might it be that you're afraid of what my mother will do to you when she finds out you knocked me out?"

His skin paled. "Of course not."

Saint was only afraid of one thing. No beast or man could make him quiver in fear like Adelaide Blackburn.

"You will be at the wedding."

It was not a request, and from the look on his cousin's face, he knew it. "Your father already informed me that I needed to be there."

"Good, we need a show of solidarity."

Saint shrugged. "I'm off."

And with that, he left. As Nico walked up the stairs to his house, he thought of his cousin and his reasons for coming to London. Just the idea that he had come to London was disturbing enough. He rarely left the small village where he lived and avoided just about every person. While the Blackburns might have avoided society, they did not avoid the regular gatherings throughout the year for the Alliance. Saint and his family did. Always.

He shut the door behind him and realized that his energy was completely drained. No one was around save for a footman.

"Tell my father and mother that I am staying in this evening."

The young man nodded, and Nico decided that for once, he was going to indulge in a long night of sleeping. Lord knew that he would need his rest for the day ahead.

* * * *

"Do you know anyone here?" Diana asked Cordelia as they looked out over the ballroom. The wedding guests seemed to be enjoying the festivities. Champagne was flowing and the food seemed to be never ending.

She glanced at her sister then at the milling crowd. "I know you."

Out of the corner of her eye, Cordelia thought she saw her sister's lips twitch. "What I meant is do you know any of these people, other than the ones you have introduced me to?"

Cordelia shook her head. "No."

When she was a girl, she had spun dreams and fantasies about what her wedding day would be. The dress Adelaide had ordered was a vision and something any woman would want. Pale ivory, simple in its design, but it made her feel beautiful. The silk clung to her body, and the shade was perfect for her skin tone. Adelaide had known exactly what she was doing. Cordelia brushed her hand against the fabric and delighted in its sleek feel. Any woman would be thrilled to have a dress designed by Monique.

Something tickled the back of her throat again. That

panic had been plaguing her since she had found herself compromised.

She took a deep breath and looked up. Her sister was correct. Cordelia barely knew a soul in the room. She had walked herself down the aisle since there had been no one to give her away. The only family member she had at her side barely knew her.

She was a stranger at her own wedding.

Tears burned the back of her eyes. For the first time in years, she ached to have someone she could share things with. Her sister was not someone Cordelia could tell her secrets to. Not anymore.

She blinked and brought herself back to the present. Her sister was staring at her oddly, and she realized she had spent several minutes standing there without saying anything.

"I know some of these people. Or I should say, I know of them, who they are. They are a bit above my social circle. And, of course, everyone knows Gray."

Cordelia glanced at Nico's friend who was surrounded by a group of men. No matter where Gray went, there seemed to be people following him. It was a bit embarrassing how many matchmaking mamas seemed to try to get his attention.

"I met him the other night. He helped with our…situation. He is the highest ranking member in the room. Although I sense that he defers to Nico for some reason."

Her sister glanced at her, then back out at the people. "I do not think you understand just how powerful your husband is."

"Of course I do. He controls a lot of the aristocracy because his family has lent money to most of them. And many of them still owe him."

Diana shook her head as her eyes grew shadowed. "It is not only that. Do you see how these people react to him? He gave them less than three day's notice of the wedding, but here they are. And they come from different factions within society."

"Most of them have a title in front of their name."

The sharp look her sister gave her told Cordelia she heard the irritation in her voice. "You have a title."

"A lot of good it did me."

"That's true," she conceded. "But never forget that you have the blood of the Earls of Collingsworth flowing through your veins."

She turned to face her sister. "Have you been drinking?"

"Whatever do you mean by that?"

"If you want to pretend that I wasn't the bastard of the family, that's okay, but do not ever throw me in with the rest of you. I find it annoying."

Diana opened her mouth to argue with her, but Nico came to her rescue.

"Darling, I have some family I need to introduce you to." He lifted her hand to his mouth, brushing his lips over her flesh. When he looked up at her, the banked fires she had seen in his eyes earlier were still simmering. When he straightened, he did not relinquish her hand. Instead, he pulled it to his arm and faced Diana. She did not miss the silent message he was giving her sister. He let her know that he was by her side now that she was his wife. She swallowed and blinked a few times. It had been so many years since someone had taken the time to protect her, and Nico seemed to have been doing it since the night of the ball.

"I hope you do not mind if I steal her away, do you, Diana? My mother was looking for you. She wanted to talk to you about something, but I am not quite sure what."

Diana looked like she wanted to argue, but Nico had made it impossible.

She studied them for a moment, and Cordelia wondered what was going through her mind. There was something in her expression that Cordelia could not decipher. After a long pause, she nodded.

"Of course."

Nico lead her through the crowd, and once again, she noticed people moved out of his way without even realizing it.

"Thank you."

His lips twitched. "For what?"

"For saving me. I was not in the mood to hear about how wonderful it is to be related to my brother and the rest of the family."

"You think I saved you? I think not. I was worried about your sister. You looked like you wanted to hit her. And while we did marry under a scandalous cloud, I did not want a scene at the reception. I believe that might be too much for my mother to accept."

For a moment, she didn't know what to say, then she chuckled.

"Ah, I like the sound of that. It is your wedding day, my bride. You should be happy."

"Of course."

He led her over to a gaggle of men and women and started to introduce her. They had a receiving line, but many of these people had been late. When he got to the end of the line, a massive man dressed in a kilt stepped forward. She had to lean her head back to be able to see his face. She thought Nico was tall and powerful, but this man was amazing.

"Saint, I would like you to meet my bride, Lady Cordelia. Cordelia, this is my cousin, Alistair the Earl of St James."

"Oh," she said, recognizing the name. "So wonderful to meet you."

He looked at her, his eyes the same shade as Nico's, but somehow mesmerizing. His unbelievably long auburn hair was slicked back and tied behind his head. Then his lips curved, and he smiled. He had been an attractive man before, but now he was stunning.

He took her hand and raised it to his mouth. Unlike his cousin, he kissed just above her skin. "It is I who should be saying that. I did not know what to expect when I found out Nico was getting married, but I would say that he picked well."

His Scottish burr was so heavy it was very difficult to understand him, but for Cordelia it did not matter. The accent was enough to entrance her.

"That's enough of that, Saint." Nico huffed. "And you can let go of my bride's hand."

His cousin's smile widened as if he knew what he was doing.

He released her hand then glanced around the room. "I understand you have a sister?"

She nodded. "She is with Mrs. Blackburn."

"Do not bother, cousin."

Saint shook his head. "No worries, Nico. I just want to see what had Malik so enthralled. By the by, I will be stopping by tomorrow to discuss my findings."

Before he could leave, Nico stopped him. "Talk to my father. I do not know if I will be in tomorrow."

The tone in his voice told her he didn't plan on leaving their bedroom.

Saint gave him a salute and wandered off, apparently in search of her sister.

"I cannot believe you said that to him."

Nico gave her a lopsided smile that had her heart seizing. It lightened his usually serious expression. It made him look years younger, as if he did not have a care in the world. How did a woman deal with that?

"If I hadn't, he would have been here early in the day wanting to discuss business."

"And what did he mean about your friend Malik? And why do you keep calling me your bride?"

"First, Malik was a little...taken by your sister."

"Really?" She searched the room for her sister. She

found her next to Adelaide. Then she looked for Malik. He was across the room with a few men, but he watched as Saint ambled up to them and did the pretty. It only took a few seconds before Malik was making his way over to her sister. "I would have never guessed."

"Well, he is. I am not sure what he is going to do about it."

"I can assure you there will be nothing from Diana. I might not know my sister well, but I do know that she will not marry again."

Nico nodded.

"And the bride moniker?" she asked.

"You are my bride."

"I am also your wife."

His lips curved slowly, and the heat in his eyes flared hotter. *Lord.*

"You are not my wife yet."

She swallowed as her heart started a wild tattoo against her chest.

"Oh?"

He nodded without taking his gaze from hers. He leaned closer, so close that she could feel the heat of him. "But you will be by tomorrow morning."

If her face could get hotter, Cordelia was sure she would die. She could not form a word in response. He had dissolved every thought from her head.

"Nico, I need to talk to you."

It was Gray who stood beside them, but neither of them acknowledged him.

"Blackburn."

She tore her gaze from his and realized that something was bothering the young duke. "Nico, Gray needs you."

She could tell her husband did not care, but he did look at Gray. When he saw his expression, Nico's entire manner changed.

"I will return shortly, love," he kissed her hand as his

mother and Diana appeared by her side.

"Everything will be all right, Cordelia," her mother-in-law said.

She nodded, agreeing with her mother-in-law though not knowing what she was talking about.

"Why don't we get a drink and talk to some of Nico's aunts?"

She agreed, but she could not seem to stop worrying about the look on Gray's face. Just what did the duke want to talk to Nico about? She glanced at the hallway where Nico and Gray had disappeared.

She had a feeling that she would never truly know her husband.

* * * *

The door shut behind Gray, and Nico was surprised to find that his father and Malik were already in attendance.

"What is going on?" he asked.

"There has been another attack," his father said.

"Where?"

"Mayfair." His father shook his head. "This Born is getting more and more gutsy. The fact that we know now of two peers of the realm who have been changed…I wonder how many more have? This is not a good development."

"Did the Made get taken care of?" Nico asked.

"Yes, he's dead, thanks to the woman he attacked."

"She's a Carrier?" Nico wondered how a woman was able to fight off a Made in Blood Lust.

"Yes, and an earl's daughter. Lady Elizabeth," Gray answered.

"Lord. She killed him?"

Gray nodded. "She is not all that well after the attack. He raped her, or at least started, but she had taken to carrying a stake with her apparently. She struck him in the chest."

"Where is she now?" Malik asked.

"She is at Doctor Bingam's house. He is caring for her."

"For her sake, we need to keep this quiet," his father said. "Do you think we should have your mother take care of her?"

"She will need a woman, and Bingam is a confirmed bachelor," Malik said.

He nodded. "What did you do with the Made? Was he someone we know?"

Gray's lip curved in disgust. "Yes, that damned Baron Walton."

"Ah." The baron was known for his debauchery. He had even been rumored to have injured a few whores...one he was said to have killed. He was one man Nico had refused to lend money to. He was filthy, but because of his title he was allowed to do what he wanted.

"Well, no one deserved it more than he did. I have a feeling knowing the baron that he was in the Devil's Temptation."

Just then, the door opened slowly, and a head popped in. It was Saint, and he didn't look happy.

He slipped in and closed the door behind him. "Not nice leaving me out there with all the Carriers trying to match up their daughters." He apparently sensed the mood. "What happened?"

"Another attack," Nico said. "The woman survived. The man did not."

Saint's eyes widened. "Truth? I don't know if a woman has ever survived one of those attacks. Can you think of any Samuel?"

His father shook his head. "Not only that, she fought him off and killed him."

"The Made was taken care of, but he is definitely the kind of man who would frequent the hells," Nico pointed out. "It would be best to really infiltrate that one. We need more people."

His father shook his head. "The Alliance will not give us

any more."

"Then we need to find them," Nico said. "I can think of a few tonight we need to talk to."

"No, you don't, son." He glanced at his father. "I know more than anything you want to find the bastard who is doing this, but you are married and until you mate with her, you will be off your game."

Saint chuckled. Nico shot him a quelling glance.

"It is true, Nico," Malik said. "Add in the fact that all eyes are on you now because of the wedding, and it makes you a target. Let your father, Gray, and I talk to some of the others."

"I can help with that," Saint offered.

"I don't want people to be threatened," Nico said.

"Some of them need to be. Because if what you are saying is right, the Born is not going to stop now. Even if he is, it might be something we deal with more often."

He wanted to argue with his cousin, but Nico knew it would do no good. Nico had worried what Saint had said would come true. Once some devious Borns understood what they could do by turning humans, it could be disastrous for their kind. Humans would not take kindly to the results, and they would once again be hunted.

"But threatening them will not work, and you know that. I agree we have a huge problem, and the threat is growing by the day. Still, we need to convince them it is the right thing to do."

After a little more discussion, everyone filed out but his father. He said nothing, just studied Nico.

"What?"

"You do know your life is now changed?"

"Is this where you give me some fatherly advice?" he asked, worried that was just what his father was about to do.

"No, not truly. I know that Cordelia does not understand her situation, and while your mother thinks we should have told her before the wedding, I disagree. You will have your hands full tomorrow morning trying to explain everything. Just don't forget you have a family to help you through."

He nodded.

"And remember, a woman does not make you weak. In fact, binding with the right woman can make a man stronger than he ever expected."

With that his father left him alone. It was the first time that day he had several moments to himself. His father knew of Nico's declaration not to bind. It was not something he ever wanted to do. He would have disagreed with his father's comment, but did not out of respect. Binding with a mate made you vulnerable. She would become the center of his world.

Worry had his head throbbing. A regular Carrier would be upset if he did not bind with her tonight, but Cordelia knew nothing of their world. And binding to him would not be advisable. It was possible he would be injured in this war he felt approaching. He could not risk her life that way.

He walked back to the ballroom and immediately found her. It was easy enough for him. Even before drinking from her he was empathic to her presence. He watched her and wondered what she was thinking. The expression on her face was one of amusement, and much better than the sadness he had witnessed earlier. Her loneliness had struck him hard, and his protective instincts took control.

She must have sensed him. Her gaze met his across the room of people. The crowd melted away, and it was as if only the two of them were there. He could not stop the smile that curved his lips thinking of the night ahead of them. She had already proven to be a match for his sensual needs, and he looked forward to teaching her. Her cheeks pinkened, and for the first time that day, his heart felt light.

With determination, he made his way through the crowd. It was time he claimed his mate.

Chapter Ten

Cordelia stared at herself in the mirror. Who was the woman staring back at her?

She recognized pieces of herself. The long tangle of curls dripped over her shoulders. That was normal. The blue eyes, the same face, but there was something different. She knew that part of it was the nightdress she was wearing.

Adelaide had insisted on buying her the most decadent silk negligee she had ever seen. What was she thinking? She had never really paid attention to such things before. Plain linen had been fine for her, until she found herself married.

The neckline dipped low between her breasts, revealing more than it concealed. It was not even stitched up the side. Instead, it tied closed, easy to undo.

She shut her eyes. It had been bad enough shopping for her nightclothes with Adelaide. Having her try to explain what would happen on her wedding night had been painful. Cordelia had come to the realization that her mother-in-law had no embarrassment talking of personal things.

She opened her eyes and looked at herself again. Her hands were fisted on the table in front of her. Her ring sparkled in the light. It wasn't new. The design spoke of another era, and she wondered at the age of it. It looked as if it had come from another world. Two bands of gold twisted together, then knotted in the center. A ruby sat atop the knot. There was wording, but she could not read the ancient text.

"I hope you like it. It has been in the family for many years."

At the sound of his voice, she turned around and saw him standing behind her. How such a big man seemed to move without making a sound was beyond her. And at that moment, she truly couldn't think of anything. He was wearing a pair of silk pants and a robe. He had left it untied, allowing her to see his bare chest.

"Cordelia?"

"What?" She tore her gaze away from his chest and then raised it to meet his. "Oh, the ring. It is very beautiful."

"It was my grandmother's."

She held her hand against her chest. "Oh."

She did not know what to say to that. It meant so much more to her now, but she had a feeling if she said that to Nico, he would ignore it, or worse, pity her. She barely knew the man. His entire life was a mystery to her, but there was something about him that made her want to be with him.

"Such a serious expression," Nico said, drawing her attention back to him. "What are you thinking about?"

She wanted to lie and say nothing because that is what another woman would do. She could not. Cordelia was horrible at lying, and for some reason, she knew she could not lie to Nico.

"That I don't know you."

He nodded. "I don't know you either, but that is not so different from other married people much of the time."

She sighed. "Yes, but for a man it is different. You have more power, more freedom."

He frowned as he swirled the brandy in his glass, stopping to take a drink. "You will have your freedom."

She blinked. "What do you mean by that?"

"I am not a man who thinks that you have to answer to me all the time."

"And you do not have to answer to me."

Which meant, as she knew most powerful men always did, he would have his affairs.

"I can see wheels turning in that pretty head of yours, but I think that you need not worry about those things tonight. We can work out the details on how we will get on later."

He took her hand and raised it to his mouth. His breath feathered over her flesh a moment before they made contact.

The small gesture sent a sizzle of heat racing up her arm and then spread throughout her body. He looked up at her. His smile dissolved as his eyes turned dark. Her own body was already responding. It was odd that this man could make her want things she had never even fathomed before meeting him.

Not true. She had thought about the marriage bed but had never thought she would have to worry about it. Now she was ready to jump in headfirst, although there was a little bit of fear along with the excitement.

"I would love to know what goes on in that head of yours."

She smiled. "It is never all that interesting."

"I find everything about you interesting."

At first, she wanted to push aside the words. He couldn't truly mean it, could he? Most men disdained her thoughts or that she had a mind of her own. But from the serious look on his face, he really cared. Cordelia could not help the thrill of knowing that, at least to Nico, she was interesting. And, at this moment, that was all that mattered.

"Come," he said gently, and tugged her along to the bed. He waited for her to sit down and then took the place beside her. This time there was no hesitation in him. He leaned next to her and kissed her neck, right on the pulse point. Instantly, her body heated as she felt something strange and exciting tug at her. Nico continued to kiss her neck, then kissed a path up to her mouth. He cupped her face and without closing his eyes, he took her mouth.

She felt his tongue gliding over her lips then he pulled back. "Open up for me, love. Let me inside."

She didn't hesitate. She opened her mouth and closed her eyes. His tongue darted in and she could taste the brandy he'd had at the reception.

He eased her back on the mattress as he hovered over her, still kissing her. All her worries seemed to slide away as her body took over her mind. Heat as she had never before felt went racing through her blood. Her body pulsed with a need she did not know she had ever had before. His fingers traced her jawline, and she wanted them to move lower. Her breasts ached, her nipples almost painfully so. She arched up, offering her body to him, wanting to feel his hands move over her flesh.

As if he understood, he slipped his hand down her neck to her breasts, his mouth following the same path. She thought he would pull her flimsy nightdress away, but he did not. Instead, he set his mouth atop the fabric and teased her nipple. The sensation of the wet fabric sliding over her was amazing. She had thought it would give her some kind of relief, but it did not. Instead, as he continued to alternately lick and suck at her, the ache in her breasts increased. Before he was done, he had teased both her breasts. Her stomach muscles tightened as he slid his way down her body. He made easy work of her gown, pulling it up and over her head. Then he kissed a path down her belly. With each touch of his mouth, her stomach quivered. He nipped at her skin, then licked it.

Heat surged, and her head spun.

Just as several nights ago, she was shocked, but she now knew what to expect. He set his mouth upon her sex as he slipped his tongue inside of her. The tension in her stomach tightened. Everything in her wanted something, some kind of release into pleasure, just as she had in the library days before. She lost all sense of time. The only thing she was aware of was the feel of his tongue against her most private parts. She grew slick with anticipation, and her heart was galloping out of control. Biting her bottom lip, she tried to hold back the moan vibrating in her throat.

Nico must have sensed it. He growled against her, the tremors skimming over her flesh. He said nothing as he moved his mouth up to the tiny bundle of nerves. She flinched as a jolt shot through her. He slipped a finger into her, then bit down gently. Then, in the next instant, the tension burst free. A rush of heat danced over her nerve endings as she slipped her hands into his hair. Wave after wave of ecstasy crashed through her, and she was helpless to do anything but accept it.

As she floated down, she opened her eyes. Nico had thrown off his robe and was clawing at his pants. It was so unlike him that for a moment she couldn't react. This was not the practiced seducer she had known from a few nights ago.

"Nico?"

When he looked up at here, his eyes were brighter, somehow more entrancing to her than before. With more confidence than she was feeling, she reached up and cupped his face. For a moment, he did not do anything, but then he turned into her palm. He closed his eyes and drew in a deep breath. The act of it was simple, but she felt shaken to her core. It was something so basic and primal.

She felt his mouth open against her palm and then the flick of his tongue. Cordelia shivered.

"I can't seem to get you out of my mind."

He said it as if he were confessing some horrible sin. And maybe he was. The man had been a confirmed bachelor until that afternoon.

"Is that such a problem?"

He looked down at her. "There are things about me, things I must do that you will never understand. In truth, I doubt you will ever understand me."

There was something behind the words that she couldn't quite detect. And before she could, he leaned down against her again.

He bent his head and took her mouth again. The urgency was there, but it was somewhat tamed as he had regained his control. His tongue invaded her mouth. It was still a bit odd, but the heat that he had built before started to rekindle. Her body was apparently ready for more…of what she did not know.

He continued to kiss her as he slipped between her legs.

The ache he had satisfied before was back, pounding through her blood. She felt something prodding at her sex then felt the intrusion. She had grown up in the country and had spent time around horse breeding, so she expected this. She felt full, as if she would not be able to handle it.

But as he continued to kiss her and touch her, any worries she had slid away. He pulled back from her for a second and hovered, his mouth over hers.

"I'm sorry, Cordelia."

She did not know what he was apologizing for until he thrust further into her. A sharp shard of pain wound through her, erasing some of the pleasure. But then he moved again and the pain began dissipating, being replaced with the pleasure of having him inside of her.

"Nothing but satisfaction now."

She opened her eyes and found him staring at her again. She slipped her hand up to the back of his head and pulled him down for a kiss. This time, Cordelia opened her mouth immediately. He dove into her and she sucked on his tongue. A shudder moved through him. He groaned and began to move faster and faster. The bed squeaked and shook with the force of his thrusts.

Nico was mumbling to himself as he kissed a path down her neck. She felt the first scrape of teeth against her flesh, then the flat of his tongue. Something moved through her, as if she had moved into a dream, her flesh numb. She felt a prick into her flesh, and for a moment she thought he had bitten her. Nico thrust into her one more time, sending her over into ecstasy again. Cordelia arched up against him, screaming his name. Nico stilled, groaning with gratification as he poured himself into her.

Her body continued to feel as if she were floating on a cloud. Nico collapsed on top of her. He was so heavy, but it didn't matter to her. She would tell him to move in a minute.

It was her last thought that night.

* * * *

Nico watched her sleep, his body fulfilled for the moment. For a woman who seemed so animated at times, it was odd to see her still. He brushed back a silken curl from her forehead. She frowned in her sleep, and he couldn't help but smile. She looked so cute. Nico knew that she would not like that term, but in this he could assure himself he was correct. She turned to him and cuddled closer.

He wrapped his arm around her and pulled her against his chest. She was his mate now, officially. Tomorrow, the explanations would be given, but for the moment, he enjoyed the way she had her head on his shoulder, and her small hand over his chest where his heartbeat.

He knew then, without any doubt, he would protect her to the death. He just hoped that when he explained what her new life would be, that she would understand why he had married her first.

In their world there was no way around it. They were mated, and she would have to accept it.

Chapter Eleven

Malik looked down the hallway and watched Gray pace. He had been like this since Malik arrived.

The door opened, and Gray came to a stop. Malik stood. The diminutive figure of Dr. Bingam slipped out the door, and he shut it behind him.

He looked at both men with surprise.

"She's alive and more than likely will stay that way," Dr. Bingam said.

"But she has not regained her senses," Malik said. He did not have to be told. He knew an attack like the one she had dealt with would take days, if not weeks to recover from.

The doctor shook his head. "Sleep is best. Have her parents been notified?"

Malik looked to Gray. A look of disgust moved over his expression. "Yes. They have told me they no longer have a daughter."

Now he understood. The bastard parents thought they had lost a commodity. It was not that much of a problem in their world for her to no longer be pure—but to have been tainted by a Made could be devastating.

"Can you tell us anything else?" Gray asked.

"She's a fighter. A lesser woman would have just submitted, but this one did not. And she saved herself. After I had the midwife in last night, I am almost certain she wasn't raped. She fought back so hard that he didn't have time to finish his task."

"What should we do?" Gray asked.

"I think it's best to get a woman to look after her. That way she will not feel so threatened when she wakes up. And I am sure that your family or the Blackburns will help her once she heals. She will need a new life somewhere."

From the look on Gray's face, he did not look like he would allow her to leave. Before the duke could embarrass himself, Malik stepped in.

"With Mrs. Blackburn in town, I am sure she can take care of her when she is well enough."

"Yes, of course. Mrs. Blackburn. Well, I am off. The Fredricksons are expecting me."

The doctor left them alone. Malik waited for Gray to say something, but he just kept staring at the door.

"I can go by to see Nico, although I'm fairly confident he won't be happy about it. I can bring back Mrs. Blackburn. She was a comfort I think last night even though the woman was barely alive."

Gray nodded without taking his gaze from the door. "Empathy from another female Carrier will help."

"Gray."

He didn't even acknowledge Malik.

"Gray."

He finally turned his attention from the door. "What?"

"I'm going to the Blackburn's home right now. I will bring his mother back with me."

Gray nodded. "I guess that will be best."

"Is there something wrong?"

Gray shook his head. "No, just...the woman. To think what she has gone through and survived—most men would not have been able to think in a situation like that. Admirable."

Malik nodded. "Remember that when she awakens."

"Why?"

"I have a feeling she isn't going to be very receptive to any of us for a long time."

With that he headed off to the Blackburn's townhouse. Interrupting Nico's honeymoon was not something he looked forward to, but once he was done with it, he might be able to get some sleep.

* * * *

Cordelia awakened slowly. She stretched her arms over her head and winced. She was sore in places, especially between her legs. She opened her eyes and found the room dark. There was a little bit of sun peeking through heavy drapes.

It took just a second for Cordelia to remember where she was. Nico's house. No, her house. She lived here now. How did she go from being plain old Cordelia to being Nicodemus Blackburn's wife?

Before she could answer the question, the doors opened and a maid's head poked in.

"Ahh, Lady Cordelia, you are awake."

She slipped into the room. Cordelia started to sit up but then realized she wasn't wearing anything. She pulled the bed linens up to her neck.

"Mr. Blackburn told me to let you sleep, but it has been hours and Mrs. Blackburn—meaning his mother—said to check on you."

She was plump and young, probably no more than twenty if that. She had blonde hair, bright green eyes, and one of those healthy complexions you usually only saw on country misses.

"My name is Bessie, my lady. Mr. Blackburn assigned me to you."

"Nico…where is he?" she asked, trying to pretend not to be utterly embarrassed—as if being completely naked with people walking around was normal for her.

"He's talking with Malik."

For a moment, the use of Malik's given name surprised her. But she had never heard anyone use another name for him.

"Mr. Blackburn wanted me to help you with the facilities. He wasn't sure if you had used the plumbing."

She nodded, wondering what she was supposed to do

now. Cordelia had grown up with servants, but it had been years since she had a personal maid. In fact, it was before she had reached the age of thirteen.

"Ahh…"

The maid looked at her as if she were waiting for Cordelia to say something.

"I need a robe."

"Oh," her eyes widened at the comment. "Of course."

Bessie scurried over to the wardrobe and pulled out the black silk robe Cordelia's mother-in-law insisted on buying her. She laid it carefully on the bed. "I will meet you in the bathing area."

With that, she hurried off again. Cordelia sighed and tried not to be embarrassed. To avoid thinking about it, she picked up the robe and slipped it on. After tying the sash, she walked in the same direction as Bessie. It took her longer than usual. The pain between her legs had increased. She stepped into a passageway that led to a bathing room. On the other side of the room sat a copper tub. Water was pouring out of a pipe extended from the wall.

"Goodness."

"I am amazed Mr. Blackburn did not show this to you last night. But, being a man, he had other things on his mind."

Cordelia's face started to burn. When she said nothing, Bessie glanced around.

"Oh, I am sorry, my lady. I am sometimes too talkative for my own good."

Cordelia cleared her throat. "No worry."

She smiled. "That's good because I can tell you I was excited when Mr. Blackburn appointed me to take care of you. The truth is, there are a lot of people in our world who would kill to help a mate of a Blackburn."

The odd speech caused Cordelia's mind to freeze. What was she talking about? In their world...mate?

She opened her mouth to answer her, but Bessie turned

off the water. "I put some good salts in here that should help you. I am sure you are a bit tender."

Cordelia nodded. "Thank you."

"I am going to go down and order some food for you. I am sure you are famished."

Before she could say anything, the young woman curtseyed and hurried out the door.

"Well," Cordelia said to an empty room.

She decided to make use of her privacy and slipped off the robe. Gingerly, she stepped into the tub. At first it was a bit hot, but she ignored it. Once she sat in the scented water, she sighed.

"Oh my."

The heat helped her muscles relax, her mind to drift. She moved her head from one side to the other and felt a tug on the right side of her throat. She lifted her hand and felt an indention in her flesh. She slipped her fingers over the two tiny marks wondering about them, but the bath was too tranquil. Within moments, she was dozing.

* * * *

"The girl is awake?" Nico asked.

Malik nodded. "No."

"But Dr. Bingam thinks she will recover?"

Malik nodded. "He examined her, as did the midwife. They believe she wasn't raped."

"At least there is that," Nico's father said.

"Her family has disowned her."

"Bastards." Nico did not understand how parents could do such a thing to their child.

"I never cared for them." His father frowned. "Your mother will come up with something by the time she recovers. That might be a while, since I am sure her body needs rest. She needs to sleep. It will give her time to heal, physically and mentally. I cannot even imagine what she has been through."

"Dr. Bingam said that we should just let her sleep, and when she comes to, we are to give her tea and some gruel. It seems to be helping her. Gray is a bit..."

"What?" Nico asked.

"I think he is getting a little obsessed with her. I am not too sure that is a good thing."

"Obsessed? In what way?"

Malik shrugged. "I am not sure, but it is just odd the way he acts like he is her protector."

Nico filed that bit of information away. "Is there anything else?"

"Yes. I thought having your mother there would help."

"Excellent, Malik," his father said. "Adelaide will be happy to help."

"Good. If that is all, I would like to see my bride and not be disturbed."

Before he could leave, Malik stopped him. "There was another killing last night. Not two blocks from Gray's house. The Alliance is not going to be happy about it."

"No, but are they going to do anything about it?" Nico asked sarcastically.

His father shook his head. "Our problem is that we are too set in our ways. It is not doing any of us any good, especially not in a time like this. They do not want to look at the idea of someone doing just what Vlad did. Worse, there is a chance he has better knowledge. You know he has to wonder what happened to Hurst."

Nico knew that, knew that he should be worrying about it. His mind was on something else entirely.

"Talk to Gray to see if he can find some younger men to help us. Then we might be able to plan some kind of surveillance on these areas. Also, tell Gray I want him here tomorrow to discuss this. I want to map out the killings and abductions. Maybe we can find some kind of pattern."

"That sounds like an excellent idea, son."

Nico's mind returned to his mate. He'd only been away from her a few minutes, and he already missed her. "I am off. I have been married less that twenty-four hours, and I would like to at least spend a little more time with my bride."

He left without waiting for an answer. Malik was worried. Nico knew that and was worried too. There was nothing they could do without some organization. That would take a day or two, and hopefully they would at least have some breathing space before their killer struck again.

He took the stairs two at a time. There would be some explaining today, but he was sure that she would not remember being bitten. The serum from his fangs had taken care of that, and she would be healed. Still, he could not allow her to operate within his world without knowing what he was…what she was. Soon, her own abilities would start to appear, and that would be frightening enough even knowing what she was.

By the time he reached the bedroom door, Bessie was slipping out of it.

"Oh, Mr. Blackburn. Lady Cordelia is in the tub, dozing a bit. I set the food tray on the table in the sitting area."

"Thank you, Bessie."

She curtseyed, which he had never seen happen in his house before, and scurried down the corridor. He chuckled. He guessed having someone of royalty in his house was changing a few perceptions.

Nico made his way to the bathing room and then stopped in the doorway. She had her head resting on the edge of the tub. All her glorious golden hair hung over the edge. The warm, humid air added a curl to it that he found he liked.

"Are you going to continue to stand there?" she asked.

"I didn't want to intrude on your privacy."

She opened her eyes. "If you were worried about that, you wouldn't be here. I would like to finish then I will join you in the bedroom."

Being this close to her so soon after their initial mating

was awakening all his primitive instincts. It was in his genetic makeup to want to be close to her. In fact, he couldn't leave her alone if he wanted to. But he didn't. There was a part of him that knew it was a function of their mating ritual. But there was a part of him that was intrigued by her. There was so much he did not understand about her. He was sure once he did that the novelty would wear off.

"Nico?"

He shook himself free of his thoughts. "I thought I might join you."

Her face had been flushed from the hot water, but now it turned brighter. "I don't think that is a very good idea."

His body was ready for another joining. He did not need to feed from her just yet, but his teeth were already trying to descend. It would not be good for her. Cordelia would probably already be weakened by the feeding he took last night.

He approached the tub and she turned around. Nico knew that he was probably pushing her too much. Normally he took his time. He was known as a connoisseur of women, one who knew how to seduce a lady. But with Cordelia, he didn't seem to think straight. Not since the moment he had her in his arms on the dance floor.

He pulled off his shirt and tossed it onto the floor. Then, he squatted behind her and reached into the bath water. It was lukewarm at best, telling him that she had been in there for a while.

"You might want to get out," he suggested. His voice had deepened. He couldn't help wanting her, needing her.

"I will if you leave."

She said it so primly that he smiled. It was very unlike Cordelia.

"I have seen you naked, my love." He pressed his mouth against her neck. She shivered.

"Not in the daylight."

She sounded mortified.

"Love, I plan on seeing you in the daylight and the moonlight. I would think you would appreciate the fact that I want to."

She stilled and her spine straightened. "So, I should be grateful that you married me and want to actually bed me?"

He knew that tone. He had heard it from his mother a time or two just before his father was verbally demolished.

"That is not what I meant."

"It sounded like you did."

He threw his arms up. "I cannot believe that you are starting a fight with me about this."

She smacked her hand against the water. "Of course, it is always the woman's fault."

She pushed away from him and stood. He couldn't respond because his tongue was glued to the top of his mouth. He had seen her naked, just as he had acknowledged, but as she said, he had never seen her in the daylight. Water sluiced down her flesh. Her body was a work of art, full, rounded, and beautiful with the morning light dancing over her slick skin.

Cordelia grabbed a towel and wrapped it around her body. He was already so far gone that he growled. She looked up at him, and her blue eyes narrowed.

"Did you say something?"

He could not speak coherently. He shook his head.

She marched off out of the room and into her bedroom. He was helpless to do anything but follow.

"I am sick to death of English men thinking women are lucky to be married. Did I ask to be compromised? No, I did not. I was extremely happy with my life the way it was."

"You were? And how were you living your life?"

She stopped in her tracks and stared at him. "Excuse me?"

"How were you living? I know that your brother was not supporting you, and Diana was not. So, where was the money coming from?"

"That has nothing to do with what I was talking about. I will not be treated as if I should be thankful that you married me."

The linen towel was plastered against her body, and he licked his lips. He could make out the outlines of her nipples. He could remember the way they tasted…how it felt to slip his tongue over the hardened tip.

"Nico, are you listening to me?"

He shook his head again and started to walk toward her. She was amazing before, but now she was magnificent.

"Nico!" She backed up and stopped when she hit the edge of the bed.

"I cannot help myself, Cordelia."

She rolled her eyes and snorted. "Truly."

"*Truly*. You have always intrigued me, but now…well, I like a woman who has some backbone. I sense that we will have many fights in our future."

Before she could respond, he grabbed her and tumbled them both on the bed.

Chapter Twelve

Nico landed on top of Cordelia, who squeaked. She didn't truly struggle, but then he didn't give her a chance to think. He only took a moment to enjoy the way her soft curves felt against his body before he put his plan into action. He captured her mouth in a long, wet kiss, enjoying the way she moaned against his tongue. She had been a virgin the night before, but she was definitely a passionate lover.

He forced himself to pull back and settle his weight on his elbows. Her hair was fanned out over the bed, her skin rosy from her bath, her lips swollen from his kisses. He had never been struck mute by a woman in all his years, but one look at her and for a moment, he forgot his name. When he met her gaze, he could only say one thing.

"You are beautiful."

"You don't have to say that, Nico."

"No. I do. You are beautiful. You should see yourself."

She started to look away, but he knew this was important. He set his finger against her chin and gently turned her face. "You don't believe me?"

"I know my shortcomings. You don't need to lie to me. We will get on better that way."

He could deny it—tell her just what he was feeling at the moment. But he wasn't sure exactly what he was feeling at the moment. Instead, he would show her.

He kept his eyes open as he kissed her. Hers were impossibly blue, as if they were endless. Then he pulled her bottom lip into his mouth, grazing his teeth over it. She sucked in a breath then released it slowly. He slipped off her to the side and tugged the wet fabric away from her.

"I must have done something right in my life," he said beneath his breath. He looked up at her, and she was watching him warily with a hint of desire darkening her eyes. She was a woman who did not know her worth. If Nico could, he would beat her father for his treatment of her.

Without breaking eye contact, he bent his head and took her nipple into his mouth. She shuddered as he bit down gently. As he continued to tease her, he slid his hand down her stomach to her sex. He first skimmed his fingers along her slit, then slipped them between her folds. She was already wet with desire, something he knew was just a primal reaction to him, her mate.

But he could not stop the way his heart reacted. Knowing she wanted him as much as he wanted her was one of the greatest aphrodisiacs for him. He kissed his way down her stomach. Her flesh was sweet, delectable. He was not a man who had hidden his needs, but with Cordelia, she brought out something in him. He did not know how to explain it to someone else. He just needed her. Now.

As he settled between her legs, he enjoyed the musky scent of her arousal. It called to him as no other had before. Already, his body was ready, primed to take her again and again. But she needed him to be gentle. With that in mind, he set his mouth against her sex.

The taste of her exploded across his tongue, and his incisors throbbed with the need to feed. He did not require another feeding, but he wanted that connection during their mating. It was too soon after last night, but his body did not give a damn. He thrust his tongue into her. She gasped and then moaned his name. She slipped her hands through his hair, molding them to the back of his head. He teased the little bundle of nerves as he slid his finger back into her sex. She jolted against him and moaned again. He could taste her need, her passion, and it urged him to take her. Never had a woman reacted to his lovemaking the way she did. Her reactions were so honest. There was no coy gestures or practiced flirting. With Cordelia, she did not hide her raw passion, and it fed his own.

He took her to the edge, but did not thrust her over into her orgasm. Instead, he pulled back and moved up her body. He wanted to be inside her when she gained her release.

Nico slipped off the bed and pulled off his pants. Then, he climbed back on the bed, drawing himself up to his knees, pulling her hips up and off the bed. His movements were rough and unrefined, but she did not seem to care—nor did he.

"Cordelia."

She opened her eyes slowly, lazily, as if she would expend too much energy by opening them. When she finally met his gaze, he thrust into her. The moment her wet heat surrounded his cock, he almost lost it. There was something about Cordelia, something that made him just want to lose himself inside of her and stay there for days.

He wanted to go slowly, but found himself unable to control his compulsion. Why would it be any different than their entire relationship? He had never had any control around her, and for once in his five hundred years, he did not give a bloody hell. He thrust into her again and again. He barely registered that she wrapped her legs around his waist. It did not take long before she was coming apart beneath him. The ripples of her release moved over his member as he thrust into her faster and harder. When he could no longer control himself, he let go. As he poured himself into her, he leaned down and ravaged Cordelia's lips.

Moments later, he collapsed on top of her. He knew it was unrefined of him, but he could not seem to drum up the energy to move. He expected complaints from her but instead, she wrapped her arms around him. For the moment, he was happy, happier than he had ever been before in his life.

Finally, he could pull himself up and look down at her. The sight had the air backing up in his lungs. Her hair was damp and even curlier, her face flushed with exertion, and there was a small smile curving her lips.

He gave her a kiss, this one slow and almost sweet. Her eyelids fluttered, then opened.

He forgot his name again. Then, he shook his head and rolled them over on the bed, pulling her closer to him and covering them with a sheet.

"We truly shouldn't lie about in bed," she said with a strange mixture of embarrassment and lazy sensuality.

He kissed her forehead. "We can do whatever we want. We're newlyweds."

"Indeed." Her voice was already fading. When he heard her even breathing, he smiled…then followed her into sleep.

* * * *

Cordelia lay in bed, feeling completely and absolutely decadent. Her husband—and she would never get accustomed to using that word—was feeding her fresh fruit. And she was naked. He'd put his pants on, probably for her sake. She was too embarrassed to tell him that it was of no use. Now that she had seen him completely nude in the daylight, she wasn't so sure she would be able to think of him any other way.

"What are you smiling about?" he asked.

"Nothing."

He shook his head. "No, I know that look. You hide a lot behind that sweet smile, but I know you have a devious mind."

She blinked. "I do not."

He chuckled. "Yes, you do. I have a feeling a great many inappropriate things run through your head when you are at a function."

She tried to remain aloof, but it was impossible. She could not resist his grin. It made him appear younger than she had ever seen him. Nico always seemed to carry the weight of the world on his shoulders.

She smiled and shook her head. "As if you are any

different. You do not like it any more than I do. I am sure you think horrible things, too."

"I do, but I don't try to hide it as you do."

"That is true. In fact, I have a distinct feeling that there are very few people who will attempt conversation with you when you don your 'approach me and die' look."

His cheeks flushed, and she had the distinct feeling he was blushing. "I tend to hate the city."

"Indeed?" She cocked her head and studied him. He was definitely embarrassed. "What are you doing here?"

"Fate?"

She laughed. "I don't believe in fate."

"I thought women always believed in things like that."

She sighed. "Maybe some women, not me."

Not after her childhood. No woman would believe in fate after what she had endured. Her father and brother had stripped away any fantasies she had about life in general—and especially men.

"Well, you should."

She didn't want to talk about it. Her family life mortified her, and she hated Nico knowing that about her. Cordelia knew he did, but admitting it to him face to face was a bit too much. "Normally, you are not in town, but you are now. You said you don't like it?"

He shook his head. "Too many people, too dirty. I prefer the country and clean air."

"And that is where we will be going this week?"

"No. I have business to attend to in town."

She wanted to ask more, but she had a feeling that Nico did not want to reveal more than that. She reached up to scratch an itch on her neck, and her fingers moved over the two indentions she had found earlier.

"Nico, did you see this? I can't tell what it is."

If she hadn't been paying attention so closely, she would have missed the way he stiffened.

She dropped her hand and studied him. "Nico?"

"There is something I need to tell you."

She said nothing, the warm, happy feelings dissolving at the distant look on his face.

"There is a bit about my life that I have not told you."

He did not continue. She shivered as a chill slunk down her spine and into her soul. Was he a money lender? Or worse, a white slaver?

Inwardly she admonished herself. A man with a mother like Adelaide Blackburn did not make money from the flesh trade.

"Go on."

He sighed. "My family and I are not normal like you. Well, you are like us, but you don't realize it."

Again she was struck into silence. She opened her mouth then closed it. She could not seem to come up with a response to that.

He moved away from the bed and started to pace. "We...are not entirely human."

He hesitated again. Panic fluttered in her stomach. Cordelia was not a patient woman, and now she was at her wit's end. Not entirely human? What the bloody hell was going on here?

"Just tell me," she said.

"We're a family of vampires."

"Vampires?" she asked.

"Yes. I was drawn to you because you have the gene that makes you a Carrier. I mean, that isn't the only reason I'm attracted to you. But, you are predestined to be married to a Born."

She lifted her hand to feel the indentions on her neck.

"And those. I could not help myself. It is part of the mating ritual. You will just have to accept it."

She could not seem to follow the conversation which Nico seemed to be having mainly with himself.

"Nico," she said, moving to the edge of the bed. She grabbed her robe and pulled it on, not taking her gaze from his pacing. "Nico."

He stopped moving and looked at her.

"Tell me what you are going on about."

"I'm a vampire, as is my father, and now that you have mated with me, you will birth more."

* * * *

The Made looked out the window and took the information in. In his youth he had been impulsive, reckless. Now, though, he listened to the news that Nico Blackburn had married with ease.

Or, at least, he let those around him think so. Inside, he raged.

It wasn't enough that he had to be a success at everything, now he had a Carrier for a wife, one that apparently came from strong stock. Would the man's luck never end?

"You should have taken him down when you had the chance," his mother said. He ignored her as he did most of her suggestions. One mistake he would never make would be to listen to a woman. They were good for bearing children and little else, just as his father had said. It was why his father had never bonded to his mother.

"I have not had a chance. I can assure you if I had, I would have driven a stake through his heart."

She opened her mouth to speak again, and he shot her a look. "I would suggest you find something to do. I am not in the mood to discuss any of your ideas."

She pursed her lips, a sure sign she was not happy with him. Then, without a word, she left him alone.

He would have to find out if Nico bonded with his mate. If he did, he would be as easy to kill as his brother…but he would make sure that the bastard was there to watch her die.

Chapter Thirteen

Nico could not discern Cordelia's reaction. She stared at him, no expression on her face. For the longest of moments, he thought she might faint.

"Vampire?" she asked, her voice barely above a whisper.

"Yes."

"You married me because I can birth vampires?" she asked.

"Yes."

She started to back away from him. "And your parents are vampires?"

Relief started to edge out his worry. She was starting to understand. "Yes."

He followed her steps, and she stopped by the door. "Stop stalking me."

"I am not stalking you. You are running away."

She took another step then stopped. Her spine stiffened. "You tell me you are a vampire and then expect me not to be afraid."

He hated hearing her say she was afraid, but before he could reassure her he would never harm her, there was a knock at the door.

"Go away," he shouted at the same time she said, "Come in."

The door opened, bumping Cordelia in the back. She pitched forward, and Nico caught her to keep her from falling to the ground. He righted her. Cordelia wrested her arm out of his hand and shot him a dirty look. His mother poked her head through the opening.

His mother smiled at him reassuringly. "I see you told her."

She looked at his mother. "Told me?"

"What we are. He told you." His mother nodded, slipping through the door. "I have a feeling Nico did not explain it quite right."

"That you are a family of vampires?"

Cordelia's voice had grown smaller each time she spoke. He didn't like it. Not one bit. He would rather have her yelling at him.

His mother took the comment the wrong way. Her smile widened as she stepped into the room. "There. That is all settled."

"Settled." Now, Cordelia's voice was barely audible. His mother finally realized that there might be something wrong.

"Yes, dear. I can answer any of your questions."

"Cordelia, you look ready to faint," Nico said.

That snapped the glazed look out of her eyes, and her spine straightened. "I am not about to faint. What do you take me for? I am not some silly-brained woman who faints at the slightest of shocks."

"But of course not, my love."

She shot him a look that told him he was in more trouble than he had expected.

"I think I need to have a moment alone," she said, her voice measured.

"Cordelia—"

"Why don't you leave us alone, Nico? I am certain that I can make sure your new bride does not run away."

His mother's tone told him she was not happy with him. He didn't care.

"I think Cordelia said she wanted to be alone."

"Bloody hell, just go away, Nico." This came from the loving woman he had just been feeding fruit to in bed. Now she was treating him as if he were unwanted. Nico looked at his mother, then back to Cordelia, and knew it was better to retreat. But he would not leave until he made his point.

He stepped closer, slipped his hand around her waist, and pulled her to him. She opened her mouth, but he didn't give her a chance to speak. He slammed his mouth down on hers, thrusting his tongue in. It was hot, wet, and thoroughly arousing. By the time he stepped back, they were both breathing heavily.

"Just remember where we left off."

With that, he turned and marched off to his bedroom.

* * * *

The silence that followed Nico's exit almost deafened Cordelia.

"Well, I see that Nico is not that different than his father."

Cordelia choked.

"Oh, there I am again with my plain speaking. It embarrasses Nico quite often." She walked to Cordelia, took her by the arm, and pulled her along to the bed. "Have a seat, dear. If you have any questions, ask away."

Cordelia sighed and blinked against the tears burning the back of her eyes. "I just don't know where to start."

"Well, I am sure you think we are odd."

She felt a giggle tickle the back of her throat. Cordelia tried to clear it, but it didn't work. The laugh exploded from behind her lips. Even she heard the hysterical edge to it.

"Odd is not the word I would choose."

She felt her mother-in-law's study. She turned her head to look at her.

"Ask anything you want, dear. I told Nico he should tell you before the marriage, but the Blackburn men are not patient. I've had seven hundred years with Samuel, and he still has little to no patience."

"You are telling me you are seven hundred years old?"

Adelaide rolled her eyes. "No. I wish I was. I am approaching seven hundred and fifty at the moment."

"And you have had only one child in all that time?"

The smile that her mother-in-law had worn faded a bit.

"No. I had another son, Demetrius. He died along with his mate almost thirty years ago."

"So you do not live forever?"

She shook her head. "No. There are those that choose to go on, then there are those who are killed. A stake to the heart."

She said the last bit in a whisper, as if saying it would make it happen.

"You are telling me I am a vampire?"

She laughed. "Oh no, dear. You are a Carrier, the only ones of our bloodline who can birth vampires."

"Birth vampires? That sounds strange and slightly archaic."

"I know that modern literature has us as slaves to blood, that we are all Mades, and that we have no hearts. But we do. We are as alive as you and your friends."

Cordelia sighed and closed her eyes, lifting her hand to rub away the headache that brewed there. "I can hardly understand it all."

"There is a lot to take in, dear, but you will definitely be able to handle it."

She opened her eyes and could not help but ask, "How do you know that?"

"How? Why dear, you enticed Nico. I have to say I never thought that boy would mate."

"Boy?"

Her smile widened. "He is my youngest, the baby, and I will always see him as a boy."

"How old is he?"

"Five hundred years old."

"And you think I can handle a man like that? Handle this?"

The hysteria was back in her voice. A week ago she was writing for a column, and her only concern was making enough money to survive. Now she was married to a vampire and his mother was telling her he had been alive for five hundred years.

"You can. As I said, something about you drew Nico to you. He couldn't resist you."

"I think you might have our relationship confused. There is no love."

"Oh, for us, love comes second many times. Especially for the males. Borns fight mating because it is for life. Would you want to pledge yourself to a woman who wasn't right for you?"

"I wouldn't want to be pledged to a man like that."

She stared at her for a moment then threw back her head and laughed. "Oh, I think we will get on well together."

"I now have to have blood?"

"No. You are a Carrier, a female who has the gene to birth the Borns. There are Mades, but that can be dangerous. And, you must have a very prominent birth father for you to pull at both Hurst and Nico the way you did."

"Hurst?" Then his behavior hit her. "He's a vampire."

"He was Made, which is why we almost lost him."

Her head started to spin with the unfamiliar words, the strange world she was now a part of. Just what the bloody hell would she do now?

"Why don't you get dressed? Nico can explain a lot of this later. I do not want to confuse you. I am pretty sure Malik will be back soon, too. We had an incident that I need to help with."

"An incident?"

"A young Carrier was attacked. She needs some motherly care, and it seems her mother...well, I shouldn't use that word. Her family has disowned her. I must make sure she survives now. I am a healer, my special talent. And you will have yours."

Adelaide rose and walked to the door. "Wait. Mine? You mean talent?"

"Yes. Now that you have mated, whatever skill you have will grow stronger. I would take no longer than half an hour, dear. Nico might come up here and tear the door down. Nico is not going to want to be separated from you for long so close to your first mating."

With that, she slipped out the door. Cordelia kept staring at it, her brain almost numb. She was married to a vampire, and now she would birth them.

Bloody hell, why did she always find herself in situations like this?

* * * *

Nico watched his mother talk about his bride then glanced at her rabid audience. It included his father—who was enjoying the story a bit too much—Malik and Gray. They all seemed to take a particular interest in the way his bride handled the information.

At the moment, he didn't truly care about what they thought of him. He tried to fight the urge to run up the stairs. He knew it was instinctual, primal, but he hated being away from Cordelia. It would not do for her to think he could not handle their separation, but at the same time, he almost did not care.

"I think she will be fine, Nico. You should have explained things before the wedding," his mother said.

"Then she would have run away. You and I both know that. Her reputation would be in tatters. I could not let that happen."

His mother looked at him for a few moments and opened her mouth, but he was saved by Cordelia.

"I see that you brought in troops."

He glanced at her, and his body responded immediately. He could not help it, nor did he care to. All he wanted to do was to strip off the day dress she was wearing and feel her flesh, then feed off her again. The need he had for her was madness. It grew stronger each time he saw her.

"I like a girl with a little fight," his father said with a

chuckle. "I hope you are not going to hold it against all of us that you were not told."

"What good would that do? I would still be married to a vampire."

Malik chuckled. Nico frowned at him, but Malik just grinned. It was bad enough this was playing out in front of his family, but having both he and Gray here was making it worse.

"Mother said she explained it all to you."

Cordelia looked at him, but he couldn't read her feelings. He really didn't have to. She was definitely not happy about it.

"I think I will have more questions about us later, but the main one I have is about Hurst."

The air stilled around them, and he found himself wanting to flee. He didn't want to scare her even more than she already was.

"What would you like to know?" he finally asked.

"He is Made."

Of course she didn't need an explanation on that. She was not a stupid woman. She was lush, beautiful, and he knew just how she moaned his name. His body reacted to the thought, his blood traveling quickly to his groin.

Dammit.

He shook his head, trying to bring himself back into the conversation.

"I sense there is something else you are not telling me."

He hesitated, and of course no one came to his aid. They left him dangling there, flailing in the wind.

"Cordelia—"

"Nico, please do not treat me like a simpleton. I have not run away screaming in the street so please, tell me what you can of this Made business. I understand from your mother that Hurst is Made, and he almost died."

"It isn't a pleasant tale."

She glanced around at the room then looked at him. "I

have had many an unpleasant tale in my lifetime. One more will not make a difference."

"Cordelia, have a seat, and I will tell you," he said, keeping his distance. He already captured the faint scent of her, and his body was humming. He needed her more than he expected, but he could control it. It was normal...or at least he hoped it was. He also prayed that once they settled down, he would be released from this insane need he had for her constantly.

He sat in the chair opposite of hers and explained the last few weeks. The room was quiet, and no one interrupted him throughout the entire telling. Even his bride. He was surprised she did not, but he could watch her taking in all the information.

"So, he had to be taken care of. He is somewhat recovered, and Malik will help him through the next few months."

She glanced at Malik. "You are Made?"

He nodded.

"From Egypt?"

Malik's eyebrows shot up, and he gave Nico a warning look. He was right. Cordelia was extremely intelligent. He had not told her everything, but she would find it out if they were not careful.

"Yes, Malik is from Egypt," Nico said.

She barely spared him a glance then turned to Gray. "All the Dukes of Queensbury have been vampires?"

Gray gave her a smile. "We prefer the word Borns."

His voice was solicitous enough to irritate Nico. In fact, his teeth started to descend, but not because of lust. Anger and possessiveness wound through him, heating his blood. He was an inch away from attacking Gray when his father said, "Settle, Nico. Gray is not after your bride."

Cordelia turned her head, and her eyes widened then narrowed. "Really, Nico. I am not in the mood to have one vampire in my life let alone a second, and a titled one at that.

I really do not have time for such foolishness."

His father chuckled, but Nico ignored him. He did pull his possessive instincts into check.

"Is there anything else you need answered?" he asked.

"Is this normal? The making of vampires?"

"Why do you ask?"

She didn't like his question. He knew she was smart enough to understand he had not answered hers.

"I think if there had been a group of Made vampires running the London streets, I would know. I have never heard anything of the like. Add to the fact there is a sense of urgency whenever you talk to Malik, and I assumed there were problems."

"I told you she was smart," his mother announced with a wide, satisfied smile.

"There are some problems, but they are not truly anything you need to worry about."

In that moment, he felt her shift away from him. "But of course. Now that I know all of this, what am I expected to do?"

"Expected to do?"

"There must be some kind of duty I have."

"What your wife is asking you is if you have any duties for her," his mother said.

He had something he wanted from her, but he didn't think he should mention that in front of the others. Cordelia must have sensed which way his thoughts went because she blushed.

"What I am asking is what kind of social duties do I have?"

"None."

She rolled her eyes. "I know that normally you live in the country, but here in town, we will need to make the rounds. And I can help with the investigation."

"Absolutely not."

He said it so adamantly, he knew the others caught on to

him. He could not have her investigating his past, the things he had done. She would be appalled at the assassinations he had carried out in the last few months. Cordelia was a strong woman, but knowing her husband was a murderer might be a bit much to handle.

"I just suggest that because I know a bit more about society than anyone here."

"I doubt you know more than I," Gray said, smiling again.

She sniffed. "But of course, Your Grace. I do know that you like brunettes with green eyes, but then, I am sure most do. Oh, and remember, I know that you are a member of the Cock and Bull."

Gray's mouth dropped open. "Bloody hell."

"I am assuming your mother is alive, even though they say your father is dead?"

Gray nodded.

"She would probably not be happy to know that you play such dangerous games." Cordelia's expression never changed as she threatened the duke.

Nico smiled. He couldn't help it. His mate was intelligent and didn't mind letting people know it. It made him like her even more.

She turned to him again. "I want to know what I am getting into when I go about in society. I don't know who is one of our kind. I do not want to make any mistakes."

He was captured by the comment of being "their kind." She did not say "your." The fact that she was already thinking that way was good.

"Mother will help you through society for that. You will be recognized by many of them without telling them."

She nodded.

"If you do not mind, I would like to talk to Nico alone."

The request caught him unaware.

"We can go to your room."

She rolled her eyes. "I think not. We won't get any

discussion done there."

His father chuckled again and stood. "Rightly so. We have other matters to address, and we can do that in mother's parlor."

Within moments, they were alone.

"What is it you want to discuss?"

She sighed. "I need to know everything. I sense you are holding things back from me."

He was, but he could not let her know that. The baser side of their kind was not pleasant. "I cannot tell you everything."

"No, I need to know."

"What?"

"My sister, she is a Carrier? My mother was one, too? But what of my brother?"

"You did not have the same father. He was born of a human father, but you were not."

He thought she would be embarrassed about her mother, but she was not. "I don't know who my father was. But does that make Diana…"

He nodded. "If Diana doesn't not mate with a Born, it does not matter."

She sighed and nodded. He hated that she looked so dejected. "What is it, Cordelia?"

She shrugged. "It is just a lot to take in."

"Your problem is that you think too much, my love."

She shot him a narrowed look, her blue eyes sparking fire. "I do not like you using that name for me."

"You don't?"

"I am not your love. I do much better living in reality. You did not marry me because of love, and I do not love you."

He rather doubted that, at least on her part. A woman like her could not give herself as freely as she had the night before if she did not care for him a little. She had not been able to hide her feelings when he was touching her. So open, so generous. Need pounded through him as the memories of their lovemaking washed over him.

She was still talking but he did not hear it. He saw her mouth moving, but the words did not register. Instead, he rose from the couch, walked to the door, and turned the lock. When he turned around, Cordelia was staring at him as if he had lost his mind. He had. He couldn't think straight. Not here alone in the room with her. He could still taste her passion as if he had just taken her moments before. His teeth descended. His body felt more alive than it ever had. He needed her. Now.

"Nico?"

Her voice had deepened, and the sound of it danced over every blasted nerve ending in his body. It was painful and arousing at the same time. He said nothing, but pulled her up off the chair and into his arms.

Before she could say anything else, he tumbled them both to the floor. He took the brunt of the fall, pulling her down on top of him. Then he quickly rolled them over the thick Aubusson rug so that she lay beneath him.

Her eyes were wide, her face flushed, and her mouth parted. Nico could not resist, even if he wanted to. And why would he want to? She was his mate, his to take, to feed from.

"I know it is madness and at the moment, you are not that happy with me. But, Cordelia, I want you."

He held his breath, waiting for her to deny him. She was aroused. The scent of her teased his senses. He closed his eyes and drew in a deep breath, allowing it to fill him. His teeth were completely descended. When he opened his eyes, he found her smiling at him.

"Cordelia?"

She slipped her hands up over his shoulders then wound her fingers through his hair. She pulled his mouth down to hers. "If you want me, then take me, Nico."

Chapter Fourteen

Cordelia did not know if Nico was happy or not with her brazenness. For mere seconds, she held her breath. She could not deny the craving she had for him. It was insane, but the urge to mate, to have him take her, took over every instinct she had. Then, his lips curved, and he dropped his mouth on top of hers. There was a sense of urgency but not as frantic as the time before.

At least not from him. Passion was already pounding through her, and he had barely touched her. Was this what he spoke of? The primal need to be his mate? It was consuming her every thought. Joining with him was all that mattered. Her body hummed with the need to have him ravish her. If she took time to think about it, she would be frightened, but he stopped all thought when she felt his lips on her jawline.

He kissed his way down her neck then slid his mouth over her pulse point.

He huffed against her skin. His breath feathered over her hot flesh, and she swallowed a moan. She wanted nothing more than to be taken, every nerve in her body sensitive to his every move. It hurt just to lie there and feel his breath on her skin.

"Bloody hell, you drive me insane, Cordelia." Every word was ground out as if the admission was hard for him to say. It was even harder for her to hear. It called to everything she had suppressed for years. So many times she had denied being like her mother, but at the moment, she understood her mother's predilections. If she ever felt like this with any of her suitors, Cordelia understood her mother's actions now.

He traced his tongue over the vein as if trying to sense where it was, as if he could taste her blood through her flesh. She felt the graze of teeth, and she could not help but stiffen.

He paused.

"I'm sorry. I am not accustomed to that."

He continued on.

She tried to relax but she could not. Even with her body telling her this was right, that it was no different than the night before, she had to ask, "Will it hurt?"

He shook his head and looked up at her. What she saw had her heart almost stopping. This was the feral man of the darkened room their first night together, the man who had taken her last night. He was speaking the truth when he said he needed her. His eyes shown with need and were almost otherworldly looking.

"I drank from you last night. There is a serum that is injected first that will help with the pain. But I can wait if you need me to."

Of course he would. Nico might have lost his head around her once or twice, but he was first and foremost a gentleman. He was her husband, and she wanted the full treatment.

"No, do it."

He shuddered as if he had been released from a bond and bent his head. He licked her skin again, and she felt it go slightly numb. But instead of drinking from her he worked his way down her body and shoved her skirts up. He tugged her drawers off and tossed them behind him. Without a word, he pressed her thighs wide and put his mouth on her sex.

Cordelia jolted at the touch of his mouth against her. She was wet, so wet she was embarrassed by it, but she easily forgot about it when he slipped his tongue between her folds. Pleasure spiraled through her as she shivered against his mouth. Each time his tongue thrust into her core, her hunger deepened. Again and again, he took her to the edge, but before she could experience her release, he would pull back, teasing her with his teeth and mouth.

She was barely able to think by the time he rose to his knees. She wanted—no needed—release so badly, she physically hurt. Every fiber of her being ached. He undid his britches and lifted her hips.

"Cordelia, love."

She raised her gaze to his and in his eyes saw the need that filled her reflected back. Then, with one hard thrust, he was inside of her. She came apart right then, unable to hold back, not wanting to. She convulsed as her release burst through her. Nico continued to move within her and bent his head to feed.

He licked her flesh, then she felt the tiniest of pricks against her neck. The moment he began drinking from her, she exploded again. She screamed his name, bucking up against him so hard he growled against her neck. Ecstasy flooded her body, claimed her senses. The feel of her blood being drawn into him was at first strange. Then, in the next instant, she felt the connection to him, the pleasure of giving him nourishment, and another level of arousal shifted through her. Before she could prepare herself, a second release was upon her. It left her gasping, her body rearing up against his, and she lost herself in the pleasure he gave her. Nico thrust into her one more time and moaned her name as he poured himself into her.

He pulled his fangs out of her neck, and she winced at the feel. It wasn't so much that it hurt, but just the odd feel of teeth beneath her skin. He licked her neck again and the flesh there numbed. With a sigh, he pulled out of her, then collapsed beside her on the rug. He slipped a hand over her waist and tugged her closer to him. His body felt as if he were on fire.

"I do not think I can keep up with you," he said, his words muffled against the carpet. She looked around. The drapes were closed, but there was a bit of light peeking through. Just beyond the door, she heard people walking down the hall and the murmur of voices.

"Bloody hell, what am I doing?" she asked.

He chuckled. "Making love with your husband in the

middle of the day."

He pulled himself up to look down at her. The feral look had faded, but there was something else there, something that left her oddly confused.

"I think that everyone will allow us time for fun like this in the middle of the day. We are newly wed."

He said it with such sincerity, she almost laughed.

"I guess so. I don't think they know what we were doing in here."

He chuckled. "My sweet, you are exceedingly loud when you make love. I have no doubt everyone heard you in the house...possibly all of London."

She felt her face heat. "I was not that loud."

"You were. I am convinced you are a temptress, weaving some kind of spell on me. 'Tis as if I am not five centuries old. Like I said, you might be too much for my old heart."

"And you do have hearts?" she asked before she could stop herself.

He nodded as he pulled one of her hands into his then kissed her knuckles. "Yes, we have everything you do."

"I felt it beat before, and I wondered." Then she hesitated. Her family had never been happy with her endless questions. In fact, she remembered spending most of the afternoon locked in a closet after asking Alex too many.

"No, ask."

She glanced up. "What?"

"Ask me what you want to."

"I am not sure where to start."

"We are built like humans. We all are born the same way, live the same way."

"But you never die unless you are killed."

"That is not entirely true. There is a time when we can choose to go into the afterlife, but the timing depends on the couple."

"According to the gothic novels, vampires cannot be out during the day."

He rolled his eyes. "Please, do not believe that nonsense. We can be out in sunlight, although too much of it might leave us with a rash and it does drain our energy."

"Will I..." she paused. How could she put into words what she wanted to say?

"I told you to ask me anything."

The sincerity in his eyes had her looking away. A lump had formed in her throat, and for the barest of moments, she wanted to believe her fantasies. Cordelia was always a woman who dealt better with reality. She knew this was a marriage forced by conditions they had no control over, and falling for a man like Nico Blackburn was a mistake. She barely knew the man...and even an eternity would teach her little.

She pushed away those thoughts and looked at him.

"Cordelia, ask." There was an edge to his voice now, even as he tried to keep his tone mild.

"I feel like I am in the dark, and I do not like it. It is one of the reasons I read when I was a child. After Father fired my tutor—"

"Your father fired your tutor?"

She nodded. "After that, I had to teach myself. So I read anything I could get my hands on."

He was frowning at her.

"This is a little disturbing."

"There is so much to learn and usually people learn from birth. Since your mother did not know apparently, she told you nothing."

"My mother died in childbirth."

"Ah. Do you have any idea who your father was?"

She shook her head. "Father used to call me his Scottish bastard, so I am assuming he was from Scotland."

His eyes sparked with anger but before he could respond, a knock at the door interrupted him.

"I am sorry, my lord, but Malik has told me to interrupt. There has been another attack."

Nico glanced toward the drapes and saw what she did. It was still light out. If someone was this brazen, it was not a good sign. Still, he hesitated. It made her feel better that he thought twice about leaving her. They may not have married for love, but respect and passion were good enough for her.

"Go," she said.

He leaned down to kiss her, but he did not close his eyes. Instead he stared into her as he brushed his mouth over hers. The gentle kiss had tears burning the back of her eyes. Then he rested his forehead on hers.

"We need a real honeymoon," he said, his voice ragged.

"You cannot mean you want to..." she trailed off at his knowing look. She cleared her throat. "I may not know much about your world, but this seems slightly more important."

He stood, a smile curving his lips. He helped her up off the floor. "After this is over, I will take you away, and we will spend three weeks in bed."

She felt her face heat and he laughed. He waited for her to right her clothes then opened the door. A footman stood there.

"Sir, Malik is in the dining room with your father, the duke, and your *relation*."

She bit her bottom lip, trying not to laugh. She knew Saint was the only one who could probably bring out such open animosity from a servant.

Nico turned and kissed her, in front of the servant. "I hope not to be too long."

"No worries, Nico. I understand it is urgent."

He smiled, and she felt her heart jump. She watched him walk down the hall and sighed. The first thing she had noticed about him was the way he walked through a room. Several months ago, she had watched him stride through the ballroom as if he didn't care what people thought of him. And now that she knew him better, she knew he really didn't. He was so self-possessed, so sure of himself.

"Lady Cordelia?" the footman said.

She realized she had been standing there staring after her husband. "Yes?"

"Mrs. Blackburn would like to see you in her morning room on the second floor."

"The second floor?"

"Second room on the left, my lady."

"Thank you, James."

The footman looked surprised when she remembered his name. She started up the staircase, thinking back to her husband. He really kept her off balance. One moment he was the imposing businessman, and the next he was enticing her into making love in the library. She loved the way he made her laugh. It had been so long since she had genuinely laughed at anything. In less than twenty-four hours, he had slipped beneath her reserve. Of course she was falling in love with the man.

She stopped on the next to the last step as it hit her.

She was falling in love with a man she didn't know, and worse, he wasn't even a man. He was a vampire.

"Cordelia?" her mother-in-law said. She saw her standing just a few paces away from the stairs. Cordelia shook herself.

"Yes?"

"Are you all right?"

She nodded slowly.

"You don't look well. Do you need to lie down?"

She shook her head. "No, I just need a little tea I think."

She followed her mother-in-law down the hall and into her parlor. As she did, her mind worked through the ramifications of being in love. She could stop it, she was sure of it. She did not know him well enough to be in love. Goodness, she didn't even know enough of this new life to contemplate being in love with a man who married her out of pity. They could say anything they wanted, but that was the truth of it. Nico would have survived the scandal. She would not.

"I'm a little worried about you. It isn't easy acquiring any family, but this…well, it isn't what you expected."

Cordelia sighed. "True. I wish I knew more about my birth father."

As she poured the tea, Adelaide looked at her. "You know nothing of your father's family?"

She shrugged. "Just that he was from Scotland."

"That is something. We can start looking there," she said, handing Cordelia a cup.

"Start looking?"

"I think we need to find out where you came from. Believe me, Nico has never been a man to lose his head. In fact, it was worse after Demetrius died. So locked down, but you blow into town and he is suddenly found in a compromising situation."

She blushed again. "I am sorry for that."

Her mother-in-law laughed. "Don't be. I am happy to watch it. His father and I were wondering if we would ever have grandbabies. With you, I know now that I will. But, with that said, I can assure you that it is important to find out who your father is."

"Why?" she asked, afraid of the answer. What if they found out her father was a horrible person?

"My dear, we should all know where we come from. And, your sire must have been a very powerful Born. You had both Hurst and Nico trailing after you. To be honest, I am amazed you have not been claimed before now."

"I am positive there were not many Borns in my area. This is my first real year in London. I had been here off and on for other things but not an entire season."

"Well, let's get down to work. You said your father was from Scotland? And you are eight and twenty? I think we need some help sorting out who was in London at that time."

Cordelia sat back and watched as her mother-in-law formulated a plan of attack and noted that she and Adelaide were probably more alike than either of them realized.

* * * *

Nico tried to concentrate on the conversation but his mind kept wandering. It was very unlike him, especially when the stakes were so high. He could not get his mind on the subject when he could still taste Cordelia on his tongue. He wanted to take her away. The cottage he owned in the lake district would be perfect. They could spend their days and nights making love, only stopping to eat and sleep. He could handle a month of days like that. Or more.

"Nicodemus, you might want to pay attention," Saint said.

He looked around the table and realized that his father, Gray, Malik, and his cousin were all staring at him. He shook himself and leaned forward.

"So, there was another killing?"

"A male human this time. I have a feeling one of the Mades tried to turn him," Malik said. "We know that does not work well."

Of course it didn't. A Made would never be strong enough to turn a human. It always ended up with the human dying as they slowly bled to death.

"Was it cleaned up?"

Gray nodded. "We got to it before the human authorities, but the rumors are definitely swirling through the lower classes. Fear is growing. At some point I am hoping the Alliance will step in."

"Don't hold your breath," Nico said as he looked at Malik. "You are sure it is another Made who did it?"

Malik nodded. "I doubt it was his idea. The Born who turned him probably gave him instructions."

"I just wish we had an idea who that is. It would be easier if we did," Nico said.

When everyone around the table lapsed into silence, he looked at them. There was something else they were not telling him.

"What is it?"

His father, who had been uncommonly silent until then, stood and walked to stand beside him. He reached into his pocket and handed over a familiar necklace.

Nico looked at the ruby necklace and knew what the inscription said. He glanced up at his father, who suddenly looked his age.

"What is this?" he asked, anger and irritation filling his voice. It was the betrothal necklace his brother had given his wife. It had not been seen since his death.

"It was left at the scene of the attack. We think it is a sign."

"I killed Neal."

"Are you sure?" Saint asked. "You were half out of your mind before we got to you. The fever raged through your body and you almost died. Did you see him die?"

Nico closed his eyes, trying to block the memories of a hundred years ago, but they came rushing back. The feel of pressing the stake through Neal's heart still haunted him. He had killed more than a few Mades in his time, more to put them out of their misery and protect Carriers. But this was different. This was a Born and one of his best friends. Killing him had not been easy.

But Saint was correct. Neal had given him some kind of concoction that had made Nico ill, and his memories were hazy at best.

"Bloody hell," he whispered.

He opened his eyes and looked at his friends and family. "It is either Neal Pearson seeking revenge or someone very close to him."

"Either way, son, if we are right, you are the reason he is here. I have a feeling he will stop at nothing to ruin you."

And that meant his friends and family were in the crosshairs.

"And more than that," Malik said, "some of this will

have to be explained to your new bride."

"What?" he asked, his rage turning into panic in a split second. Even without asking he knew the answer, but he did not want to face it.

"Nico." Malik waited until he looked at him. "There is one thing we know about Neal and his form of revenge. He *always* goes after the women."

Which meant that by marrying Cordelia, he made her a target of an insane killer bent on making Nico pay for imaginary transgressions.

Neal would not stop until Cordelia was dead.

Chapter Fifteen

The next afternoon, they assembled in Nico's library to map out the attacks. Nico knew he was missing something. There was some little bit of information that was just out of his reach mentally. He knew as soon as he discovered it, this would make more sense. At the moment, though, it did not.

Neal had been his best friend for a while. They were the same age and had some of the same interests. Or so he thought. Now he was not sure of that. Everything Neal did in the end was colored by his actions before his death.

Before Nico killed him.

"So, you think that this is Neal Pearson?" Gray asked.

Nico shook himself out of his funk and looked at the map they were working on, then up at Gray. "Yes, I do. Not many people know about the necklace. It has been missing since my brother's death."

"But you killed him, correct?" Gray asked.

He nodded. "I thought I did."

"There have been experiments." Saint stood and began pacing the room.

Everyone looked at Saint.

"What?" Nico was shocked. Experimenting with life and death?

Saint stopped at a window, looking out at the street. "I have heard there are a few people that have reported experiments on almost-dead Borns. I have not been able to find anything."

And that meant a lot. Saint was a giant of a man, but he had a scientific mind and he was actually brilliant. From the tone of his voice, he thought the story might be true. And if the cynic could be convinced...

"Raising Borns from the dead? That sounds ridiculous,"

Gray said.

"Don't be so hasty in your judgment, Gray," Malik said. "Borns have done some horrendous things in the past collectively, but individually, they have been even worse. Get another Born who is upset over losing a loved one, then they will do anything."

Saint snorted and crossed his arms over his chest. "If he is insane."

Malik smiled. "You should know you don't have to be sane to be brilliant."

Saint snorted again, but said nothing in retaliation. "There have been rumors of that for the last fifty years or so. More in the last ten about reviving the dead."

"So someone could have revived him?" Gray asked. "I cannot say that the Alliance is going to be happy about this."

"No, but I did not say it was successful. I highly doubt they were, but I didn't want to rule anything out." Saint returned to the map.

"Would there be anyone who would want the bastard around?" his father asked.

Nico shrugged. "He was an orphan, but there was Charlotte, his mate—if you can call her that. He had very few friends."

His father nodded. "I think it best if we make some discreet inquiries to find out about her and her people. She was a Carrier?"

"I think she was. I knew little about her." Nico's memory of that time was faint, like his brain had tried to forget it all.

"That's odd," his father said.

"What?" Everything about Neal had been odd.

"Most Borns like to parade their mates around once they have mated and bonded, but you are saying he did not?" His father looked confused.

"It is hard to know exactly what he was thinking at the time. The man never seemed to have a plan, but we all know that he did." Nico couldn't keep the irritation out of his voice. As his friend, Nico should have known. But, he had not. He'd never had an inkling of where the bastard had been from. There were rumors after he died about his parents, their murder...and that Neal had been responsible. But Nico had chalked it up to gossip.

Gray turned his attention to the map. "Let's look at the killings. I have marked off on the map that Malik made where the killings have occurred here in London."

"These here, what are they?" his father asked, pointing at the map.

"These are the first killings. They are women, no men at this point," Gray said.

"And now, these are men?" His father pointed to a different area of the map.

"We can't say for sure if they were attacked by a Made." Gray ran his fingers through his hair. Talking about the killings was obviously hard on him.

"They were." Malik said, certainty ringing in his voice.

"You know?" Nico asked.

"I know this one, right outside the hell. We were there when they found the man. The scent was unmistakable." The look on Malik's face was one of disgust.

He did not have to ask Malik what he meant. He had smelled it, too. There was a distinct odor to a newly Made that often caused Nico to become ill.

"Do you not see the pattern?" Hurst asked quietly. He had not said a word since he arrived.

"What?" Gray looked up, surprise on his face.

He set his finger on the map. "This is your townhouse."

"Yes." Nico studied the map, looking for what Hurst saw.

"These are the killings," Hurst said, moving his finger to the markings they had made. "He's surrounding your house."

"Bloody hell," Gray said. He looked at the map. "He is coming after you, Blackburn."

"Why would he do that? Revenge, yes, that might be a reason. But why now? It has been one hundred years since I killed him." Nico shook his head. "What am I saying? It isn't him. It is someone who knows the story."

"We kept that secret. Very few people know the true story," his father said.

"But they know, Father. Some of the details have probably made their way through the gossips." Nico knew the way this town worked. Nothing stayed a secret for long.

Before his father could respond, there was a knock at the door. Without waiting for an answer, it swung open. His mother marched in with Cordelia behind her.

"Good afternoon, gentlemen," his mother said with a smile. "Nico, Samuel, we are going out."

"Out where?" Nico asked from behind the desk, trying to pull the women's attention away from what they had been working on. He did not need his mother or Cordelia getting involved.

"We are going over to Bingam's house to spend some time with Lady Elizabeth."

His father caught on also and came forward. He kissed his mother on the cheek. "You will take a footman with you."

It was not a request. It was an order. Those usually did not go over well with his mother, but she smiled and patted his cheek.

"I daresay we need to take several. Cordelia and I are definitely not stupid," his mother said with a smile.

He glanced at his wife to see her reaction. She smiled, and a bit smugly at that. Nico did not say a word as he approached her.

"You will be careful." Again, he ordered, just like his father.

"I guess I could defy you, but that would be stupid. And I will remind you, husband, that the only time I was not careful, I ended up married to a vampire."

He sensed their audience, but he ignored them. It was

not hard to do. Whenever Cordelia was near, little else matter to him. Even before he neared her, he could scent her blood. It called to him like a siren's song.

He gave her a kiss much as his father had his mother, but whispered just loud enough for her to hear, "Do not take too long, or I'll come after you."

When he pulled back, her face was delightfully pink. Her eyelids fluttered then she looked up at him. She might be able to hide a lot of things, but her attraction to him was not one of them.

"I don't like to be threatened." Her breath whispered over his skin. He knew from her cheeky tone she wasn't angry.

"Be careful." Nico leaned down and kissed her nose.

She nodded and followed his mother out the door. He watched the sway of her hips until she was out of view. When he turned around, the entire room was watching him.

"What?"

"It seems that our leader has truly fallen." Saint said.

"What the bloody hell are you talking about? Leader?" He paused. "What do you mean fallen?"

His father returned to the map, a grim expression on his face. "Boys, I think we need to work on the map and get our strategy more refined before the ladies return. If I know my wife, and I do, she is formulating a way to get back here in time to find out. It is best we keep them as far away as possible."

They all agreed.

* * * *

Cordelia followed Adelaide up the steep staircase, trying to push the thoughts of Nico aside. She had been smiling since they left the townhouse, and it would not do for her to walk into a room with an ill woman looking like that.

The maid led them down a short hallway and through the

door. The room was dark, but well-appointed, with a large bed, a sitting area, and a private bathing area. Apparently vampire doctors could afford these things.

She suppressed the giggle that threatened. When had her life become so strange?

"She was awake part of the morning, but mostly she is still sleeping," the maid said quietly.

"I can hear you over there, Abigail." The voice came from across the room.

The maid smiled. "And she is a wee bit cranky."

"You are being generous. I am being a raving bitch. You can say it," said the woman in the bed.

The accent was refined, telling of her time spent at finishing schools and fine tutors. As they approached the bed, she recognized the woman. She had seen her at a few balls and musicales in the past few months. They had not circulated in the same social circles, but she had heard that the woman was strong minded, or as men called it, overly opinionated.

Cordelia's mother-in-law approached the bed with a smile on her face. "Good afternoon, dear. I'm Adelaide Blackburn."

When Cordelia finally got a good look at her, she had to swallow her gasp. Her face was ravaged. Two days after her attack, yellow and purple bruises marred her face, as did a swollen eye. Her lip had been split, and when Cordelia looked closely, she saw that there were faint bruises around her neck.

Her eyes fluttered, but she could only open one.

"I see you did not run screaming from the room." The woman gave them a weak smile.

Adelaide tsked. "Of course not. I raised two boys. And, being as old as I am, I have seen much worse." She kept her voice brisk and official, with a touch of warmth. Cordelia's admiration for her mother-in-law grew. "This is my daughter-in-law, Lady Cordelia."

Elizabeth looked at her, and Cordelia smiled. "Good afternoon."

"I am not sure there is much good about it, but it is nice to have visitors."

Adelaide patted Elizabeth's hand. "Oh, but it is good. You are alive. That is more than any woman who was attacked by a Made has had the joy of saying. Do not waste it."

She glanced at Adelaide. "I have been disowned by my family and now there are whispers that I am tainted."

"How do you know that?" Cordelia asked, moving to the other side of the bed.

"That duke thinks he talks softly, but he does not."

Cordelia snorted and she saw Elizabeth's lips curve. She winced.

"You should be careful, or your lip will bleed again," Adelaide said in a motherly voice. "I think it is time to eat."

Elizabeth's face paled. "I am not sure I can."

Adelaide sat on the edge of the bed beside Elizabeth. "You can and you will. Cordelia, please order her some tea and dry toast. It is very important that you eat."

Cordelia hurried to do Adelaide's bidding. She assumed she was being dictatorial because it was the best way to deal with a sick person who did not want to heal. And she had a distinct feeling that Elizabeth hoped that she would die. If not, she was going to help it along.

After speaking to the footman outside of the door, she came back in the room.

"What do you care what your stupid parents say?" Adelaide asked.

She rolled her eyes. Cordelia had thought her family was odd until she married. Now she had a vampire husband and a mother-in-law who had no problems speaking her mind.

"They are my family." Tears pooled in Elizabeth's eyes.

"They sound like they are idiots. Now, I must go down and give the cook my healing herbs for your tea. Cordelia, dear, come talk to Elizabeth."

With that, Adelaide walked out of the room.

Cordelia took her mother-in-law's place. "I hope that she did not upset you too much."

"No, it's just...to be completely shut out of my family. I feel as if I am at sea."

Cordelia shrugged. "The only contact I have with my family is my sister, and there isn't much."

Elizabeth took Cordelia's hand. "Your mother, does she approve?"

"My mother died in childbirth. I did not even know I was a Carrier until after I married Nico."

Elizabeth sighed. "I have never gotten along with my family very well. I never actually fit in with them."

Cordelia sighed. "I know how that is. I came here on my own this year."

"Without your family? What did they say?"

"I doubt very much Alex knew I was gone for the first couple of weeks." Her brother wasn't exactly a caring person.

"Oh, Alex, the Earl of Collingsworth."

"Yes." Cordelia smiled. "See there are things that can be worse than having your family disown you."

Elizabeth smiled, then winced.

"I am sorry. I will try not to be funny." Cordelia didn't want to cause the poor girl any more pain.

"No, it is much better than the duke and Dr. Bingam. They are both so dour. They look at me as if I am a puzzle to solve. I do not like it."

"I do have a question." Cordelia hoped she wasn't being too personal.

"Yes?"

"Did you fight off a Made? All by yourself?"

Elizabeth grew serious. "Yes. And I would do it again if I had to."

"When you are feeling better, would you teach me how to fight? I really don't know how to." If she'd learned anything in the last few days, it was how vulnerable she was in this new world.

"And why would you think you need to now? You are married and mated. Blackburn should take care of you."

"I am sure he will, but I want to plan for anything." Cordelia had spent too many years on her own to allow herself to rely solely on a man.

"I will be happy to, but I am not sure I know where I will be when I am better."

"Why don't you move into Nico's townhouse?" she said.

"What?"

"You can move in with us." It would be nice to have a friend in the house.

"That is an excellent idea, Cordelia," Adelaide said as she walked in. A footman followed, pushing the teacart. "Now, we will have something to eat and leave you to rest. I would like for you to move in by the end of the week."

Elizabeth gave Cordelia a pleading look. "I have learned that it is best to just go along with anyone who has Blackburn as a surname."

"But of course. Come, sit up, dear. Cordelia, could you help her?"

She did Adelaide's bidding, doing her best to keep from hurting Elizabeth. Still, she could tell it bothered her a bit.

As the three of them sat there waiting for Elizabeth to eat, Adelaide chattered on about nothing in particular. Cordelia played along, taking her cues from her mother-in-law. By the time Elizabeth had eaten one piece of toast and drank a cup of tea, her eyes were drooping.

"I think we need to leave Elizabeth to sleep, Cordelia." Adelaide stood from her chair.

"I am sorry," Elizabeth said, her voice slurred.

"Don't be, dear. You get your rest, and we will come back tomorrow."

As they left the room, Cordelia could already hear Elizabeth's even breathing.

She followed her mother-in-law out, and they sat in the carriage. Cordelia knew she was holding in her thoughts until they were in private, and it did not take long for Adelaide to explode.

"I want to strangle her parents."

There was enough anger in her voice to tell Cordelia it was a good thing they were not near Elizabeth's parents.

"How can anyone ignore what has happened to her? How can they leave her?"

Cordelia shrugged. "Not all families are like yours."

"Ours," she said without taking her attention away from the window.

"What?"

"It is ours now. You are part of the family." Adelaide sighed and looked at her. Her anger drained, but now she saw the pain. "I cannot understand leaving a young woman like that to fend for herself. Not with her background. We do not look at virginity the way the rest of society does. A woman does not have to be a virgin when she marries, but because she was ruined by a Made, and worse, survived by her own hands, she has been left out in the cold by her parents. They are reprehensible."

"Maybe they will change their minds."

"I doubt it. But they will regret it. I will have Nico ensure they do not have a very successful business season."

Cordelia was surprised by her mother-in-law's words. She was always so kind to the people around her. "You would do that?"

Adelaide looked her in the eye. "She is their daughter, and they have disowned her. And, let's remember, for something that was not her fault. No, they deserve what they get."

"Remind me never to make you mad."

She studied Cordelia for a moment then she threw her head back and laughed. "Every day I am reminded that Nico chose very wisely."

She opened her mouth to say that Nico did not choose her, but the carriage shuddered to a stop.

Something tickled at the back of her neck. Something close to panic.

"Why are we stopping? We could not have made it home so fast."

Before her mother-in-law could respond, there was a shout.

"Oh, that does not sound good," Adelaide said, leaning toward the window. A sense of foreboding filled Cordelia. She would never be able to explain it to anyone if they asked, but the sense that something was very, very wrong swept through her.

"No, don't." She closed her eyes as a wave of nausea washed over. "You need to stay here."

There was a struggle on top of the coach. It jolted from side to side. There was a loud gunshot and the door opened. A nasty looking fellow leaned into the cab.

"Here she is, fellows!"

The short, fat little man was dirty, as if he had been rolling around the streets. When he smiled, yellow teeth took up half his face. His eyes were small and so brown they were almost black. Fear rolled through her as he reached for her, his fingers grasping at her skirt and tugging. She could not do anything but act on instinct. With more force than she thought she had, she raised her foot and kicked the man in the stomach. Her mother-in-law started hitting him with her parasol.

"Bloody hell," he screamed, falling back and releasing her skirt.

Before the door closed, the carriage was taking off into the gloom of a late London afternoon.

Chapter Sixteen

Nico and Malik were sitting in his library, enjoying a brandy, when a commotion rose in the hall.

"We need someone dispatched to get Dr. Bingam right now," Cordelia said, her voice rather loud and echoing down the hall.

At the sound of his wife's voice, Nico was on his feet and hurrying out the door. Sheer terror raced through his blood before he finally saw Cordelia standing in the hall. She was directing the footmen to bring in one of the guards.

She must have spotted him out of the corner of her eye. Without hesitation, she ran to him, and he wrapped his arms around her.

"What happened?" Nico looked around at the chaos surrounding him. Obviously, something very bad had happened.

"We were attacked and John was shot. We need to bring him into the library."

He nodded and waved the men into his library.

He kept his arm around her waist, but he ushered her into the room. John looked okay. He had a bit of blood on his sleeve, but being a Born, he had a strong constitution.

"What are you doing sitting up? We need Dr. Bingam to look at you," Cordelia admonished John. She shook off Nico's arm, and he did not like that. In fact, he almost pulled her back against him, but realized that would not go over well. She was standing over John, her hands on her hips.

John didn't know what to do from the look on his face. He wanted to tell her to leave him alone, but because she was the lady of the house, and more importantly, Nico's wife, he would never tell her that.

"Cordelia." He waited until she looked at him. What he

saw broke his heart. Fear still darkened her eyes. "John is a vampire. He is not going to die from a flesh wound."

She glanced back down at John, and her face flushed. "I am sorry, John."

He shook his head. "Do not worry, my lady. It is nice to have you concerned about me."

She nodded but said nothing else. Nico could tell she was barely holding on to her emotions. Her embarrassment was easy to see, but he could also sense she was still recovering from the aftereffects of the attack.

John left, and for the first time, he noticed his mother was being calmed by his father. Not much upset his mother, since she had nerves of steel. For her to be so upset, it must have been bad.

"Tell me what happened."

Stuart, the driver, stepped up. "Sorry for this, sir. We did not even see the problem until it was upon us. They used a ruse to stop the carriage. A false accident," he said, his voice ripe with self-disgust. "I should have seen it. The gunshot was an accident from what I can tell."

"What were they after?" he asked.

Stuart looked at Cordelia.

He nodded. "Thank you, Stuart. You can go now."

Stuart nodded and closed the door behind him.

Nico took a few moments to bring his rage under control. He did not want his mother or Cordelia to think that he was mad at them. But, the extra time did not seem to work.

"What the bloody hell is going on!"

His mother gave him a withering look. Cordelia's eyes widened, then narrowed.

"Do not take that tone with me, Nico. It isn't our fault. It was starting to get dark, yes, but it wasn't that dark. And we escaped with no damage."

"Except for John."

She frowned. "Of course. John."

She looked toward the door.

"Don't even think about going to check on him again. He's fine." He glanced at his mother. "Borns or Mades?"

Cordelia answered. "These were not vampires."

"How would you know?" Malik asked bluntly. Nico had forgotten his friend was still there.

"Give me some credit. The one man we saw was not a vampire. He was short, probably shorter than I am, and he was dirty."

"We are not immune to shortness or filthy in our ranks," Malik countered. "In fact, Mades could come from any walk of life."

"Of course. But his eyes were not green like yours. And he did not have the strength. The man who grabbed my dress was not a man who could have broken down a door," she retorted, her eyes hot with anger.

Nico glanced at his friend and noticed his lips twitching.

"So, they were human. But why?" Nico asked.

"Could the bad Made have hired him?" Cordelia asked.

"Possibly, but I don't think so. He would want someone who is beholden to him for more than some gold pieces," Malik said.

Before they could discuss it more, there was a knock at the door.

"Come," he said.

"Lady Diana is here to see her sister, and she is in quite a state," James said. Before Nico could respond, Cordelia's sister rushed in to the room.

"There you are," she said and ran to Cordelia. For a moment, Nico thought she might hug Cordelia, but at the last moment, she stopped. "You are not harmed."

Her voice was filled with relief.

"What are you talking about Diana?" Cordelia asked. "You look like you ran all the way here."

"Alex sent a footman with a note saying you had been abducted."

Silence filled the room. He shared a glance with Malik, then he looked at his wife. It took only a moment for her to understand just what had happened. At that moment, he wanted to wipe away the pain he saw shift over her face before she hid it.

"You say you received a note from your brother? He is in town?" Nico asked.

Diana nodded, not taking her gaze from Cordelia. "I did not know until his footman showed up with the note. I am just happy that it was all some kind of sick joke."

He shared another glance with Malik. This had not been a joke.

Nico turned to Cordelia. "Why don't you, mother, and your sister take some tea? Malik and I have some business to discuss with my father."

Both his mother and Cordelia gave him knowing looks. "Of course," his mother said finally, but her tone told him that she knew exactly what was going on. Diana followed his mother, but he grabbed Cordelia and pulled her to stand in front of him.

She was looking down at the ground. He slipped his finger beneath her chin and raised her head to meet his gaze.

"Whatever your brother did does not reflect on you."

She looked into his eyes, and he had the idea that she was trying to read his thoughts. Then she nodded and followed his mother and her sister.

As soon as the door shut, Malik asked, "What do you know about your bastard brother-in-law?"

"That he's the only one who is the true son of the late earl. And that he owes everyone in town," Nico said. "Not to mention that he left his sister to her own devices here in London."

"If he knew she was here," Malik commented. "I have a feeling your wife did just about anything she wanted to."

"I think we need to pay him a visit."

"Do you know where he is staying?" his father asked.

"More than likely he is in the townhouse now."

Malik nodded. "Let's go take care of him."

* * * *

Cordelia was looking out the window when the tea tray arrived. She knew it was too late to have afternoon tea, and they had already had tea earlier, but Adelaide was of the belief that everything could be solved with a good cup of tea. It had worked on her sister. Diana was the typical British lady, stuffing her emotions down until it was like they did not exist.

When she burst into the house earlier, it was the first true emotion Cordelia had seen her sister display since she'd been married.

"Do come and have a little bit to eat, Cordelia," Adelaide said.

She wanted to say no and keep pouting. How could you face people who knew the worst about your family? Her brother had sent people to abduct her. For money.

"Cordelia?"

She finally turned and did her mother-in-law's bidding.

"I do not know what Alex was thinking. He never did have a proper sense of humor," Diana said.

A nervous laugh escaped before she could stop it. Diana looked at her as if she had lost her mind.

"Sorry, but only you would think there is a proper sense of humor."

"What do you mean by that?" Diana asked. There was an edge to her voice but Cordelia did not heed it.

"I mean that there is no proper sense of humor. There is no guidebook that says what is right and what is wrong."

Diana sniffed. Cordelia realized she might have hurt her sister's feelings.

"I am sorry, Diana. I did not mean to be cruel."

Diana shook her head. "No you never do mean it."

There was a beat of silence that stretched into awkwardness. Cordelia sat forward and placed her hand on Diana's knee. "I truly am sorry, Diana."

Diana looked down at Cordelia's hand, and there was a moment where Cordelia almost pulled it back. But Diana laid her hand over Cordelia's.

That seemed to give Diana the courage to speak. "You do not truly know how cruel he could be. I know he wasn't that nice to you, but when we were growing up..." she trailed off, shut her eyes, and shook her head.

"Go on." Cordelia had never seen Diana so upset.

"Alex took delight in scaring me. And father egged him on."

"Oh, Diana."

She looked up at her. "Do not pity me. Do not. Mother did chastise Alex, when father wasn't around."

Cordelia was truly not surprised by this information. "He is not a nice person."

Diana gave a watery chuckle. "That is an understatement."

Cordelia squeezed Diana's knee. "You do realize this was not a joke?"

Diana's eyes widened. "What are you saying?"

"Some men tried to abduct me earlier."

"But, how did Alex know?" Then comprehension filled her expression. "Oh."

"Yes, oh."

"We must do something."

"What can we do?" Cordelia asked as she shrugged and pulled her hand away from Diana's.

"Do not worry. Nico and Malik will take care of it," Adelaide said.

She glanced at her mother-in-law. She had forgotten she was there.

"What?"

Adelaide smiled. "Nico. He is over there to give your

brother the talking to he deserves."

Alarm moved through her. "Adelaide, you mean Malik and Nico went over to the townhouse? Why didn't you tell me?"

She shrugged. "I thought you knew."

"Knew?" Alarm ballooned into panic. "I did not know."

She shot up out of the chair but did not get far. Diana grabbed her by the arm.

"Cordelia, what on earth is going on?"

"If I am correct, my husband and his friend just went over to our brother's townhouse to kill him."

"Oh, they won't kill him." Adelaide corrected. "But he won't ever try to get someone to abduct you again."

She looked at Diana. "He will kill him if we don't go over there."

Diana nodded and stood. "Although, there is a part of me that thinks we need to just leave them to it."

She stopped, and Diana ran into her back. She turned and looked at Diana. "No matter what you think of my husband, he is not a killer."

Diana looked confused. "You just said you were afraid he would kill Alex."

How could she make her sister understand? "Out of anger. Otherwise, he would not think of it. Alex is a horrible person, but he is a peer of the realm. No matter how powerful Gray is, Nico would be in trouble if he were to kill our brother."

Diana grabbed her by the hand. "Let's go."

* * * *

No one answered the door when Nico knocked.

"He probably fired the staff," Malik commented. His attention was on the street behind them.

"More than likely. Cordelia kept the staff on somehow, but Alex probably could not keep up the payments."

"How did your wife pay them?"

Nico knocked again. "What? How did she pay them?"

Before Malik could answer, the door was pulled open. The man who stood there bore no resemblance to his wife or his sister. His hair was the color of mud, his eyes small and black, and he was short. At least a head shorter than Nico himself. He was disheveled, as if he had just risen from bed, but he was wearing evening clothes. Alex had been drinking for most of his adult life and probably before then. He was bloated, his enormous stomach hanging over his waistband.

"What do you want?"

He was not standing that close to Alex, but he could smell the soured liquor on his breath. It was so strong, Nico had to fight the need to step back.

He squinted at Nico, then looked over his shoulder at Malik. When his gaze came back to meet Nico's, Nico noticed how glazed Alex's eyes were. He doubted his brother-in-law had been sober much in the last twenty-four hours.

"Who the hell are you?"

"Nico Blackburn."

He did not introduce Malik. He saw no reason to. "May I come in for a chat?"

Alex hesitated but finally relented. Nico followed him in, waiting until Malik caught up with them after closing the door. In less than a week, the house had become dirty. He must have gotten rid of the staff immediately after he came to town.

He led them to the same breakfast area where he had met with Cordelia. There was no fire in the hearth, no warmth.

"Keep control of your emotions," Malik said just loud enough for Nico to hear.

Nico looked at him. "Have I acted out of control?"

Malik shook his head. "I've known you long enough to know you are just waiting."

Waiting? Nico wondered what that was supposed to

mean. "For what?"

Alex spoke before Malik could answer. "So, you're the poor bugger who is attached to our little Scottish bastard?" Alex said.

Anger shifted through him and sparked into rage. One minute he was telling Malik that he would control himself, and in the next, he was holding his brother-in-law by the neck as Alex clawed at his hands.

"I would advise you that Nico does not like you using that name," Malik said calmly.

Nico had no intention of being calm. "Were you the one behind her abduction?"

"He cannot speak, Nico," Malik said.

With an angry shove, he pushed Alex back into the chair with such force, it almost toppled over.

"Tell me," Nico said through gritted teeth.

"I didn't think it right," Alex answered. "She married you, a commoner, without approval of her family."

Nico was quickly losing his patience. "Your oldest sister was in attendance, and I myself sent you a note."

"I did not approve," Alex huffed out as he leaned over to grab a bottle of brandy. "As the brother, I should have been contacted for approval."

"And so you decided to have your sister abducted to get money from me?" Nico suspected the man was crazy.

Alex snorted. "Good lot that did me. She has been a blight on our family since the day she was born. Must be the Scottish blood coursing through her. Cursed she is."

"I think you might want to rethink your opinion on your sister, Alex," Malik said.

Her brother blinked, looked up at Malik and sneered. "I do not have to answer to the likes of you."

Malik glanced at Nico. "Do what you want."

"I hope you got her unsoiled." Alex sneered. "With her mother's blood, I cannot say I would be surprised if she wasn't."

That pushed Nico over the edge. The bastard drank and whored his sisters' money away, and he sat there passing judgment on her. Without hesitation, he stepped forward and took hold of the bastard's collar again. The crack of Alex's nose beneath Nico's fingers was loud and satisfying. He kept hitting Alex, until he felt someone tugging on his arm. Through the haze of anger that clouded his vision, he heard his wife's voice.

"Nico, please stop, you are going to kill him."

He turned, still holding Alex by the collar. "What?"

He was trying to come to terms that his wife was there when she yanked on his arm.

"Please, stop."

Nico shook his head, trying to clear it. She released his arm and then cupped his face in her hands.

"Let's go."

He released Alex, who dropped to the floor with a loud thud. Alex was coughing and sputtering, gasping for a good bit of air.

"I will have you arrested by God."

Cordelia released Nico and looked around him at her brother.

"You even think of saying anything about my husband to the authorities, I will let everyone you owe money to know that you are in town."

His eyes widened.

"That's right. I will also let it be known that you have nothing to your name."

With that she turned around. "Let's go home."

He noticed for the first time that Diana was in the room. "Come, Malik, Diana, let's do as Cordelia says."

They settled in the carriage. No one said a thing for a few awkward moments.

Diana broke the silence. "Well, things do seem to happen around you, Cordelia."

"Diana, I do not think my wife needs to hear that right

now."

Diana looked at him. "Of course."

Cordelia felt the need to defend her sister. "Don't berate her, Nico. Diana was just trying to help. She was never good at silences."

Diana gave her a thankful smile. "True."

"Would you like us to drop you off at your townhouse, Diana?" Nico asked.

Diana smiled. "That would be wonderful. I do believe I will stay in tonight."

"No, come with us. We are not going to do anything, and we can have dinner. You too, Malik." Nico offered. He sensed Cordelia's study, but he did not look at her.

"That sounds wonderful. Thank you," Diana said.

Malik answered with a low growl.

Cordelia leaned back in her seat, wondering what her husband was up to.

* * * *

Dinner had been a test of his wills, Nico thought. Cordelia had held her head high, not once letting on to anyone else that she was close to falling apart. As he followed her up the staircase, he wondered just who the woman he married was.

It was an odd thought considering the intimacies they had shared over the last few days. Still, there was a lot to her that he didn't know. When she reached the door, she reached for the knob at the same time he did. His hand landed on hers. She bowed her head.

"I can open doors for myself, Nico."

It was an odd statement. "Of course you can, but it doesn't make you weak to accept help."

She nodded and said nothing else. Nico opened the door and waited for her to step into her room. He followed her, shutting the door behind him.

"Did my brother say anything horrible?"

He wondered at the tone, but he answered. "No. Nothing I did not know before."

She looked at him over her shoulder. Most people would say it was a coy gesture, but he saw the earnest look on her face.

"So he said horrible things you already knew?"

"Why are you worried about what he said?"

She shrugged and sighed, walking over to the window. "My brother is not a nice man."

"No, but London is littered with men like him."

'Yes, and they think they have a right to everything."

"Is there something else I should know about your brother?"

She shook her head but did not look at him. "Knowing what a bastard he is should be enough."

He sensed there were things, things she would never reveal to him, and it made him so tired. So bloody tired. They couldn't truly know each other while they were in London. With the case hanging over him, he couldn't concentrate on her and her needs.

"What he is has no reflection on you."

"I always thought it odd that he acted as a bastard when the rest of us were bastards in the truest of ways."

"Your brother has no character."

She shook her head. "A loveless marriage. My father had to marry, and he wooed my mother. Her family was rich as Croesus and had money to spare. So, he married her. Then he ruined her life."

Nico did not know what to say to his wife to comfort her. He couldn't imagine what her life must have been like as a child.

Her voice had grown very quiet. "I wonder what would have happened if she had never met him. If she had a life that was worth living."

His heart broke at the sadness he heard in her voice. She

wasn't a woman given to melancholy, not that he knew of. But being confronted by her brother and his actions might be a little too much for her.

"Cordelia—"

"He paid them, didn't he? My own brother hired the men who tried to abduct me?"

He could lie, but she needed to know the truth. "Yes."

She dropped her head against the window.

"It is no reflection on you."

She turned to him then, and he could see the unshed tears in her eyes. "How can you say that? I share blood with him. If someone in your family did that, what would you think?"

Tears spilled over. "I tried. For a very long time, I tried to fit into the Collingsworth household, but by the time I was seven, I understood. I would never be accepted. By him, by my father. And the worst of it? Being considered a bastard. I would never try what he tried today."

Of course she wouldn't. Cordelia did not take the easy way out.

"And, to bring Diana in on it. That is lower than I thought he would go."

"Then why did you protect him when you got to his house?"

She frowned at him, her brow furrowing in confusion. "What?"

"You pulled me off him."

She rolled her eyes. "It had nothing to do with him and everything to do with you."

He needed to know. Did she think him a monster? He would not blame her. She had been thrust into an unknown world where everything she thought was true wasn't.

"Did you think I would kill him? That I am like the Mades who are running the streets?"

"What are you talking about?" Confusion was plain on Cordelia's face.

"I worried that you thought I could not control myself."

"Of course you couldn't. You were ready to kill him."

"I can control my temper."

"No you cannot."

Frustration boiled over. "I am not an animal."

Her eyes widened. "Yes, I know that."

"Then why did you stop me?"

"Because, I did not want my husband to go to jail for killing my brother. I might not have wanted to get married, but I definitely do not want my husband in prison."

Something close to relief rushed through him. The fact she sounded so irritated told him she was telling the truth. He reached for her, pulling her into his arms. He needed her so much. More than he would admit to even himself.

She came to him easily, tilting her head back and offering her lips up to him. He wanted to taste…to tease…to conquer. It wasn't about that, not this time. This time was to show her just how much he cherished her.

He kissed her slowly, biting at her lips. She hummed and closed her eyes. The sound of her approval washed through him. Had he ever worried about another woman accepting him? He did not think so. But this woman, he desired her in a way that was not normal.

If he thought more about it, he might worry, but instead he wanted to show her what she meant to him.

He kissed a path down her neck. Drawing in the scent of her and the sweet smell of her blood, he shuddered. He had been feeding for hundreds of years, but he could not remember ever needing someone this much. He licked her pulse point, then grazed her neck with his teeth. She shivered and moaned. Carriers had the need to provide nourishment to their mates. It was primal. Cordelia probably didn't even know what was compelling her.

He broke her skin and vein, drawing a little of her blood into his mouth. The taste of her essence danced over his taste buds. His inner beast roared to life, demanding he take more.

It took all his control to fight it back. This was about Cordelia.

He pulled back and watched as her lashes fluttered, then she opened her eyes. He bent and picked her up.

"Nico," she said, but did not finish. He did not let her. He swooped in for a kiss, trying to pour every bit of his hunger for her into it.

He walked her to the bed and set her on her feet. Cupping her face, he kissed her again. Then, he slipped behind her and undid the buttons down her back. As he pushed the fabric apart, he encountered bare skin. He sighed and sent a prayer to his maker for giving him such a wonderful wife. Her flesh was smooth as porcelain. Unable to resist, he touched his mouth to the back of her neck. Slowly, he moved his way down her delicate spine, pulling her dress down as he went. Soon she was completely naked. He laid her on the bed and joined her.

"Nico?" He could hear the question. What was he doing? If he told her, she would never believe him. So, he showed her.

He bent his head and tasted her then—licking and nipping her flesh until he lost himself in her soft curves and scented skin. When he set his mouth on her sex, the flavor of her desire shot through him. His teeth were actually throbbing, aching with the need to feed. It only took moments before she was gasping his name, her body shivering with her release.

By the time he made his way back up her body, he was consumed with a hunger only she could satisfy. When he reached to undo his trousers, he realized his hands were shaking.

He made quick work of his own clothes and joined her on the bed. He entered her in one hard thrust, and she moaned his name. Waiting was not an option. Every primal urge was pushing him to feed. He continued to thrust inside her as he punctured her skin, sinking into her vein and drawing her sweet blood out. It rushed through him as he continued to thrust inside of her. The sensation of reaching his orgasm while drinking from her had his head spinning. He pulled his fangs from her throat, licking over the punctures to ensure they would heal properly, then he collapsed on top of her.

She lay beneath him, the scent of her still filling his senses. With great effort, he lifted his head and looked down at her. Her eyes were closed, her flesh dewy, and she was smiling.

"Don't ever assume that I look at you through your relations."

She opened her eyes and looked at him. A long moment passed as she studied Nico. Then she cupped his face with one hand and gave him a sweet, slow kiss.

"Thank you."

He had thought she might say something else, but for now, it was enough.

* * * *

"I hate this bloody place," Saint said. Malik glanced at him but dismissed him again. Saint wasn't happy unless he was complaining. It was something that Malik had learned well over the last week.

He could not blame his friend, though. This hell was one of the worst he had ever been inside. It was nice enough, had all the things most of the *ton* wanted in their hells. But, the debauchery went beyond what either he or Saint liked. Malik had certain tastes, but this place definitely lean toward the extreme.

"So you talked to Lady Diana," Saint asked. "Is she like her sister?"

He didn't like the tone in Saint's voice. "Yes, and no, she is nothing like her sister."

"Hmm, she is quite beautiful, but she has not mated.

Odd." Saint's mouth formed a faint smile.

"I have a feeling that Diana still does not know what she is," Malik answered.

There was a beat of silence. "So she has no idea that she is a Carrier?"

He asked it so loud, a few people glanced at them. "Keep it down, Saint. No, she does not know, and for that matter, Cordelia did not until she married. Since Diana has said that she will never marry again, I don't think it is of much importance."

"But, being a widow, she might be up for a good bit of fun."

"I highly doubt that." Malik tried to keep his temper under control.

"You never know."

Irritation crunched down his spine. He knew that Saint was doing it just to get a rise out of him. It didn't seem to matter. At the moment, he wanted to do nothing more than punch the damned smile off his face.

He opened his mouth to talk, but something moved across his senses. Something that smelled like blood, and a lot of it. It was wrong, though, as if it were tainted.

"You smell that?" Saint asked. His voice was strained. Malik understood. The wave of nausea did not surprise him.

"Outside."

Saint nodded and followed. He felt the gaze of every Born and Made in the room. He ignored it.

When they reached outside, the scent almost overwhelmed them both.

"Bloody hell," Saint muttered. "What is that?"

They walked down the street and into a darkened alley. Even in the dim light, they could see the bodies lying on the ground, the figure standing over them. They were men, not women, dead on the ground.

The vampire looked back over his shoulder at them. Blood dripped from his fangs and down his chin.

"*Suprema!*"

It echoed down the alley. It was only a matter of time before people detected them. He had never done it, never killed another Made, but he knew without a doubt this was one gone wrong. He had slipped over the edge and was trying to make his own vamps.

He pulled out the stake, but before he could act, Saint had his out. The Made approached them, slowly at first, then he ran at full speed. Saint stepped in front of Malik and without hesitation, Saint pulled his arm back and stabbed the Made through the heart.

The only sound from the Made was gurgling as he fell to the ground. He convulsed a few times, then went still.

"This is a bloody mess," Saint said as he looked over the three bodies.

"What was he doing?" Malik asked. "Could he have been feeding and lost control?"

"Does it matter?" Saint's voice sounded as weary as Malik felt.

Malik nodded. "But, I guess we can figure that out. First, we have to make it all disappear."

* * * *

Nico listened to the tale. He did not interrupt. When Malik finished, he thought about the implications.

"Do you think he was confused?"

Malik shrugged. "It could be. Maybe his Maker did not keep control of him or explain. If they are surviving now, it seems that whoever planned this—"

"We know who it is. It's Neal."

"Well, if it is Neal, then he might be over his head."

"And they are running around on their own trying to survive," Saint said with a nod. "That would make sense."

"Do you think he was a pederast?" Malik asked.

"As in he didn't understand what his body was telling

him to do?" Nico nodded. "It could be."

They had some Mades and even Borns who preferred their own sex. It wasn't taboo in their world as it was in the human world, but for a Made with no direction, if he were inclined that way…it would be confusing.

"He could have also been directed to do it." He looked at Malik who appeared older than he had ever seen his friend look. "It would be impossible to tell his Maker no."

"Thank you for cleaning it up," Saint said.

Malik nodded. "I am not sure about Saint, but I am ready for my bed."

"Agreed. I think we will skip tomorrow night. I am just too tired to deal with another trip to that damned hell."

A few moments later, he was left alone to his thoughts. He had left Cordelia in bed, sleeping like an innocent. She was, in so many ways. He wanted to shield her from this, to make sure that nothing ever touched her.

He rose from his chair and walked to the window. He wished it was just a few problems, just a few Mades in an attempt to take over their world. That would be easy to deal with. This…this was something different.

Neal was planning something. Last time Neal planned something, it left his family in mourning. He could not let the bastard win. Not this time.

This time Nico would make sure he felt the last beat of Neal's heart as he died.

Chapter Seventeen

Nico watched the dancers at the ball and tried to ignore the frustration pounding through him. It had been a month and they were no closer to finding Neal.

"You mustn't frown so much, Nico," his father said.

"You sound like mother." He knew he was being rude, but he couldn't stop himself.

"You look angry and frustrated."

He tried to smile, but he knew it looked false. "I do not look frustrated."

"Yes you do. If there is one thing we know about that bastard, it is that he is watching you. More than likely Neal is in this ballroom, and he is taking delight in your behavior."

He rolled his shoulders and ordered himself to relax. His father was right. Neal was a bastard, one of birth and of character. He had befriended Nico in hopes of getting into the Alliance and making connections. It did not happen. Not because he was a bastard by birth—there were enough of them around the Alliance—but because with Neal, there had always been rumors about him, about the fact that his birth father was insane. His sire had disappeared years before and had never been heard from again. Of course, part of it had to do with the fact he was Scottish by birth. Many of the lowlanders and English did not trust the Borns from the north.

"You should be paying more attention to your bride. She is conquering the *ton* with ease."

He glanced around the room and found Cordelia. His father was right. She fairly glowed with new confidence, and unfortunately, too much of her showed in the dress she was wearing.

"What was Mother thinking when she ordered that dress

for her?"

"It is modest compared to some."

Yes, but her neck was exposed so...enticingly. The dress was brilliant red with a little too much of her breasts on display. Still, she had walked down the stairs earlier and he had forgotten how to speak. She looked like a diamond of the first water. He could scent her blood from across the floor, and it was driving him a bit batty. Every time he drew in a breath, the urge to march across the room and drag her away almost overwhelmed him. It would not do, especially since this was their first official ball as a married couple. They were stuck there. He ground his teeth together trying to keep his incisors in check.

The actions of the *ton* had not made it easy for him. From the moment they arrived, she had been surrounded by both vampires and humans. The women had tried to gain her attention—the same women who had ignored her only weeks earlier and had treated her like an outcast. The men, well, there were one or two of them Nico would be talking to.

Then his eye caught on Saint working his way through the crowd. The fact that his cousin had not disappeared to the north to hide in his castle told Nico their problems were very grave.

Then he realized Saint was going to ask Cordelia to dance.

"I guess I should see to my bride."

"Indeed," was all his father said as Nico strode off to meet her.

He reached her before Saint did, and the knowing look his cousin gave him told Nico he had been doing it on purpose.

"Hello, my dear," he said.

Cordelia smiled at him. It was a full grin that showed her dimples. "Good evening."

Nico would never admit to the fact that she had his heart skipping a beat or that his head spun a bit from her attention.

For a few moments, he did not say anything. Everything around them seemed to disappear, and it was as if they were back home, alone. A hum of need wound through him, flowing through his own blood. The one message that he heard from his inner beast was to take. Take, conquer, ravish.

Saint cleared his throat, and Nico realized that the people circled around his bride were staring. Cordelia blushed prettily because she knew exactly what he had been thinking.

He pushed the thoughts of seduction aside, for now. He held out his hand. "I would greatly appreciate a chance to dance with you this evening."

The string across the bow signaled the start of the waltz.

"But of course." She looked at her circle. "Please excuse me."

She put her hand on his arm, then jolted when she saw his cousin. "Oh, Saint, I did not see you."

"I was just keeping an eye on you, Lady Cordelia."

"An eye?" Nico said.

"Yes, and if you know what is precious, you would make sure to stay close."

It wasn't a threat or even a warning. It was more of an advisory. Saint had a fantastic sense of intuition. Something bad was right around the corner, and he wanted Nico to know. Nico glanced at Cordelia then at Saint, who nodded imperceptibly to tell Nico he had felt something off about Cordelia's safety.

He led her to the dance floor and drew her into the waltz.

"What on earth was that about?" she asked.

"Saint has...visions. He is worried about you."

She nodded. "We really did not need to come out tonight. We could have stayed home."

It was his choice. He did not like putting her on display for the *ton* or Neal Pearson. But he knew without a doubt that they needed to be out and about. Even though, now, he could not remember why it had been important.

Cordelia moved through the dance effortlessly. "No one

expects me to be that active. My family was known for their debauchery. Not many of them, cousins included, are seen about in society."

"Mother thinks it is important."

"And I am sure it is best for the bad Born to see us. You do not want to be seen as retreating."

He glanced at her as he worked his way around an old duke and his young daughter.

"Retreating?"

"I do not know much, Nico, but you seem to be worried a lot lately, and I'm thinking that possibly this has more to do with you. Also, there have been meetings at our house. I know it is not this Alliance that I hear talked about. That is much bigger and I have a feeling, ruled by more than just a handful of Borns."

She was too smart for her own good.

"It is also good for your reputation."

She rolled her eyes. "At the moment, I don't care. I would much rather be at home."

The thought had his heart warming. Right now they were stuck in London, searching for Neal under every rock. His cousin and his cohorts had not found one lead on Neal, but they were all positive he was the man at the center of everything. The death toll was rising, and now even the human authorities were giving them problems.

"Do you think we will have to stay that long tonight?" Cordelia asked, breaking into his thoughts.

"We need to stay at least until dinner."

She sighed. "All right."

They danced for several moments in contented silence before she spoke again. "Do you have anything new on the investigation?"

"No, not really."

It was true. Dead bodies had been littered over most of London's stews, but there was not one bit of evidence that Neal was still alive. The bastard had outdone himself this time.

"If you would tell me a little more, I might be able to help."

"Absolutely not."

Her eyes widened slightly, and he realized that he had talked quite loudly.

"It isn't safe for you to be involved."

She did not like the answer but she said nothing else about it. As the dance ended, the dinner bell rang, and he knew he had been granted a reprieve. He knew she wanted to discuss the investigation, but he could not allow that. The less she knew the better.

* * * *

Two days later, Cordelia was summoned to Nico's library in the middle of the day. As she walked down the hallway, she wondered what her husband would want from her. Nico had been the same passionate lover at night, but he had been a bit distant during the day. No more daytime trysts in the library or even in her room. The one thing she did find wonderful is that he slept with her every night. She knew the ways of the world. Husbands and wives in the upper classes rarely slept together. Nico barely spent time in his own room now.

She reached the doors and found them open. When she stepped into the room, she found her editor from the paper there, Mr. White.

"Cordelia, it seems that your employer was worried about you." Nico's voice did not sound very welcoming.

"Oh, Mr. White, I am so very sorry that I forgot to contact you."

The elderly gentleman smiled. Every time he looked at her like that, it reminded her of Tibbens, the gardener her family had when she was a youth. He used to sneak her sweets when her father wasn't looking.

"I see that congratulations are in order."

Mr. White didn't sound angry, but there was an edge of concern in his tone. Nico was mad, that was for sure. She could feel the anger rolling off him as she walked across the library to address Mr. White.

"Thank you so much. I do apologize. Everything happened so fast that I did not have time to contact you."

Mr. White sighed and shook his head. His blue eyes twinkled behind his spectacles. "I hate to lose you, Lady Cordelia. You are my best writer, but I wish you luck."

He gave her a hug. "Make sure he treats you like the prize you are," he whispered in her ear.

Before she could respond, he pulled away.

"I apologize for the interruption, Mr. Blackburn." With a nod to Nico, he left them alone.

It took a few moments for her to compose herself. She knew that Nico was not happy. She turned to face him, and he was as distant as he was before they married.

"Would you care to explain?"

"I needed money, Nico. You of all people can understand why I would have to work."

"I understand that. I cannot understand why you would not tell me you were working."

She blinked at his tone. She had heard him unhappy, teasing, but she had not heard him with anger vibrating beneath the surface as if he could barely hold onto his temper.

"I don't truly know. With everything that happened, it slipped my mind."

"Are you working on another article?"

She widened her eyes. "What?"

"Are you writing another article? I think the question is easy enough to understand."

"What would I be writing an article about?"

"Vampires."

She stared at him then rolled her eyes. "I would not write

an article and expose you or your family. What do you take me for? Even if I had wanted to—which I do not—no one would believe me."

He ground his teeth together. She could actually hear them move against each other. It was starting to become a nuisance. She hated that she heard conversations and the sounds on the street in the middle of the night. Every day, the ability grew, and she found herself more and more aggravated by it.

"So you *did* think about it."

"Nico, stop it. You are starting to irritate me."

"You. *You* are irritated?" He stalked from behind the desk, his frown threatening. "I think I have more of a right to be irritated."

She took a step back from him, then stopped herself. She crossed her arms beneath her chest. "What are you talking about?"

"A strange man just showed up at my house demanding to see you in person because he wanted to make sure you were not in danger."

Her heart softened. Mr. White had never been that talkative, but he had been a fatherly figure, one who paid more than he should have for her articles. She knew he did it to help her. She would always have a soft space in her heart for the man. A confirmed bachelor, he had never wanted to marry, but he had taken her under his wing as if she were his own daughter.

"And do not get that dreamy-eyed look on your face. I want an explanation."

She blinked. What on earth was he talking about? "Want an explanation?"

"I demand one."

"I explained myself earlier. I worked for him, writing articles about the *ton*." Why was he so upset about the fact she had been employed?

He studied her for a moment, his teeth mashing together.

"Oh, will you stop that. I can't stand hearing you grind your teeth together." The noise was driving her mad.

"I was an assignment."

That was the problem. She nodded. "Yes, you were. There was a question about where your money came from. Of course, I did not know you had hundreds of years to acquire it."

Her voice was almost as loud as his was.

"And so I was just an assignment you felt you needed to seduce."

She frowned at him, confused. "Seduce? Really Nico, do you think I knew what to do with you? You're the one who made the advances."

"But now I know what really attracted you."

"What is that?" He'd admitted he was first attracted to her because she was a Carrier. Did he suspect her attraction was also based only on instinct?

"My money."

She wanted to roll her eyes and laugh. Why would anyone want Nico just for his money? Did he not see his appeal? Apparently not because he was staring at her as if she was a snake in his garden.

"Your money? Nicodemus Blackburn, you are a numbskull."

He paid no attention to her name-calling. "I demand to know if my money is why you followed me into the room that night."

She could see the anger in his eyes but couldn't stop herself from saying what she was thinking. "In a way it was."

He took a step closer and towered over her. "Explain yourself."

"First, stop looming over me." She waited until he took a step back. "Second, if you did not have the money, I would not have been following you for a story. And I was hiding from Hurst. I did not know where you had gone because I was trying my best to avoid him. But I can assure you that your money would not be enough to compensate for your personality."

She shouted the last of the statement. He blinked and took another step back from her. He looked confused and a bit wary. Good. She was sick of men pushing her around. First her father, then her brother, and now Nico.

"You were not totally honest."

Honest? He was one to talk.

She snorted. "I think not saying I was working as a reporter is a little bit less of a fib than you not telling me I was marrying into a family of vampires."

"I—"

She didn't want to hear any more excuses from him. "No. I am done with this conversation. Really, Nico, if you think a woman would put up with your temper, your mood swings and secretiveness because of your money, you are not as smart as I thought you were."

"What do you mean?"

How could she get it through his thick head? "Your personality makes it very hard to like you, let alone love you. Nicodemus Blackburn, you do not have enough money to make me pretend to like you. You are bossy and you often irritate me so much that it takes everything I have not to throw something at you." She marched toward the door. "Even if you had as much gold as Midas, it wouldn't be enough to make me pretend to like you."

She walked out the door, slamming it hard enough that the figurines on the back wall shelves jumped. She heard them jangle against each other.

Cordelia ignored the looks the staff gave her as she walked away from the room. The nerve of the man. She stomped up the stairs. Was the man blind? For over a month now, she had been enthralled by him, and he questioned why she was married to him?

It had started as a marriage of convenience, but she was in love with the stupid man.

She burst into her room, happy that the maid was not there. She shut the door and walked over to her bed. She was so tired. Nights out until the wee hours of the morning had her body aching for a good rest.

Now she had nothing to do. She was exhausted from their time out in the *ton* the last few nights, but sleeping all day was not something she liked to do. From an early age, she had worked in some way or other. She was testy and overemotional because she needed something to do.

Her mother-in-law had offered to help Cordelia find her birth father. He might not want to know her, or he might have moved on, but she needed to know where she came from. With a sigh, she decided to take Adelaide up on the offer and set out to find her father.

* * * *

What in the world had come over the woman? Nico was still staring at the door several moments later. The emotional outburst was so unlike her. Or what he knew of her. He knew her family life had been horrific from the little tidbits she had told him. Being called the "Scottish bastard" growing up was far from the ideal environment for a girl to be in. Now, though, he wasn't too sure that she had told him that much. She had allowed him a peek into what had formed her into the woman she was today, but he had no idea what else lay behind the shield.

A writer. Of course it made sense. She would never take payment to be someone's paramour, and she would never put herself on the marriage mart. The first, because she had too much backbone, and the second, because she knew her background. Normally, she would have never married someone like him.

Not that he was a prize. He shook his head. They needed time together. He had kept her in the dark for the most part about his world. He did not need her to know about binding.

Someday she would probably figure it out. Binding was the ultimate in mating, where you bound your life forces together for eternity. When Nico lost his brother, it had been because Demetrius had lost his mate. They had been bound the night of their wedding. It had been his brother's death sentence.

He shook away the thoughts and realized it was getting late in the day. He hadn't heard from Saint or the other men working the stews today. As if summoned by his thoughts, the door opened without a knock. Of course it was Saint.

"This plan isn't bloody working."

Nico blinked. Saint was abrupt most of the time, but this was beyond his usual behavior. "Indeed?"

"We need to find Neal."

Nico sighed. "Yes, but a man who is dead…how can you find him?"

Before Saint could answer, Cordelia came marching back in, irritation still rolling off her in waves. She opened her mouth to yell at him, but she noticed Saint pouring himself a brandy.

"Lord…er—Saint. I did not know you had arrived." She gave Nico a nasty look.

"I only just arrived, Lady Cordelia."

The monster of a man who rarely displayed any kind of manners smiled at Cordelia.

Nico frowned at her. "We were working on the case."

She ignored his admonition. "I am looking for your mother."

"I believe she and my father should be here for dinner."

"Fine."

She looked at Saint. "It is nice to see you. Please join us for dinner."

He nodded, still smiling until she left. Saint grinned at him.

"Ouch, cousin, you have a woman there you better be careful of."

"You did me no good. What is all that smiling anyway?" As soon as the words were out of his mouth, he wanted to kick himself. He sounded jealous, and he wasn't. Not really.

"I have learned to be very careful of a mated Carrier. They can be…dangerous."

"You do not act like that around others."

"She will have the sight."

Saint said it with enough conviction that Nico paused.

"How do you know?"

"We know each other. We can sense the gift in someone else. It is just going to get worse now that she is breeding."

"You can sense it? What a bunch of…wait, what did you say?"

He shrugged and took a healthy drink of his brandy. "She's breeding."

"You're sure?"

"Positive. There is a reason she is so…unsettled I guess is the best word. Her emotions are going to get the better of her."

"Did you take a blow to the head? She cannot be breeding. We have only been married a month."

"That means nothing, Nico. You know that a Carrier is very fertile right after the first feeding." Saint studied him. "This is good news."

"It makes her an even larger target." Learning that his mate was carrying one of their offspring should have made him happy, but with Neal on the loose, he only felt fear.

"True. I think we need to formulate a new plan. This one is not working and after a month of Mades leaving behind a trail of Carriers raped and murdered, the Borns are getting very restless. There is talk of segregation again."

Too many Mades were important in their society and had earned the place, Malik being the most important.

"I will call on Gray. Hurst is ready to make his way about in society now, so we might need to reintroduce him. It might help."

Saint nodded.

"Have you told her of this? That there is a threat to her and you?"

Nico shook his head. "She knows some, but I don't want to horrify her with every detail. She knows to be careful, especially after her brother tried to have her abducted."

Saint shook his head. "You will never learn, Nico. She knows. Or she will. Then, there will be hell to pay."

"What do I tell her? There is a man who killed my sister-in-law because he wanted my brother to suffer a long and tortured death? And now this same man is after her and wants to kill her to punish me?"

"And kill you."

He said nothing. How could he admit to Cordelia all the danger he'd brought into her life?

"You have not bonded with her. Nico, what on earth are you thinking?"

"That I do not want to leave her vulnerable. If we are bonded, her life is more at risk."

Saint studied him for a long time then shook his head. "That is not what you fear, but I am not in the mood to argue. I believe I will get notes around to Gray and Hurst, and then we can have our meeting tonight. I am ready for my own bed and the Highlands out my window."

He left Nico alone to his thoughts. Just what was Neal up to? The man was a viper, one ready to infect anyone with his venom. Making an army of Mades would be a plan Neal would love. It was perverted, and it would send fear racing along the upper classes of Mades.

But, why was he waiting? Was it to drive them crazy, to pretend that it wasn't him? After one hundred years he had surfaced, but what was the reason? Why did he wait?

With a sigh, Nico sat down at his desk and started to work on the books. If he was going to have a meeting tonight, he would have to deal with the Blackburn business first.

* * * *

The man known as Neal Pearson to most, but to his mother as Michael, watched the rain patter against the window of his townhouse and thought about his next move. It had been three months since he had put his plan into action. The Mades were terrorizing everyone, and Nico Blackburn had no idea who he was.

"What is your next move?" his partner asked. He hated the man, hated that blasted Scottish accent that reminded him of his youth. But he had no choice.

"I am not sure at the moment. We need the leaders of the Alliance here."

"There is talk of a meeting in a few weeks. They want to remove the Blackburns from the quad council."

He smiled. "How amusing. The one man who sees what is going on and they want to get rid of him."

"And once the council finally comes to London. The plan?"

He hadn't told him much. The Scottish laird was helpful at the moment, but soon he would have to take a stake to the bastard. Neal knew the only reason he was there was to try and take over the council.

"Then we move the Mades in. With their allegiance to me, I will be able to overthrow those old men on the quad."

"And then we will have our seats."

He said nothing.

"Pearson?"

"Yes, we will have our seats."

But in truth, he wanted nothing to do with the Alliance. The only plan he had was to destroy their council and watch Nico Blackburn suffer for what he had done.

It would be the sweetest of victories.

Chapter Eighteen

Dinner had been uneventful, much to Cordelia's surprise. She had expected Gray and Saint to attend. The men had become permanent fixtures in their house the last few weeks, as well as Lady Elizabeth, who had moved in with them as planned. But when she found herself face to face with Hurst, she could not hide her dismay. He looked changed. His eyes were now green and he was thinner. She was embarrassed that she hesitated before taking his hand. His looks were not the only thing different. His manner was more measured, quiet, and reserved.

Now, two hours later, she found herself seated in her mother-in-law's parlor. Lady Elizabeth had gone to bed after dinner and the men had left them to huddle together and make their plans.

"I hate that they will not include us, too," Adelaide said.

Cordelia glanced at her. She could tell by the way Adelaide pursed her lips that she was irritated. She did not realize until that moment that her mother-in-law understood they were being left out of the discussions.

"I know. They seem to think we are too stupid to know what is going on."

"It isn't that, dear."

"Indeed?"

She shook her head. "That is part of the problem. They do not want us involved because they think we will be in danger. All men want to protect, but vampires, they are worse. Much worse. And now that this threat is growing, they will become unbearable."

"But there are things we could help with. Men are not infallible."

"Yes, but they do not know that."

Cordelia shared a smile with her. "That is true. Still, there are always rumors swirling about. Things we could find out for them."

"Is that how you became a writer? Looking for the rumors?"

She shrugged. "Nothing I said wasn't true."

"I am not faulting you for surviving. A lesser woman would have done something easier. For example, being a courtesan."

"I do not think that would be easier than being a reporter."

"Oh, but dear, it is. You don't really have to work at that, as long as you have the right partner. And if you will forgive me for being a little insensitive, but with your mother's reputation, there would be a great many gentlemen in London who would be happy to take you up on any offer. No, instead, you wanted to forge your own way. I have to admire that."

She shouldn't be surprised, but she was. Not by her mother-in-law's blunt comments or that she had understood Cordelia so well. But she was a deeply private person.

She pushed her irritation aside. "I did want to ask your help in something."

"Anything," she said, smiling.

"You offered to help to find out who my father is."

"That is an excellent idea. There wouldn't have been many Scottish noblemen around then, or any other time. Your mother did not go to Scotland, did she?"

Cordelia shook her head. "I doubt it. I did not know her, but then, she was one for society. I doubt she would have gone to Scotland in the middle of winter, either."

Her mother-in-law nodded. "Of course. That makes sense. I will have to ask around. That was a busy time for us."

"Oh?" Cordelia asked coyly. She was not trying to pry, but Nico had done little to reveal his past to her. And his explosion this afternoon highlighted that. He claimed to know little of her, but she knew less of him, and he had been alive a lot longer than she had.

"Yes. Demetrius had just married Magdalen and we were so busy."

"Demetrius, that was Nico's brother? Older brother?"

"Older. He was older than Nico by about fifty years. I had difficulty giving birth again after Demetrius."

Cordelia nodded. "They were killed?"

Pain moved over Adelaide's expression, and Cordelia hated asking her. She did not want to cause any discomfort to the woman who had accepted her so readily.

She opened her mouth to change the subject, but Adelaide stopped her.

"Yes. They were. They were bonded as most spouses are, and she was killed. That caused Demetrius to die, but it was slow as he felt her life force drained from her."

The idea of knowing your wife was dying, feeling every pain she had as she died, was horrific. Cordelia blinked against tears.

Then she caught on to a term she had not heard. "Bonded?"

From the expression on her mother-in-law's face, she had just realized she said something wrong.

"Yes. After a time, you are bonded."

"After a time? Is there no ritual?"

She sighed. "Yes. The Made must offer his blood. Then, your life forces are together for eternity and into the afterlife."

Cordelia let the information sink in. Nico had not bonded with her. It made sense because they were not a love match. True, she highly suspected that she was in love with the man. She would not have lost her temper that afternoon if she wasn't. He had not told her, though. He probably didn't want to explain why he had not bonded with her.

"Cordelia, it is a very serious matter. No Born does it

lightly."

"You do not have to make excuses for your son. I know we are not a love match. What I hate is being in the dark about your world. He rarely tells me anything. What little I find out is snippets. I have no problem with not being bonded." She blew out a breath. "That's a lie. It bothers me a little. What I hate is feeling as if I am a stranger. I have spent too much of my life like that."

"I will help you."

She glanced over her shoulder and smiled. "I would appreciate it. I just want to make sure I can find my place."

"We will start tomorrow on finding out who your father is. Your sister should have some kind of idea."

Cordelia sighed again, now feeling as if she could sleep a thousand years. She really hated dealing with Diana. She had stayed in London, which was very uncommon for her sister.

"Yes. I guess I could invite her for tea tomorrow."

Adelaide nodded. "That sounds wonderful. I think you better go to bed. You do not look well."

"Thank you. I think I will."

She hesitated.

"Go on, Cordelia. I will tell Nico."

Cordelia walked down the hall to her suite. Each step she took made her even more tired. By the time she was in her room, Cordelia felt ready to drop. With great effort, she undressed and then donned her nightdress.

Slipping into bed, she pushed away all thoughts of her new life and drifted off to sleep.

* * * *

"We are going to have to start patrolling more," Gray said, his voice ominous.

Nico nodded but his mind was on his wife. If Saint were to be believed, he was about to be a father. Every time he had a stray thought, it was about her or the baby they would share together.

"Nico, are you paying attention?" his father asked.

Of course he wasn't. Again. He had been married just over a month, and he didn't seem able to tear his thoughts away from the woman.

"I think we need to call on the Alliance for this," Nico said. "We need younger vampires out on the streets. If we don't have them, we can't protect women."

"And we need to stop the number of Mades he is producing," Gray added.

"I doubt it is just him," Saint said. "More than likely he has one or more people helping him."

"Why? He is a pariah in our society. Who would help him?" Gray asked.

"There is always unrest, those who would rather not want the Alliance to have control of things. There are also a number of Mades he could manipulate. That might be why we are finding the blood drained of the men," Saint said.

Nico nodded. There was a slight knock at the door, then his mother came in. Everyone rose around the table, but she waved them back down.

"No, dear, I came by to tell you Cordelia is not going out tonight. She is too tired and really needs a good rest."

"Of course," he said.

"I take it you are going out tonight?" His mother looked like she knew the answer.

He was, but now he didn't want to. It might be best to stay in and rest himself. Next to his wife.

"I think I might stay in." Yes. That sounded like a much better plan.

She gave him a knowing look and a kiss on the cheek.

"I am going to retire myself. I feel every one of my seven hundred and fifty years tonight."

Then, she left them alone.

"I am going to contact father," Gray said. "I think that he

needs to rally some of the council members around this cause. If not, we might find ourselves with a war on our hands."

Malik shook his head. "We already have a war on our hands, Gray. Do you not see it?"

Gray sighed and nodded. "There are more than a few reports of people disappearing, and I know for a fact that Viscount Emery had an encounter with one the other night. The Made insinuated that there were a few more running the streets."

"Not just a few," Saint said. "I would say that there is a chance he is reaching the hundreds now. He might have heard how you saved Hurst and started doing the same to save his."

Malik shook his head. "And if he knows that, he will have them under his thumb. He will have a bloody army of Mades ready to do his bidding."

Malik knew exactly what he spoke of. He had witnessed it twice, and Nico knew that his friend still had nightmares.

"Contact your father. I think we can drum up some more support and make it impossible for the bastard to make his army stronger," Malik said.

He fell silent, and Gray was watching him. "What?"

"The thing that is bothering me is why? I can understand why he would come after me, but what is his plan for the world of the Borns? Neal is a Born. He wanted to be on that damned Quad so badly. He doesn't need a massive army and he doesn't need to come after me. So, I am confused."

"Who gives a damn?" Hurst asked, his voice quiet. He had been silent for most of the time, watching the men as they discussed the situation.

"What do you mean?"

"Why do we care why he is doing this?" Nico could hear the aggravation in Hurst's voice.

Nico understood Hurst's irritation and the fear Nico knew Hurst was trying to hide.

"We find out his reasons, we can possibly guess his next move," Nico said calmly.

Hurst lapsed into a brooding silence.

"I am going to go out tonight," Saint said.

"Let me drop Hurst off at the house and I will go with you," Gray said.

"I want to go." Hurst spoke quietly, never leaving his chair.

They all turned back to Hurst.

"No, too dangerous," Gray said. "You are newly turned, and we do not know what will happen."

"I want to go. I want to help find this bastard."

Nico opened his mouth to disagree, but Malik said, "Let him come."

He studied his oldest friend, the one he was closer to than even his own brother. Malik was the only one who knew what Hurst was truly going through right now.

"You think he can handle it?" Nico asked.

Malik looked at him. "I can keep an eye on him. He might remember something, help us in some way."

Nico nodded. "Then it is settled. He will go with you." He looked at Hurst. "Be careful, because he might be a target. By now, Neal knows Hurst survived. He will be worried about what Hurst remembers, and he might want to kill him."

Malik nodded. "Remember, old man, I can take care of it. I will stake my life on it."

"I am going tonight." Nico should be there. He could not allow his friends to go into such a dangerous situation without joining them.

"No." Malik shook his head at his friend. "There are enough of us. Cordelia already said she did not want to go out tonight. I will get ready. I have stakes."

Hurst's face paled.

"Just as a precaution." Nico smiled.

"I hope you know what you are doing, Nico. You are his

target." Malik looked worried.

Nico stood from his chair and began pacing the room. "I do not like hiding. It is beginning to make me feel unmanly."

Saint rolled his eyes.

"Can we get on with it tonight?" Hurst asked.

"Indeed," Saint said.

Malik took the others to outfit them with stakes as Nico made his way to his bedroom. Of course, it was Cordelia's, but she had not realized he had moved into hers. He could not sleep anywhere else, nor did he want to.

He knocked softly. There was no answer. He slipped through the door, shutting it behind him. She was sleeping. The only light in her room came from the moonlight peeking through the curtains. He moved towards the bed and watched her. She was curled up on her side, her blonde curls feathered over the pillows.

He needed to change into different clothes, but instead, he stood staring at her. He didn't want to wake her up. She needed her rest if Saint was to be believed. Still, Nico couldn't resist brushing her hair back away from her face and slipping his finger down her jawline.

She mumbled his name in her sleep, then snuggled closer to the pillow. A lump formed in his throat, and he found it hard to swallow. The idea of having a child with Cordelia warmed him. An emotion he could not seem to define almost unmanned him.

For her and their future, he would do everything in his power to end this mess.

* * * *

The scent of rotting food and the stench of unwashed bodies assaulted Malik first. He hated this, and it was worse for their kind, but walking down an alley to the hell was the easiest way to go undetected.

"Why are we going the back way again?" Gray asked.

Desire by Blood

He swore violently when he stepped in a puddle.

"Because, the five of us skulking around the streets will raise attention. We want to do that in the club, not on the street. Makes us a target."

It would also make Hurst a target. The man was going to have enough to deal with in the coming years, let alone the physical attacks he would take. The fact that he was one of the few Mades he could save in recent memory did not leave Malik feeling any better. Anything is better than dying...unless you were turned by a Born against your will.

"It should be around the corner," Nico offered.

Malik nodded and let them to the door. Hell's Door was one of the better hells frequented by Mades and Borns alike. Here they did not care where you came from, just that you had gold coins to spend.

"We were here a few nights ago. There were a few suspicious characters trolling the area, not much more," Saint said.

"But they do cater to vampires and humans, so it would be the perfect hunting ground," Malik said. "He would like to go after people who were at their end, so to speak."

They started up the steps, but Hurst didn't say anything. He stood looking at the painted red door. Malik turned.

"Hurst?"

"I think I was here," Hurst said quietly.

Saint stepped closer. "You're remembering."

It wasn't a question. Bloody Scot probably already knew that Hurst would remember things. Malik was just happy he didn't see the future. He had learned a long time ago not to look at the future but live in the present.

"Let's go."

They all followed him in. Malik was given easy access. It helped that he was accompanied by three peers of the realm, one being just a stone's throw away from the throne. With a Blackburn there, it helped even more, but Malik was wealthy, and that was well known within their world.

www.melissaschroeder.net | 217

They made their way through the gaming tables and nodded to a few people he knew, both human and vampire. There appeared to be nothing out of the ordinary, but something was making him very uncomfortable. His intuition told him there was someone watching them.

"You feel it too," Hurst said only loud enough for Malik to hear.

Malik nodded.

"I don't feel that well at the moment," Hurst said weakly.

He glanced at the viscount. He looked fine, his skin flushed from the recent feeding they had given him. Hurst wasn't in danger of falling into a feeding frenzy. Instead, something was telling his senses to flee. Excitement and caution ran through Malik. That meant there was a good chance that Hurst's sire was nearby.

"Do you feel him?" Malik asked.

Hurst nodded.

"Do we need to leave?" Malik suspected they were close to finding Neal.

"I sense he wants us dead."

He would want them dead, and it wasn't uncommon for a Made to be able to feel his maker's feelings—especially if they were in close quarters.

"But do you think we should leave?" Malik asked again.

Saint frowned at them. "What are you talking about?"

"His sire is here. He's watching," Malik answered.

"Let's circulate then and see. He won't do anything here." Saint turned to scan the space.

They walked around the room, each of them playing a few hands here and there. A half hour later, they had nothing.

Nico shook his head, his expression darkening. "We could wait here all night, but I am not sure that is a good idea. We are leaving ourselves exposed. I have a feeling the bastard will not come out until he is ready."

Hurst swallowed noticeably. "He truly isn't happy you are here, Blackburn."

Nico nodded, but Malik was not ready to let it go. "Hurst, what else do you feel?"

He closed his eyes. "He is watching but not here. Or not on the floor."

"He's got an office here or a room of some sort," Gray said.

"He is furious you are in his den, and he cannot do anything. It isn't time yet," Hurst said as he opened his eyes. "This is one sick bastard you are dealing with."

Nico nodded. "We are well acquainted."

"We need to leave, now," Hurst said. The anxiety in his voice had risen, and his eyes were dilated. Malik knew better than to question his intuition. The connection to the sire had been lessened because Hurst had been fed the blood of several Borns and not the one who made him. Still, Malik didn't want to chance it. They could return later with a greater group. This was definitely the place to watch.

They slowly made their way out of the hell, and Malik drew in a deep breath. A light drizzle was falling.

"I think we should get a handsome cab," Saint said.

He glanced at Saint, who hated using any kind of closed space to travel. There was definitely something wrong.

"We would need two, and there aren't any here during this time of night. We need to walk a few blocks this way," Gray said. They walked along, and Malik felt the air change. The hair on the back of his neck prickled and a sheet of ice slid down his spine. Someone was watching them. Not just the normal criminals who hung out in the stews. No, this was the same feeling he had in the hell.

In the next moment, he heard the rush of steps behind him, and then another group came up from the alley on their right. He looked around and realized they had walked directly into a damned trap.

Chapter Nineteen

Nico heard the scrape of shoes against the cobblestone and knew immediately that they had been followed. He settled his hand on the stake he had attached to his belt and glanced at Malik. He nodded and they both turned. There were only five men, Mades from the looks of them. The one face he had not seen was Neal's.

They turned to form a circle to face their attackers.

"All we want is Nico Blackburn," one of them said. Their eyes were red, as if they had not slept. Their expressions spoke of confusion. They truly did not know what they were doing. Now, after all these years, he knew exactly what Malik had been talking about.

Nico knew it would be easier to face Neal head on, but the moment he stepped forward, Malik made a sound.

"Do not even think of it. I am not going back to Cordelia to tell her you went with Mades to a man who wants to kill you."

"Forget it," Saint spat out. "If the bastard wants a part of Nico, then he needs to come to him. Cowards don't get what they want."

Bloody hell. He knew these Mades would not kill him before they took him to Neal. He had heard that tone from both his cousin and Malik before. They both would not let him go.

"Good enough for us," the tallest of the bunch said. He was also the biggest. "We can take care of this lot and then take you to our sire."

They all thought they were invincible. They were ready to lay down their lives for their sire without a second thought because they did not know any better.

"They really are stupid, you know?" Malik said

conversationally.

And they were. The big one stepped forward and tried to take Malik. He met his blow by blocking it with his arm.

He struck the man with his right fist. The crack of bone told Nico that he had broken the man's nose. Now they all came at them. The one that took on Nico stepped forward. Nico fought him fist to fist.

He paid no attention to what was going on around him. He wanted to make sure they kept one of them alive. They needed to know where Neal was holed up.

Nico made quick work of his adversary. He gave him one last punch, and the Made fell to the ground. When he turned around to face the rest of the crew, he found that most of them had fled. The only one left was the big guy, but instead of fighting Malik, it was Hurst that had his hands around his neck, squeezing the breath out of the bastard.

"Tell me where your maker is. Tell me now!" Hurst commanded.

"You should know since he is your commander, too." The Made struggled against Hurst's hands.

The comment had Hurst squeezing his hands tighter around his throat. The Made's face turned blue in the process. Hurst would not be able to kill him, but the Made could not answer his questions. Before Nico could intervene, the Made passed out.

Hurst shoved him away. The viscount's breathing was ragged, and Nico could practically feel the rage rolling off him. He didn't blame Hurst. If the same thing had been done to him, Nico would definitely want revenge.

Both of the Mades left were unconscious.

"I can take them to my house," Gray offered. "We have room, of course."

He shared a look with Malik, knowing that they would have to question the bastards. Nico nodded.

"I better get back to the house. Can you handle them?" Nico asked.

Gray nodded.

Malik reached to pick up one of the unconscious Mades. "I'll go with Gray. Saint, you should go with Nico."

Nico frowned. "I don't need—"

"For the love of the gods, could you just do it, Nico." Malik seemed to be losing his patience. "You are the one with a wife, and your mother is there. Gray's mother is safe, as I am sure that Saint's is. There is no problem there."

Nico agreed. They helped the men get the others into a cab and then they headed on foot for home.

"You will be tested, you know this," Saint said.

"Tested? By Neal?"

"By the very thing you think you don't need."

He rolled his eyes. Saint was good at times, but many other times, he irritated Nico. He wasn't in the mood to deal with his ramblings now.

They were back at his townhouse within minutes. He was so bloody tired of this game. He wanted it to end. But he knew he had to stay to protect their way of life.

Slowly, he walked up the stairs. The thought of what he had seen that night and weeks prior to this made him damned sick.

He wanted to see Cordelia, to touch her, to know that all that was good in the world was still there. But he wasn't sure he should bother her. She needed her rest, and he smelled of whiskey and smoke. Still he wanted to look in on her at least before taking his bath. He found her just where he had left her, sleeping soundly. There wasn't a woman who could look so innocent...but he knew better. She had a wicked mind and a quick wit, and she was everything that was good to him.

He brushed the backs of his fingers over her cheek. She stirred. Her eyelashes fluttered.

"Nico?" she asked drowsily.

He should turn, leave, but he couldn't. After the last few weeks, he had grown too accustomed to having her by his side. He didn't even know when it became so damned important to have her there. He knew mating would keep them connected, and the need to be near each other was normal. But this was...overwhelming.

"I need to bathe."

She sighed and her eyes closed again. Wanting to avoid temptation, he turned to go to the bathing room. Moments later, he was slipping into a steaming hot bath. It worked on his muscles, loosening them up. It wasn't helping the cockstand that he had gotten from just staring at Cordelia.

He was starting to fall asleep when he heard her soft footsteps.

"Are you doing all right?"

The sound of her voice shifted through him. He was still running hot from the fight, and he needed time to pull himself under control.

"Go back to bed, Cordelia."

There was a pause, then he heard her move forward into the room. He closed his eyes and tried his best to keep his beast under control.

"You sound off, as if something is wrong."

"There was an altercation tonight," he said, unable to think of something else. All he could see was sinking his fangs into her neck and feeding off her as he poured himself into her.

"Oh," she said.

She made barely a noise, but he could hear her bare feet patter across the tiled floor and the way her nightdress moved against her skin. Worse, he could scent her blood. He ground his teeth together.

"No one was hurt?" she asked as he sensed her sitting on the edge of the tub. It was a bold move for Cordelia. She wasn't a prude by any means, but she had never been so forward as to approach him while he was nude.

"No. We recovered two Mades. They are at Gray's."

"Are you angry with me?"

Hunger clawed at his belly. The spark of arousal he felt

earlier was now an inferno blazing through his blood. "No. I just think…" He drew in a deep breath and counted backwards from ten. When he thought he could control himself again, he said, "Please, it would be best if you left me alone." He ground out every word, his voice harsh enough to give her the warning.

"Nico."

He finally opened his eyes. "I am riding a fine edge of control here, Cordelia. I don't want to hurt you."

She said nothing for a long moment, then she reached out and cupped his jaw. "You would not hurt me."

He tried shaking his head, but she held it still.

"You do not know what you are getting into. I'm raw. I can't be gentle."

Her lips curved. "I do not think I asked you to be."

She whispered the words, but it did not matter. He heard them, and his body responded. A yearning he did not know how to restrain coursed through him. He stood suddenly, taking her off guard. She almost fell off the tub, but he caught her by the arm, saving her just in time.

The moment he touched her, he knew he was in trouble. There was no going back, no stopping the demand his body craved. He stepped out of the tub and pulled her up into his arms. He thought she would object. Instead she wrapped her legs around his waist. He slammed her back against the wall.

"You should have left," he said as he pressed against her. "But, God help me, I can't let you go now."

Cordelia kissed him then—not sweetly as he was accustomed to from her. This time she ravaged his mouth, tangling her tongue with his and then biting his lower lip before she drew back. He licked his lip as he opened his eyes and tasted blood.

"I think I said I did not ask you to." Her gaze was direct, passion darkening her eyes. He actually quivered in reaction as if he were some untried Born on his first feeding.

He pulled back far enough to rip apart her bodice. She

gasped, the sound of it echoing through the bathing room. It deepened his need, fed the appetite only she could quench. Her breasts moved with each gasp she took, her nipples tight with anticipation.

There was a part of him that wanted to take his time, to savor the delectable treat she was. But the primal need to feed, to take, to lose himself in her took hold. He shoved the skirt of her nightdress up to her waist.

He entered her in one thrust. Her quick indrawn breath was filled with pain. She was wet, but she had not been prepared for the invasion. "I'm sorry, love," he said before kissing her.

Her eyelashes fluttered then she opened her eyes. "Don't worry."

"Only pleasure, now."

He started to move as he felt her need rise up to meet his. Within just a few moments she was with him, clawing at his back, begging him for some kind of relief. Hers came quickly. It was a wonder to watch her pleasure shift through her body as she convulsed with her orgasm.

It was not enough. He wanted more, needed more. He wanted to feel her pleasure again, to take his, to take his nourishment.

"Cordelia, look at me." She did not respond fast enough. "Look. At. Me."

She did with some effort.

"Again," he demanded as he thrust into her fast and furiously.

She shook her head as if to deny him.

"Yes." He slammed into her again and again. "Give it to me, now. Don't hide from me."

She didn't stand a chance. She screamed this time as she came, her inner muscles clamping down on him, pulling his own orgasm from him. In that last instant, he took everything he needed from her. He sunk his fangs into her neck and fed.

Moments later he pulled his fangs out of her neck,

licking it as he went. Then, with considerable effort, he carried her through the door before stumbling to the bed. She barely made a sound.

"Cordelia."

"Yes?" She did not open her eyes, but he heard the satisfaction in her voice.

"I'm sorry."

Then she did open her eyes. "Whatever are you apologizing for?"

"I was…I shouldn't have taken you like that."

"Indeed? I think you told me that several times, and I told you not to worry."

"But—"

She set her hand against his mouth. "You needed me. I did not mind. And while I might have a few bruises on my back, I would say they were definitely worth it."

"I should have been more gentle."

She smiled weakly. "Then we would not have had so much fun."

For a moment, all he could do was stare at her. Any other woman would berate him for the lack of romance, but for Cordelia, it was just fun.

"You are truly one of a kind, Cordelia."

Her smile widened as she slipped her hands up over his shoulders. "I like the sound of that."

He pulled the bed linens over both of them and fell asleep.

Chapter Twenty

Cordelia paced the downstairs parlor as she waited for her sister. The fact that her sister had agreed to talk to her was beyond surprising. Now, if she could just ask her what she needed to, and if her sister would actually answer.

"I don't think you need to be this nervous," said her mother-in-law.

"I have never had an easy relationship with Diana. She was always distant with me."

"Distant? Always?"

The tone in Adelaide's voice had her pausing. "Yes. Well, no. When I was young, she was around a lot."

"Then she married."

Cordelia walked to the window. "Yes, and in my adolescent mind, I felt betrayed. I wanted to go with her. As an adult, I know better, but then it was very painful."

"For both of you, I am sure."

"Lady Diana," the footman announced.

She turned, her heart jumping. Her sister's expression was pinched. She did not look happy about being there. Cordelia had been sure this would be the case, but her heart sank when she saw it. With a sigh, she walked to her sister.

"Thank you for seeing me today," she said with a forced smile.

"It seemed extremely important."

Her mother-in-law rolled her eyes. "I will get us some tea sent up. Cordelia, you need to make sure to ask Diana about your father."

Diana frowned but said nothing until Adelaide left.

"What is your mother-in-law talking about?"

With another sigh, she said, "I want to know about my father."

"Our father?"

"No. My father."

Diana's spine stiffened even more. "Your birth father."

"Yes. Do you know anything? You would have been old enough to remember."

Diana said nothing, but Cordelia sensed her slipping away. "Why is it important?"

"Because I want to know the man who was my true father."

"And mine."

For a moment, she could not think. She blinked as she continued looking at her sister. "We shared the same father?"

Diana nodded. "I never told you because he left, and I felt it best that you didn't know."

"Best that I didn't know? Why would you ever think that?"

"What good would it have done?"

"Done?"

Diana let out a long breath. "Yes, what would it have done?"

"Do you mean to tell me that mother had a relationship with a man for close to ten years and father didn't care?"

Diana raised one eyebrow. "This surprises you? He had a son. He could care less about anything else. As long as she did not flaunt it, it didn't matter to him."

Disgust and loathing dripped from every word.

"But, he left."

"When mother was pregnant with you. He had something going on at his estate, or something to do." Diana closed her eyes as if she could see the memory.

"And he never returned? I cannot believe you never looked for him."

"He left. Don't you understand?" Her voice wavered, and it was so unlike Diana, Cordelia could only stare at the blue eyes filled with unshed tears. "He left us and never came back. I begged him to stay, but he said he had things to do and he left. Mother was so sick those last few months...It was not fun. And then, you were born, she was gone, and he never came back."

"Do you remember his name?" her mother-in-law asked.

Diana's face turned red.

Cordelia understood how Diana felt, but she really needed her answer. "Don't be embarrassed. I asked her to help me find father."

"I called him Gavin."

Cordelia looked at her mother-in-law, whose mouth hung open. "Gavin MacDonald?"

Diana shrugged. "I am not sure. I just know I called him Uncle Gavin."

Her mother-in-law looked stunned.

"He isn't a Made, is he?" Cordelia asked.

"What are you talking about?" Diana asked.

Oh bother, she'd forgotten that her sister was there. "It's a term...one we use."

Her mother cut in. "Gavin MacDonald is very powerful."

The look Adelaide gave her told Cordelia she meant in their world.

"Do you think he could be our father?" Cordelia asked.

"Our?" Adelaide looked surprised by the revelation.

"Diana said she thinks he is her father also."

"Cordelia, really," Diana said, her embarrassment easy to hear.

"No, do not worry about such things," Adelaide said. "Gavin is a bit of a hermit, but he is very powerful, very rich. Never married."

"Never married? Not even..."

Without saying the word, she knew that her mother-in-law understood her.

"No."

She glanced at Diana and knew she would get more information out of her if her mother-in-law was not there.

"Adelaide, do you mind checking on that tea?" she asked, looking pointedly at her sister.

"Of course." She left them alone.

"Diana, why did you never tell me?"

"As I said before, what use would it have been?" Tears pooled in Diana's eyes.

"It would have explained why our…the earl called me his Scottish bastard."

Diana winced. "I did not know he did that."

"How could you? Once you married, I never saw you again." She could not hide the hurt in her voice.

"I didn't have a choice."

The pain from her childhood swelled up and took over.

"You had all the choices. You left me in that house with those two. They sickened me with their debauchery, but then, I had no choice. I was abandoned."

For a moment, Cordelia did not think her sister would say anything. Then she said, "I tried to take you."

"What?"

"I wanted to take you. Father would not allow it." Diana's voice was barely a whisper.

"He would not allow it? Why would he want me to stay? He didn't want me there." She'd spent years under her father's roof being verbally abused by him and her brother. What reason could he have for putting her through that?

"No, but he knew I wanted you. He said that if I took you, he would disown you, tell the world you were a bastard."

"Does that even matter? Everyone thinks that now."

Diana shook her head, tears now starting to dampen her cheeks. "Oh, it is a world of difference in society, Delia."

The childhood name she had not heard for years caused her throat to close up. She swallowed back the tears. "I would not have cared."

Diana said nothing for some time. Her hands were clasped tight in her lap.

"Diana?"

When Diana met her gaze, unshed tears shimmered in her eyes. "Believe me when I tell you that living with those two was better."

She wanted to ask her sister more. The thought that her life as a married woman was worse than the house they grew up in was shocking. But before she could say anything, Adelaide came breezing back in.

"Tea should be here any moment. And I talked to Samuel. He said that Gavin is actually in town."

Cordelia frowned. "You said he was a hermit."

"Yes, but he had…business here," Adelaide said.

Meaning he was here because of the recent killings.

Cordelia considered her options. "I cannot just walk up to him and ask him if I am his bastard child."

Diana made a choking sound.

"I am sorry."

"You do have a point, though. We need to have some kind of dinner or something. Maybe a small soiree, but not by you." Adelaide pursed her lips. "I will tell Grayson he must have a dinner, maybe a gathering of…" she glanced at Diana. "Of like-minded people."

"That sounds like an excellent idea." That would give her a chance to study her father before telling him the truth of their relationship.

"You are just going to tell a duke to have a dinner party, and he will do it?" Diana asked.

"Why, yes. I know his mother quite well, dear. And, as Cordelia's sister, you need to be there. I think that would be best."

Diana opened her mouth, but Cordelia stopped her. "I have learned from my husband it is better to let her have her way."

"And, look, here is the tea," Adelaide said. "I am going to get a note off to Grayson right now."

She hurried out of the room. Once they were alone,

Diana shook her head. "Does she always do that?"

"Only with the most important things. You get used to it."

Chapter Twenty-One

Nico paced the foyer and tried to control his irritation. It was hard to do when he was being forced to go to a dinner party when he should be out investigating. Worse, he wanted to keep Cordelia at home. He knew part of it was instinctual. Every vampire wanted to keep their chosen mate away from prying eyes.

"It would be better if you would bond with her," his father said.

He gave his father a sneer and went into his library. If he was going to have to deal with the elite of the bloody *ton* foaming at their mouths to meet his wife in a true vampire gathering, he needed a drink.

"What is it?" Malik asked him.

"Nothing." Nico did not want to admit his worries.

"No, something happened you did not tell me about."

Dammit. Malik knew him too well. "There is a part of me that thinks Cordelia would be better off not married to me. I have made her a target."

"You think it was better for her to worry about her reputation…and just how long was she going to survive on the pittance her brother sent her?"

"She didn't," Nico admitted.

"She didn't what?"

"Alex was sending her nothing to live on. You saw the state of the house once she had been gone a few days." Cordelia had done quite well for herself considering her options.

"So, what did she do?"

This would be the hard part for Nico to admit. "She was a reporter."

Malik looked at him as if he had grown a second head.

"What?"

"She was a reporter for one of those gossip papers, and I was her assignment."

"She was investigating you?" Malik sounded incredulous.

Nico grinned. "Yes. It seems people wonder how I made all my money."

"Ah," Malik said, but he didn't return the smile.

"What's the problem?"

"You don't think she would expose us?" Nico could see the apprehension in Malik's eyes.

"Well, as soon as I accused her of that, she said no one would believe her. And she is right."

Malik nodded, but Nico could still tell his friend was worried.

Before he could ease his fears more, something caught Malik's attention. Nico followed his line of vision and found his wife standing at the door.

He forgot how to speak.

She was dressed in deep blue, so deep that it looked almost black. It wasn't a revealing dress, but it hugged her curves. She was stunning.

After a few moments, Malik cleared his throat. It brought Nico out of his daze.

He walked to her and took her hand. "You look beautiful, Cordelia."

The smile she gave him had his heart beating harder. He found it difficult to breath, and for a moment, he wanted to take her back upstairs.

"I think we better go," Malik said.

"Yes. Your parents are accompanying Diana, so I want to get there soon."

"Lady Diana is coming to the dinner?" Malik asked. "No one told me."

She shared a smile with Nico. "I did not know that we were to gain approval from you for the guest list."

Malik said nothing else, and they were on their way.

* * * *

Cordelia took a deep breath as the doors to Gray's home opened. She had been to a few functions, but nothing that was a vampire gathering. She knew she would be judged tonight as she had never been judged before. Nico was not royalty in the human world, but from the little she had learned, they were considered that in the vampire world.

"Why are you so worried?" Nico said just loud enough for her to hear.

"Just—I don't want to embarrass you or your family."

"Cordelia." He waited until she looked at him. "You would never be able to embarrass me."

For a moment, the noise of the crowd faded away, and it was as if they were in their own little world.

"Are you sure?"

He nodded without taking his gaze from her.

"Blackburn," Gray said, interrupting the moment. "And Lady Cordelia."

She looked around and realized most of the people had been watching. She straightened her spine and smiled at Gray, who suddenly looked stunned.

"Good evening," she said, her smile growing stiffer the longer he stared at her.

"Gray," Nico said.

Gray shook himself and pulled his attention away from her. "Yes, of course, please, come. Your parents and Lady Diana are already here."

Nico worked his way through the crowd. So many people stopped him to chat that it was quite some time before they were finally on their way. "What was wrong with Gray?" she asked.

"Nothing."

She didn't believe that for a minute. "Nico, he was

staring at me like I had something wrong with me."

He sighed. "You're mated now and you sort of...glow."

"What?"

"Glow. A mated Carrier had a very powerful pull."

Before she could ask him more, they reached his parents and her sister.

"You look lovely, Cordelia," her sister said. "The dress is a perfect color for you."

She felt heat rise in her cheeks. She wasn't accustomed to so much attention.

"I believe we can say all the women in our family are quite stunning," Samuel said.

"Don't you men have something you can go do?" Adelaide asked.

"Your mother is trying to get rid of us, Nico," his father said with a laugh. "We might as well leave now."

"Behave while I am gone," he said, giving her a kiss on the cheek.

"What does he think I will do?" she asked Adelaide and Diana.

"Oh, never mind him. Men are always trying to exert their dominance over us. It is just part of their makeup. The smart women just ignore it," Adelaide said. "Your father is here."

"Mrs. Blackburn," Diana said in horror. "Not so loud."

"First, I told you to call me Adelaide. Second, no one can hear." She turned to Cordelia. "I made sure he will be seated across the table from you."

All of the sudden her heart started to gallop. "I am not sure I am ready for this."

"You are," Adelaide said. "And Diana, I made sure you were sitting by Malik."

"What?" Diana practically yelled.

"Diana, really. People are staring," Adelaide said. "Come, I want to introduce you to Countess Featherstone. She has been dying to meet you, Cordelia."

She glanced at her sister. "As I said, it is just better to follow along."

"I think you may be right."

* * * *

"Your mother wanted to be sure I invited Gavin MacDonald tonight," Gray said to Nico.

He frowned. "MacDonald?"

"Yes, I have an idea she thinks that MacDonald might be Cordelia's father," Gray said happily.

"What?" Nico was stunned by this news.

"He might be her father. You were interested in finding out at one time before you married her," Malik said.

"He's right, you know," Gray added cheerfully.

"Yes, I have been a little busy trying to find Neal." Nico hadn't given the question of Cordelia's parentage a second thought.

Gray's jovial mood dissolved. "Of course."

"I think we should go out again tonight."

"I don't think this is going to work," Gray said. "I think we need something else to draw him out."

"I have been thinking of that, and that is why I want to go out tonight." Nico had a plan.

His father studied Nico's expression then nodded. "It is a good plan."

"Risky." Nico admitted as much.

His father gave him an encouraging smile. "Yes, but you can do it. It won't be a problem."

"What the bloody hell are you two talking about?" Gray asked.

He knew that it was going to put him in danger, but it was the only way. The only reason that Neal was making vampires was to get his attention and draw him out.

"I am going to set myself up as bait."

Chapter Twenty-Two

Cordelia had to fight the urge to dry her hands on the skirt of her gown. Dinner had been excruciating. The excitement of meeting her father had made it very difficult to eat. Having her father sit across the table from her had been just too hard to ignore. It had taken all her courage to talk to him. Thankfully, Nico took pity on her and asked for a private moment with the Scottish laird after dinner.

She was clasping and unclasping her hands over and over, trying to calm her racing heart.

"You don't need to worry, Cordelia."

She looked at her husband. "How did you know I was worrying?"

"Your nervous energy is flowing off you."

"I—"

There was a knock at the library door.

"Come," Nico said.

Cordelia rose slowly from the sofa. Not for the first time, she felt her stomach roll over.

Her father walked in. Nico stood next to her and said only loud enough for her to hear, "Breathe."

She let loose a breath she didn't know she was holding.

"Laird MacDonald," Nico said.

"Blackburn," he said, his voice stern. When he turned his attention to her, his facial features soften. "Lady Cordelia."

"Please have a seat, MacDonald. Would you like a brandy?"

He nodded and took one of the two chairs opposite of the sofa. Cordelia followed suit.

"You are newly married?" he asked.

A nervous laugh tried to bubble up, but she fought it off.

"Yes, just over a month now," she said, watching Nico

hand her father the brandy.

"I understand it was hastily planned." He glanced at Nico with an evil look.

"Once I met Cordelia, I had to marry her. I knew she was my mate."

He said it so convincingly that she almost believed the story.

"Ah," MacDonald said as he nodded and took a sip of his brandy. "Your sister was in attendance?"

"Yes," she said. "She came into town just in time for the wedding."

"Did her husband attend?"

She glanced at Nico and wondered where her father was going with the questioning. "No. Her husband died several years ago."

"Ah." MacDonald swirled the liquid in his glass. "I guess you know I knew your mother. You look very much like her."

She smiled. "That is nice to know. My mother died in childbirth, so I never knew what she looked like."

"She knew, you know."

"She knew what?" Cordelia forced herself to keep her hands in her lap.

"That she was a Carrier."

She felt her eyes widen. "She did? My sisters did not know, and I know my fa—" she cleared her throat. "The earl did not know."

"So your sister is moving through a room filled with vampires and she has no idea that she is a Carrier?" MacDonald seemed disturbed by the thought.

She nodded.

He tossed an angry look in Nico's direction. "You allowed this to happen?" His accent now made it almost impossible to understand him.

"She is a widow, MacDonald. I cannot tell her to do anything. And you know in our society the women go about however they like. Being that she is seen as a widow in human society makes it even more difficult."

"I will have to have a talk with her brother."

"No," she said in a near shout. Her father gave her an odd look.

"I beg your pardon?"

"Please, don't contact Alex. Their relationship is very strained." It was the only way she could describe it. MacDonald might be her birth father, but there was no reason to let the man know just how horrible their brother was.

"Of course."

The conversation stopped there and the silence stretched out embarrassingly long. She shifted on the sofa.

MacDonald swallowed down the last of his brandy. "I am sure that you have many people to talk to tonight, so I do not want to monopolize your time."

He was leaving. Panic swelled up. She had finally found him, and he was leaving.

"Laird," she said, then swallowed her nerves and steadied her voice. "I would very much appreciate it if you could find time tomorrow afternoon to stop by for tea."

For a moment, she was not sure if she stepped over the line. In the rules of etiquette, it was just not done. But she could not take a chance that he would return to Scotland and she might never see him again.

Then he smiled. "I would love to do that, Lady Cordelia."

When he left them alone, she breathed easier.

"Are you feeling all right?"

She nodded and tried to fight down the nausea that returned. "Yes. I am feeling a little…off."

"All the excitement is not good for you." Nico took her hand.

She frowned at him. "I am not weak."

"I did not say that."

Irritation had her stomach roiling. "Yes, you did."

He gave her an exasperated glare. 'Come. Things should be settling down. People should be leaving."

She was not sure if he was lying or not, but she did not want to fight anymore. She just wanted to go home.

* * * *

Nico was worried about Cordelia. Once they arrived home, she had not protested when he said he needed to go out.

She had been fast asleep by the time he left less than thirty minutes later.

"You need to quit grinding your teeth. If you needed to feed you should have done it before we left," Malik said.

He glanced at his friend and watched the passing gas lanterns cast shadows on his face.

"I do not need to feed." But the moment he said it, memories of sinking his teeth into Cordelia's neck, drawing the blood from her veins, rose up. He could feel his body respond. His teeth ached. "I can wait."

"You are waiting too long, my friend. Although, I understand your reluctance."

"You do?"

"Yes. Bonding with a woman who is a reporter is not the thing I would want to do."

Nico felt the need to defend his wife. "Was a reporter. Now my wife."

"You hope."

Nico sighed. "It isn't that. According to Saint she is already carrying our first child."

"That's good news." The worry in Malik's voice was evident.

"It doesn't sound like you think it is."

"It is just a bad time," Malik said. "Lots of turmoil."

Nico nodded. "She was asleep almost before she got into bed. I am worried."

"You know that is normal. How does she feel about it?"

Nico crossed his arms. "I am not sure she knows."

"You didn't tell her?" Malik tsked.

"How do you tell a woman she's breeding?"

"Don't look at me, old man." Malik chuckled. "I do not mate for that reason."

Vampires, both Made and Born, could have intercourse without mating, but instead Malik had abstained for centuries. Nico knew Malik felt tainted by his Maker and he did not want to even take the chance of fathering a child.

"On top of it, I do not trust MacDonald."

"Gavin?" Malik asked.

"Yes."

"Why?"

Nico glanced out the window. "He is apparently her birth father."

"That makes sense," Malik said. "He comes from a particularly strong line."

Nico nodded. "And for years, he hid up there in Scotland and did not claim his daughter. But now, here he is, ready to do just that."

He knew he sounded jealous. He didn't care. He did not trust the bastard around his wife.

"For what reason? What would he gain by getting close to Cordelia?"

"I don't know. Money?"

Malik shook his head. "He has more money than you do."

Nico did know that. Or he thought he knew. There had always been rumors that the MacDonald fortune was massive.

"I am not certain of that. Can anyone tell us for sure?" Something about MacDonald still bothered Nico.

"What is your problem?"

"Problem?" Nico struggled to keep his voice even. "He left her with that bastard. Who does that? Not a good father, if he even is one."

The carriage drew to a stop. Malik stood. "Stop fighting it, Nico. Bond with the woman so you can get your mind back on matters."

"Of course. And what would that be?"

"Finding Neal Pearson."

He nodded and looked out of the cab. "We aren't at the hell."

"No, we are following up on a lead. There was a rumor that a man by the name of Pearson was living here."

Nico nodded and followed Malik out of the carriage. The house was in a reputable part of town, clean-looking and dark.

"Why didn't you tell me about this, Malik?"

"Saint was verifying." Malik walked towards the house.

"Why is it just us?" Nico was surprised Saint wasn't here.

"Was living here," Malik said again. "That is what I said. He's no longer living here."

"We could have come during the day."

"No. We would have been seen breaking into the house. And let's face it, you need your rest. Being out in the sunlight will deplete your energy as it is."

He would argue with Malik if it wasn't the truth. Every day he was out in the sun, he felt a little more of his energy drain out of him.

"Around back," Malik said.

They walked to the back and found the kitchen door standing open. Nico pulled out his stake. He glanced at Malik and motioned with his head that he would go first.

The kitchen had been left in a mess, as if the cook had been in the middle of preparing a meal and was interrupted. The scents of rotting food mixed in with the scent of blood. He stepped past the counter and found the cook. Her neck had been slashed.

"Not good," Malik said.

"Yeah, not good at all."

The worked their way through the house, finding the members of the household. The scent was making them both nauseous, but they continued through the entire house.

They found the last of the bodies laid out in the bedroom.

Malik lifted one of the bodies with his foot and rolled it over. Nico recognized him immediately.

"McAlister," Nico said. "He's not a very nice fellow."

"No. He's also a predator," Malik said. "It is said he likes boys."

"Yes. But why is he here?"

"We assumed Neal was working by himself, but he doesn't like to work."

Nico nodded. "He was always lazy. So, maybe he had Simmons do the dirty work and report back to him?"

"We need to get this cleaned up before anyone finds it. It's surprising no one reported it before now."

Nico looked down at Simmons. He had been murdered the most viciously. His neck was a mess, not like the clean cut of the others. "He cut them across the neck, except for Simmons. With their vocal cords severed, there was no way to scream out."

Malik studied the scene. "And from the look of them, they have only been here a few hours."

"Why would he do this?" Nico asked.

"His game is over." Malik began moving through the room, starting the ghastly task of cleaning the slaughter.

Something wrong moved through him, tightening his stomach.

Malik continued. "And he got rid of anyone connected to him."

Something propelled him to start moving. He was halfway downstairs before Malik yelled. "Where are you going?"

Nico had to go. He had to get home now. "What was the

one thing he did right before he went after Magdalen?"

"Damn. He killed all his staff."

"He's going after Cordelia."

He rushed out the front door, his worry about being detected by humans gone.

"Home, Briggs."

His driver nodded. Malik and Nico scrambled into the carriage.

"He hasn't had much time, and you have your house well-guarded. We will save her in time. He might not even be acting out tonight."

He knew Malik was trying to calm him, but Nico remembered Neal too well. "Neal was unpredictable except for two things."

Malik's face was grim.

"He always killed his partners, and he always used the women to get to the men."

He just prayed they made it there in time.

* * * *

Cordelia woke up slowly. She couldn't remember a time when she'd slept so soundly. The room was dark, but she sensed a figure moving through it.

"Nico? You know I hate when you sneak through the room in the dark."

He said nothing and kept walking toward her. As he came within inches of her, a slant of light from the bathing room illuminated his face. The man she saw was not Nico.

"Good evening, Lady Cordelia," he said as his lips curved. Something cold moved down her spine as if he were sliding an icy finger across her flesh.

"Who are you?"

"I'm an old friend of the family. The Blackburns. A pity they never told you about me."

Cordelia tried to stay calm. "What are you doing here?"

"Righting the wrongs of the past. Up, Lady Cordelia. We have a ride to take."

"No."

"Oh, I think you will come with me." The man seemed very sure of himself.

"Why?"

He held up a sharp piece of wood. Even in the dark she could tell it was a stake. "If you don't, I will kill your family."

Chapter Twenty-Three

Nico rushed up the stairs to his townhouse and burst through the door. Terror was screaming in his veins, and it was more than just worry. The fear he felt rushing along his nerve endings was not just from him.

"Cordelia," he yelled.

"What on earth," his father said as he walked out of the study. He was still in his evening clothes which meant he must have just returned.

"Have you checked on Cordelia?" he asked, running up the stairs.

"No," his father said, but he barely heard him. The only sound he noticed was the rush of Malik behind him. He hit the door full force and burst through. He found the room empty.

"Cordelia!"

Nothing but silence. He rushed into the bathing room. Empty.

"Nico," Malik said. He was holding a slip of paper.

"He has her." Nico knew what the note said without Malik even reading it.

"Yes and he wants you to meet him."

"Where?"

"Demetrius's old house."

His heart sank. Everything in him chilled at the thought. Neal had taken his sister-in-law there and killed her in front of Demetrius.

"We go." He knew what would happen to Cordelia if he did not.

"But it could be a trap."

"Of course it is. It's Neal. We just have to make sure that we outsmart him."

Malik sighed.

"Agreed. Let's send notes to Saint and Gray and tell them to meet us there."

Nico nodded.

* * * *

Cordelia shook her head, trying to get her wits about her. For some reason, everything was very fuzzy. When she opened her eyes, the room was unclear.

"So nice of you to join me again."

The voice was familiar. Then everything came rushing back to her. Her eyes finally focused. She was in a dimly lit room. The furnishings were old and there was a hint of mold in the air.

When she could finally see clearly, she noticed the man in the shadows.

"What did you do to me?" she asked then fought back a cry as pain spread from her jaw out. She tried to lift her hands but found them tied to the chair she was sitting in.

"Just a little knock to the jaw." He walked forward slowly. "Sorry about that, but I wanted to make sure that you didn't summon help."

She was still a bit dizzy and the restraints hurt. "I would not have done that."

"I could not take a chance."

Cordelia needed to keep him talking. The longer she distracted him, the better chance she had of being alive when Nico arrived. "You are Neal Pearson."

"No," he said. "I am called by many names, Devil, *Suprema*, but my mother named me Michael."

She frowned. "You have to be the man who killed Nico's brother."

"I did not do that. It was my father."

"Your…father?"

"Yes."

"If I remember correctly, Neal didn't have any children," Nico said as he stepped into the room. "He didn't favor women."

Neal stood. "Ah, finally, Nico has joined us. And yes, my father did have children."

Nico didn't look at her. "Are you alright?"

"Yes."

"How endearing. I was not sure you would come after her since…" he stepped closer and sniffed at her. There was a loud rumble from Nico. "You have not bonded. Amazing. I don't think I would be able not to bond with such a woman. Although I did learn from my mother that bonding can be a detriment. Say, if I killed her now, you would not be affected. But I had a feeling about you two."

"Do tell," Nico said.

"Something about the way you watched her. It was always so…endearing."

"You watched us?" she choked out.

"Yes, at public functions."

"So, what is your relation to Pearson?" Nico asked.

"I told you. I am his son."

"Liar." Nico seemed to be taunting the man.

Michael's face slowly turned red in anger, but when he spoke, he kept his voice calm. "I am his son. My mother was Charlotte."

Recognition moved over Nico's face. "Charlotte Bryer?"

"Yes," the man said. "She told me what truly happened."

"What truly happened?" Nico asked warily. "What do you think happened with your father?"

"Mother told me. She told me about how you used my father to blame him for the murder of your sister-in-law." His voice was tight, signaling that Nico was indeed upsetting him. She knew he was doing it to throw Michael off balance, but it also made Nico more of a target. A scream clogged her throat. Cordelia bit the inside of her mouth to keep from letting it loose.

But it did not seem to affect Nico. His mouth twitched, then curved upward. "Do tell me why I would do that?"

Michael raised his chin, looking very much like a boy trying to take on a master. "You were in love with her. To get back at your brother for marrying her, you killed her and framed my father after killing him."

"Oh, my, I am quite dastardly." Every syllable dripped with sarcasm. "Of course, your father was quite stupid, so I could see where you would fall for it."

His fingers tightened around the stake he was holding. "Shut up."

Nico continued. "He really wasn't all that smart. He was kicked out of Eton. Did your mother tell you that?"

Michael seethed, his breaths coming out short and choppy. He stalked closer to Nico. She had to bite her lip to keep from screaming at Nico. Why was he antagonizing the man?

"Nico," she said, but he did not look at her. His attention was on Michael, who apparently had forgotten about her.

"Shut the hell up," Michael screeched. "I will kill you where you stand."

"Now would work," Nico said loudly.

"What?" Michael seemed confused. She didn't blame him.

"Malik, now."

Neal lunged forward as Nico leaned to his right. Malik came through the door, a stake in his hand. Without hesitation, Malik pulled his arm back and plunged the stake into Pearson's heart.

Pearson fell back, stumbling. A look of surprise, and then dawning horror, moved over his face. The screech he released was unlike any sound she had heard before. It bounced off the walls and made her slightly nauseous. Nico rushed over and blocked her view.

He undid her restraints then pulled her into his arms. He was shaking when he drew back and kissed her.

"What the bloody hell were you thinking leaving the house?" he yelled. Then, without waiting for her to answer, he pulled her back into his arms. He hugged her so tight, she thought she might lose her breath.

"Nico," she said, but could barely hear her own voice. It was muffled in his coat.

"Do you think we can get out of here sometime soon?" Malik said.

Nico let her step back, but he did not let her completely go. He held onto her arm then pulled her to his side.

"Yes. We need to…but we need to do something with the body."

"We can take care of that," Saint said, walking through the door. He studied her as if checking to see if she was bleeding anywhere. "I see that the bastard didn't get to you."

She shook her head.

"Go on. Aunt Adelaide is going to be beside herself with worry."

Gray nodded to her but did not say anything as Nico ushered her through the door and out into the London night.

Malik followed them. Soon, they were on their way home. She was sitting on Nico's lap and would have been embarrassed in front of Malik, but she was too relieved.

"We need to kill the other Mades." Malik said it with such a cold certainty, Cordelia shivered.

"We might be able to save a few," Nico said, but she heard the doubt in his voice.

"I think they are too gone. And the ones he fed his blood to…they will be ready to kill anyone in their way. We need to send out assassins for them."

Nico glanced down at her as if he didn't want her to hear. But it wasn't like she didn't know what was going on.

"You have to order it, Nico. You have no choice," she whispered. "Mades like Malik and Hurst…they will be vilified."

"You will not do it," Nico said.

Malik tore his gaze away from the window. "Worried about me, old man?"

"No Mades should be looking. It will be too much to ask."

Malik nodded and then lapsed into silence.

She wanted to ask more, and she wanted to yell at Nico, but she apparently was more tired than she thought. The swaying carriage and the warmth of Nico's embrace surrounded her, and she drifted off to sleep.

Chapter Twenty-Four

All the lights were blazing when they finally pulled up to the front of their townhouse. Nico saw the door to the house fling open and servants and family came pouring out. So much for not attracting attention.

He waited while Malik opened the carriage door, then woke Cordelia.

"Love, it's time to wake up, we are home."

She grumbled in her sleep and cuddled closer to him, burrowing into his jacket. In that moment, he didn't want to leave the carriage. He wanted to hold her close, knowing that he had gotten to her in time to save her. And he wanted to be alone with her.

Malik stuck his head through the doorway. "Come on, Nico. Your mother is not in the best of moods, and she will start screeching soon if you do not get Cordelia out of there and into the house."

He sighed.

"Cordelia, wake up, love."

Her eyelids fluttered, then eventually opened. Her eyes were clouded, confused, then they cleared.

"Where are we?"

"Home. Let's go."

She nodded but before she slipped off his lap, he kissed her. When he pulled back, she was smiling.

"What was that for?"

He was embarrassed by it. For the first time in his life, he really did not know what to say to a woman. She had his heart in her hands and she had no idea. If she had died tonight, he would have regretted not bonding with her. He did not want to go on living without her.

He loved her more than life itself.

Nico shook his head and lifted her off his lap.

He stepped down first, then reached back into the carriage. The moment her small hands touched his, he felt the connection. Nico pushed back his emotions and helped her out of the carriage. They would have to wait until later to talk and to do what he should have done long ago.

He smiled down at her as she looked up at him.

"Get ready," he said.

"For what?"

But he didn't have time to answer. She was surrounded by a crowd, his family and he noted, hers as well. Diana and her father were in attendance.

"Let's go inside so we don't make a scene," he said.

He herded the group of servants and family into the house and did his best to calm his needs. He would have her in bed soon enough.

* * * *

Cordelia wanted to collapse she was so tired. It had been over an hour since they had returned, but no one seemed inclined to leave her alone. That is, except Malik, who gave her sister an odd look and then went to do Nico's bidding to set up the hunt to find the rest of the Mades.

"Cordelia, I would like to have a word with you in private. With you and…" her sister trailed off and glanced over at their father.

"Laird MacDonald, please, my sister and I would like to have a word with you."

She said it rather loud, and she thought she heard Nico laugh, but she ignored him. She wanted to get this over with. Her nerves had been through so much today. She was not sure she was up to this.

MacDonald smiled and nodded. She rose from her chair and felt several hands reach for her. "I do not need help," she said rather crossly. She sighed and looked around at the faces of the friends and family who had gathered to support her. Most were filled with concern, except Nico, who was smiling at her.

It was then that she realized that for the first time in a long time, there was a community…a family that cared about her. They might not be her blood, mostly, but they were her family now. All of them had been worried, and Nico…he had come to save her as if he could not live without her.

Tears burned the back of her eyes. She blinked them away. "Please, accept my apologies. I am rather tired."

Most of them nodded their heads knowingly. She stepped up to Nico's side, since he had been standing behind her chair as if he were still guarding her. She rose to her tiptoes, resting her hand on his shoulder to steady herself.

"Thank you for saving me," she whispered in his ear. "I love you."

He stilled and turned to look at her, his face with no expression, but his eyes…they were dark, mysterious, and filled with some kind of emotion she couldn't discern. As always, everyone in the room seemed to melt away as he continued to stare at her. He opened his mouth to speak, and she saw that his feeding teeth had descended. At the moment, she wanted nothing more than to go away, to be with him and no one else. But, MacDonald cleared his throat.

She felt her face heat as Nico cast his gaze upwards then back down to hers. He gave her a kiss on the nose. "After you are done talking to them, we will go up to bed."

If she had any doubts about what that meant, she only had to look at him to know. She nodded then led her sister and her father out of the room. They gathered in the front parlor. Diana shut the door behind her.

"Diana, what is it you needed?" she asked. She was trying her best to be pleasant, but she was not in the mood for this. What she wanted was to be with Nico, alone, and not come out for days.

Lord, she had turned into a loose woman.

"I wanted to talk to both of you because I think we need to face our relationship," Diana said.

MacDonald looked at both of them, his expression wary. "I knew your mother."

Diana smiled. "I remember your visits."

For a second, he said nothing. He glanced at Cordelia. The raw emotion on his face squeezed at her heart. There was no doubt in her mind. He had loved their mother.

"Please, do not say I am wrong. You were there a lot when father was gone."

MacDonald winced at the word "father," and Cordelia knew everything she wanted to know. She did not have the patience to dance around the truth.

"What Diana is trying to say is that she wants you to know that we know you are my father and possibly hers."

"Cordelia, really. Did I not teach you any manners at all?"

"Yes, but thankfully I married Nico, and now I don't have to have manners. He's rude to everyone and that allows me to do the same."

MacDonald still hadn't said anything.

Diana and Cordelia shared a glance. Cordelia shrugged. Diana approached him. "I must apologize for my sister. She really does have better manners—"

"I adored her," MacDonald said.

"Our mother?" Cordelia asked.

He nodded. "Aye. She was the most beautiful of women, inside and out."

"I remember you together, how happy she was," Diana said. "I-I loved your visits."

He glanced at Cordelia and then Diana. "I wanted to take you both away...along with your sisters. I wanted to bond with her."

Diana looked confused at the language, and Cordelia shook her head. "Diana doesn't understand everything."

MacDonald looked at Cordelia then nodded.

"Understood."

She breathed a sigh of relief. Cordelia wasn't sure if she would ever have to explain to her sister what they were, but she definitely did not want to do it tonight.

"Why didn't you?" Diana asked. Her voice was quiet and filled with tears, but there were none on her face.

"I couldn't. It killed me that she would not leave that bastard, but she couldn't, not legally, and there was your brother. But, it seems he takes after his father too much."

Both she and Diana nodded.

"I am going to stay in London a little longer. I would appreciate getting to spend time with both of you."

His eyes were shimmering with unshed tears, and she felt her own spill over. "Yes."

Diana bit her lip. Her own eyes appeared to be wet as well. She nodded.

"Well," he cleared his throat. "I need to talk to your husband about what he needs from me."

He stepped toward her then stopped. She could not let him leave like that, with this distance between them. She walked to him. Without a word, she put her arms around him. When she pulled back, Cordelia looked over at Diana and was alarmed. The woman she had never really seen upset was now crying openly.

"Diana?"

She shook her head, still unable to speak apparently. Then, without a word, she threw herself into their father's arms.

"I have missed you so much."

He patted her back and looked at Cordelia. She smiled through the tears.

Diana then pulled back. "I will be staying here to help Cordelia and would love to…spend time with you."

He nodded as a satisfied smile curved his lips. "Well, then. I will call on you in a few days."

He walked out of the room and the door shut with a

click.

"Do you want to explain what happened tonight?" Diana asked. Cordelia was so surprised by the question she almost answered. She wanted her sister again, wanted the confidant she had when she had been a child.

"Never mind," Diana said, shaking her head and sighing.

"No, I want to tell you, but...I am so tired, and Nico is not going to be happy if I take much longer."

Diana nodded. "I should have never left you."

"What?"

"I should have come up with some kind of plan to get you out of there."

For what seemed like the hundredth time that night, she felt her eyes fill up. She could not say anything. Instead, she rushed to her sister and hugged her. The familiar scent of roses surrounded her. Memories of their childhood flooded her senses.

"I missed you so, Diana."

She hugged Cordelia tighter. "I missed you too."

When she stepped back, Diana smiled, looking younger. "I will let you go tonight, but I do want to talk to you."

She opened her mouth to respond, but Nico strode in before she could get any words out. He was frowning. He said nothing as he approached her then picked her up.

"Nico!"

"Good night, Diana."

Her sister laughed. "Good night, Nico."

"Nico, really, must you act like that? Do you not have any manners?"

"No."

"That's it."

"Yes."

She sighed and wanted to admonish him again, but since she had just proudly told her sister she had no manners, she guessed she could not truly complain.

When they reached their room, he waited for her to open

the door.

"Out," Nico said to the maid waiting for her.

She flew out of the room in such a hurry, she was a blur.

"You could have just asked me to accompany you upstairs, Nico. I would have come."

He stopped in the middle of the room. He looked at her, his eyes burning with need. "Did you mean it?"

"Yes, I would have come upstairs with you."

He shook his head as his brows lowered. "No. What you said before. Do you truly love me?"

She studied him. For a quick second, she saw something that was close to vulnerability on his face.

"I would not have said it if I did not mean it."

He kissed her then, ruthlessly, as if he was trying to pour every feeling into it. When he drew back, they were both breathing heavily.

"I want to love you, to forget the world, but first we must talk."

Her body was already humming, her need for him growing with each second that ticked by.

"Must we?"

He smiled slightly but he nodded. "There are things I must tell you."

She sighed as he placed her on the bed. "If you feel it is necessary."

With a stern expression on his face, Nico placed his hands on his hips.

"I assume you know about bonding now."

She nodded, the pleasant warmth he'd created with the kiss draining out of her. She did not want to know why he could not bond with her. She knew. She just did not want to hear why from him.

"When my sister-in-law was taken, Neal tortured her until she died. My brother felt everything his wife did, then he died. It was horrible." He looked at her. "I did not want to think of dealing with that myself. I could not see myself opening to someone as Demetrius did."

She opened her mouth, but he set his finger against her lips. "I did not understand until tonight."

"Truly?" she asked. "It isn't because I was abducted? Maybe you are just feeling guilty."

"It isn't that, or the fact that you are carrying my child."

"If you...what?"

He sighed. "You did not know? Saint said you might."

"You mean your cousin knows I am...?" She waited for him to nod. "How does he know?"

"He has the sight. He says you will someday, too."

She opened her mouth then closed it.

"I am trying to tell you I love you, and I don't want to discuss what kind of abilities you are going to have," he said in a shout. "Seriously, Cordelia, do you do anything normally?"

"I find being normal boring." She sighed, her heart fluttering around the idea he had just shouted at her. "Do you truly love me?"

He nodded. "The moment I thought I lost you, that I might never see you again, I wanted to die. I knew that living without you was not an option. I needed you."

"Oh, Nico." Tears clouded her vision.

"I would like to bond with you." He shook his head. "I need to bond with you."

He slipped onto the floor in front of her, taking her hands in his. He kissed them.

"Yes, Nico, I will bond with you."

"You do not know everything. By doing this, you bind our life forces together. I will only feed from you for eternity. And, if one of us dies...the other will too."

"I know, and I don't care."

He smiled, that smile that always curled her toes.

"No turning back now, Cordelia."

She shook her head. "Never."

Nico pulled her up off the bed, then turned her around.

He made quick work of her clothes and she soon found herself back on the bed, both of them naked.

"You have the most luscious flesh."

She sighed as she felt the scrape of his teeth against her skin. It felt as if he would devour her any minute, but he kept nipping at her, teasing her.

"I do not know how I will ever be able to resist you."

He slid down further, taking first one nipple, then the second into his mouth. They were sensitive to the touch, and she gasped. He paid no attention. Instead, he kissed her stomach and then looked up at her with a smile. Without breaking eye contact, he kissed her again. Her heart felt as if it would burst. Then, he continued on, and she lost herself in the pleasure he gave her. With his mouth and his hand, he took her over the edge into erotic bliss again and again. By the time he slipped up her body again, she felt spent. He pulled himself up to his knees.

"Cordelia, look at me."

It took all her strength to open her eyes. When she did, she found him holding a dagger.

"We are to become one, until the ending sun," he said as he cut his index finger. He placed it on her lips. Without taking her gaze from his, she sucked the blood from him. The sweet, salty taste of it filled her.

He did not wait then. He entered her forcefully, thrusting so fast and hard the massive bed shook. Soon, she felt another release explode within her, and he shouted her name as he poured himself into her.

* * * *

Hours later, they still lay in bed, embracing. Satisfaction filled him. Nico now knew what his father had talked about. Having a mate, a bonded mate, was what a man needed to be complete.

"Nico, how long have you known I was carrying?"

"A week."

Her head shot up, smacking his chin. Even in the dim light he could see Cordelia's eyes narrowing. "What do you mean a week?"

"It might have been more."

"Nicodemus Blackburn, I cannot believe you did not tell me."

She turned to leave him in the bed alone, but he grabbed her and pulled her back into his arms. He kissed her on the neck as she struggled against him.

"Please, you have to forgive me, Cordelia."

"Why should I?" she asked grumpily, but she did move her head to the side to give him better access to her neck.

"Because I love you."

"Hmpf."

"And you love me."

She sighed. "There is that."

He quickly switched their positions. She was under him, giggling, as he kissed her neck once again.

"Say you forgive me or I will torture you until you do."

"Alright, I give up. I forgive you."

He pulled back and looked down at her. Her curls were a tangled mess across the pillows. Her eyes were still filled with laughter and heat, and she was smiling at him.

"Say it again, Cordelia."

Her smile turned coy. "I love you, Nico."

"I love you too, Cordelia. I will spend the rest of our lives making sure you know just how much."

"Really?" she asked as she grinned up at him. "How are you going to do that?"

"Watch me," he said as he moved down her body.

It was the last coherent words either of them said for hours.

THE END

Coming in 2013

Seduction by Blood

All of the London is convinced Jack the Ripper has returned to London, but Malik knows better. He knows the familiar scent of a Made, one that has survived longer than he should have. But, while he is pursuing the killer, he cannot keep his mind on it completely. Mrs. Diana Simpson has become too much to ignore. From her haughtiness, to the simmering passion he sees lurking behind the pain in her eyes, he recognizes his mate.

Diana has accepted this new part of her life, but she is not ready to bind herself to any man, human or vampire. Her first marriage left much to be desired and she is not ready for that disappointment again. Still, each time they are together, the passion they feel explodes and neither of them are ready for the repercussions of their actions. Especially when the new killer sets his eyes on Diana.

Enjoy this unedited excerpt from Seduction by Blood:

His breath feathered over the fine hairs of Diana's neck. The scent of him wrapped around her, teasing her senses, tempting her. In this moment, he could ask her to do anything and she would follow his command. How could this man do this to her?

"I have tried to stay away from you," Malik said, his voice deepening over every syllable. He has an upper crust English accent, but there something else there. Something that hinted at dark desires and forbidden needs. Two things she should not even think about.

She did not turn around, could not. If she did, she would definitely make a fool of herself.

"Oh?" she asked.

A beat of silence and she continued to look out over the street but not truly seeing anything. She closed her eyes the moment she felt his finger against her shoulder. She shivered.

"Yes. I am not good for you."

No man was. No man would be. She had given up on the idea of happily ever after the night of her wedding.

"You have decided you are no good for me, so nothing will happen?"

Why did she ask that? She didn't want him. Not truly.

"Nothing should happen. Not between someone like me and a lady like you."

Of course not. Men did not want her, not really. At least he was honest.

"I understand."

"I do not think you do, Diana."

He slipped in front of her. When she continued to look only at his chest, he gently placed his finger beneath her chin and raised it until her gaze met his.

His light green eyes were brilliant with need, one she had never seen in a man before. Not for her.

"I said that is should not happen," he said leaning closer. His breath feathered over her lips. "I did not say it would not happen."

He brushed his mouth over hers. She closed her eyes as he slid his hand around her waist and pulled her closer. His body heat surrounded her as he deepened the kiss. She trembled, not from fear but from the lust that pulsed through her blood.

About Melissa Schroeder

From an early age, Melissa loved to read. First, it was the books her mother read to her including her two favorites, *Winnie the Pooh* and the *Beatrix Potter* books. She cut her preteen teeth on *Trixie Belden* and read and reviewed *To Kill a Mockingbird* in middle school. It wasn't until she was in college that she tried to write her first stories, which were full of angst and pain, and really not that fun to read or write. After trying several different genres, she found romance in a Linda Howard book.

Since the publication of her first book in 2004, Melissa has had close to fifty romances published. She writes in genres from historical suspense to modern day erotic romance to futuristics and paranormals. Included in those releases is the bestselling Harmless series. In 2011, Melissa branched out into self-publishing with *A Little Harmless Submission* and the popular military spinoff, *Infatuation: A Little Harmless Military Romance*. Along the way she has garnered an epic nomination, a multitude of reviewer's recommended reads, over five Capa nods from TRS, three nominations for AAD Bookies and regularly tops the best seller lists on *Amazon* and *Barnes & Noble*.

Since she spent her childhood as a military brat, Melissa swore never to marry military. But, as we all know, Fate has her way with mortals. She is married to an AF major and is raising her own brats, both human and canine. She spends her days giving in to her addiction to Twitter, counting down the days until her hubby retires, and cursing the military for always sticking them in a location that is filled with bugs big enough to eat her children.

You can connect with Mel all over the web:
www.melissaschroeder.net
twitter.com/melschroeder

facebook.com/melissaschroederfanpage
www.facebook.com/groups/harmlesslovers/
www.facebook.com/groups/harmlessbookdiscussion
Or email her at: Contact@MelissaSchroeder.net

Other Books by Melissa Schroeder

Harmless

A Little Harmless Sex
A Little Harmless Pleasure
A Little Harmless Obsession
A Little Harmless Lie
A Little Harmless Addiction
A Little Harmless Submission
A Little Harmless Fascination

A Little Harmless Military Romance

Infatuation
Possession
Surrender

The Harmless Shorts

A Little Harmless Fling
A Little Harmless Kalikimaka
A Little Harmless Surprise
A Little Harmless Gift

Once Upon An Accident

The Accidental Countess
Lessons in Seduction
The Spy Who Loved Me

Leather and Lace

The Seduction of Widow McEwan
Leather and Lace—Print anthology

Texas Temptations

Conquering India
Delilah's Downfall

Hawaiian Holidays

Mele Kalikimaka, Baby
Sex on the Beach
Getting Lei'd

Bounty Hunters, Inc

For Love or Honor
Sinner's Delight

The Sweet Shoppe

Her Wicked Warrior

Connected Books

Seducing the Saint
Hunting Mila
Saints and Sinners—print of both books
The Hired Hand
Hands on Training
Cancer Anthology
Water—print

Stand Alone Books

Grace Under Pressure
The Last Detail
Her Mother's Killer
A Calculated Seduction
Telepathic Cravings

Coming Soon

A Little Harmless Fantasy
Southern Sins
Craving
A Little Harmless Ride
Relentless
A Little Harmless Secret

Rereleases Coming Soon

The Sweet Shoppe: Cowboy Up
The Sweet Shoppe: Tempting Prudence
Going for Eight
Chasing Luck

Please enjoy the first chapter of Melissa Schroeder's compelling paranormal series, The Cursed Clan.

CALLUM: THE CURSED CLAN

As Laird, Callum Lennon feels he has always failed to protect his cousins. Callum's impulsiveness caused the death of his father and the experience has scarred not only his body, but his soul. From that point on, he made sure to always go with the more logical choice in every matter. When his younger cousin Angus finds clues that might help break the curse, Callum begrudgingly hires Phoebe Chilton to investigate. Callum doesn't like bringing outsiders into their family affairs. Their life would become fodder for the tabloids if anyone were to find out about the curse. It doesn't help that the instant he meets Dr. Chilton he's attracted. But, he doesn't really have a choice because she might be their last hope.

An expert in archeology, Phoebe has always been dwarfed by her parents' shadow. Their high standards had her in college by thirteen and earning a second PhD by twenty-two. But her career and her broken marriage have left her needing something more than just diplomas and degrees. She wants to prove that her interest in legends, especially Celtic legends, is as important as her parents' work. When the Lennon family contacts her, she sees the opportunity to win a massive research grant. With a long-time rival breathing down her back, she jumps at the Lennons' offer her, hoping it will ensure her the grant. But uncovering the Lennon family secrets, and her attraction to Callum, could prove more than she can handle.

Forces outside the family are determined to ensure that they fail. When an old enemy threatens both the well being of the clan and the fragile new love, Callum will have to choose between believing his mind or his heart.

The Cursed Clan:
Callum

Prologue

Scotland, 1746

Death would be too kind for the Clan McLennan.

Donedella McWalton clutched her husband's faded plaid to her chest. Even as fear slithered down her spine, she knocked on the door to the witch's remote cottage. As she waited, a chilling gust of wind stole through the thrashing branches of the winter-bare trees.

From above, an owl screeched. She shivered. Before her nerves settled, the door creaked open. Donedella saw no one standing before her. She hesitated in the gaping doorway, which earned her a disembodied cackle.

"Come in, my lady," an ancient voice called from behind the door.

Donedella's heart skipped a beat. Bolstering her courage, she skittered over the threshold, eyes darting around the room. With only the light from the hearth's fire, it took a moment for Donedella's eyesight to adjust. No bats hung from the ceiling. No potion boiled over the fire. But as the flames danced, the shadows moved and dread twisted through her.

"You are Lady Donedella."

She jumped at the sound of her name and toward the voice. Donedella had imagined the woman to be older, scarier. But this woman was not much different from herself. The kerchief on her head covered what looked to be a mop of curly gray hair. Her simple peasant clothing draped over her generous figure. Even as Donedella noted the normal dress, she sensed dispassionate study from the woman who earned her keep off the misery of others.

Donedella nodded.

The witch walked forward, her steps sure and steady. She stopped within an inch of Donedella.

"You want to kill someone?"

"Nay." She shook her head. "That would be tae easy, tae nice."

The old woman humphed and paced away. Donedella watched her, wondering if the witch would do what she requested. Or could. This witch was her last chance. Her last hope. Without the woman's help, the vile McLennans would 'ner pay for their crime. Panic raced through her, curdling her stomach. She swallowed the bile in her throat.

The witch glanced over her shoulder, and Donedella almost gasped. The cold, calculating gleam in the other woman's eyes sunk into her bones, chilling her from the inside out. She fought the shiver that raced down her spine.

"For this you shall pay...handsomely?" The smile she flashed Donedella had nothing to do with pleasure.

Drawing in a deep breath, she nodded. "Aye. I'll pay anythin' to have my revenge on the McLennans."

The older woman glanced at the plaid Donedella held. She'd almost forgotten she'd brought it. "I see you have the plaid. You know what you are asking? You know that this curse is not done lightly?"

Before she could allow her conscience to get the better of her, Donedella let the pain of the last four months bubble up inside her. *The death of her beloved, the murder of her sons, and the ending of their clan as they knew it was too much to bear.* Even as she knew that the spell she sought would condemn her soul to hell, she could not stop the hate. It swept through her, whirled into her heart, into her soul, demanding vengeance.

"I want them tae suffer."

"'Tis as you wish, my lady." The fire snapped, the flames jumping as the witch nodded again and turned from her. "They will suffer, indeed."

Chapter One

Present Day, Edinburgh, Scotland

Callum Lennon dropped the file folder into his briefcase and sent his younger cousin an irritated glare. "You said she would be here at two, Angus. It's now four, and I've got a meeting on the other side of town. I'll never make it on time."

Angus adjusted his wire-rimmed glasses and studied him. The younger man graced Callum with an expression rife with his legendary patience.

Damn. Every department head claimed when they received *The Stare*, they knew they'd lost the argument. Callum supposed this wasn't any different.

"She's running a little late. It isn't her fault London was fogged in," Angus pointed out.

Callum grunted. "It's her fault for coming from London in the first place. Bloody Sassenach."

Angus smiled but said nothing in return. Everyone in the family knew Callum distrusted all things English. His younger cousins could have the luxury of an open mind. But Callum's memories were still ripe, even after all these years. But then, no man walked away from watching his family and friends butchered with a whole heart or soul.

"She's the only expert who would travel here on short notice to talk with us."

Callum raised a dark brow. "That should tell you something."

Angus continued as if Callum hadn't even responded. "And despite your assumptions, she is considered the best in the field. Her published works in archeology alone would qualify her. With her interest in Celtic legends and her ability to read so many dead languages, she's a godsend. We were lucky to catch her between projects."

Unusual restlessness forced Callum to his feet. Even as

he approached the window, he could feel worry for his cousins settling around his shoulders like a familiar cloak. Duty bound him to protect the clan at all costs, and he had fallen short of shielding them more than once.

A fine mist covered the window due to an abnormal November shower. The weather fit his mood. A burst of wind rattled around them, a sound he found oddly calming. Callum was well acquainted with the cold. For years he had lived with it in his blood, chilling his bones, freezing his soul. Each year he seemed to slip a little further into the depths of it, until he wondered if he'd ever be free. Even if they won this battle, he knew well he might have already lost the war.

Callum didn't like Angus's plan, but with everything he and his cousins had faced, he owed them this bit of hope. The other four were so optimistic about what their discovery could mean. And, hating to crush their expectations, he allowed it. It was naïve and desperate, but he understood why they wanted the quest to be true.

But it could be true.

Callum viciously squashed that voice in his head, the one that spun gold out of midair. As laird, he had to ignore the lure of fantasy and keep his feet planted firmly on the ground. If this dream shattered, as it had all the times before, and their lives returned to "normal," he would handle their pain, their loss. It was his duty to look after them.

Angus's mobile rang, breaking into Callum's brooding thoughts. After a few short sentences and a quick laugh, Angus hung up.

"That was Fletcher. They're on their way up."

He shot Angus another irritated glower, and then turned to look out the window again. They wanted this expert, but that didn't mean Callum had to be nice, especially since they were paying this woman a bloody fortune.

"Promise you'll keep an open mind about this, Callum."

"I said I would." He couldn't—wouldn't—hide his animosity or his impatience.

"Be civil to Dr. Chilton. She's the top of her field and was supposed to take a bit of a breather between assignments. She only returned from a dig last week." He paused, and when he spoke next, his tone was measured and all levity had dissolved from it. "This might be our last chance."

Pushing aside his annoyance, Callum nodded—once. Angus was right.

"I'll be professional. By God, we're paying the woman just to meet with us. I never promised to be civil."

When Angus didn't reply, Callum realized his cousin's attention was focused on the door. The anger there melted into a smile that Angus reserved only for women.

"It's so refreshing to meet a man with such honesty."

The voice—crisp and thoroughly English—held a tone of amused condescension that grated down Callum's spine. He felt the heat of embarrassment creep up his throat to his face. Knowing that their guest had finally made her entrance, he turned to greet her. The moment he saw her, every bleeding thought in his brain vanished.

Phoebe Chilton wasn't anything like he expected. He'd seen pictures of her in her file and on the back of her books, but apparently the woman didn't photograph well. If she had, he'd have been prepared to behold the Botticelli angel who stood before him.

A wealth of curly blonde hair surrounded a gently rounded face. Fat drops of water clung to the curls, which had been in some kind of an arrangement, but half of it had fallen out and was now draped over her shoulders. Pale lashes framed green eyes that reminded him of the sea. One blonde brow rose as his gaze moved to her cute, slightly upturned nose, a lush, pink frowning mouth, and a pointed chin—which she lifted ever so slightly. The shoulders of her ill-fitting, tweed, brown jacket were damp from the rain, as was her skirt, which seemed to be a size too big. The run in her hose and unattractive pumps completed the outfit.

Angus made the introductions. She didn't offer her hand. Her gaze raked over him, reeking of disapproval. Though they did not touch, her attention sent heat leaping through his veins, not only surprising but frustrating him.

When she made eye contact, she said, "I would say I was delighted to meet you, but then my mother taught me never to lie."

Sarcasm often amused him—unless it came from those on his payroll. He pushed back at the urge to respond to the woman's barb. He definitely didn't like the sharp punch of lust to his gut for what amounted to an employee—and an English one at that.

"I apologize that you overheard my comments."

She smiled without humor. "But not for saying them?"

He shrugged. "I don't apologize for my opinions."

This time she laughed. The light, joyous sound took him by surprise, as did the dance of anticipation his pulse did when he heard it.

"Forget it. I deal better when someone is honest with me. I don't need anyone to pump up my ego. It's rather big enough on its own."

Before Callum could respond, Angus gestured to the seat behind her. "Dr. Chilton, why don't you have a seat?"

She turned her attention toward Angus and smiled again. This time it reached her eyes, lighting them from within. Angus, full-grown man that he was, blushed to the tips of his ears.

"Thank you, Mr. Lennon."

As she settled into the chair, Angus spoke in a voice just solicitous enough to agitate Callum. "I think to keep confusion at a minimum, you should call us by our first names."

Her smile turned impish, dimples winking at the corners of her mouth like a mischievous fairy. "I completely understand. With three Dr. Chiltons on a site, my parents and I tend to be informal as well."

Apparently forgetting about Callum and Fletcher, Angus eased his hip up onto the corner of Callum's desk. He wore the expression of a besotted puppy as he leaned forward and rested his forearm on his leg. Callum would be amazed if Angus didn't expect a pat on the head or a scratch behind his ear.

"That's right. You sometimes dig with your parents. Your husband is in the same field, correct?"

Her happy expression faded, and her eyes lost some of their lightness. "He did. My husband passed away eighteen months ago."

"Oh." Angus straightened and cleared his throat, breaking the beat of silence that followed his comment. "I'm sorry."

She shook her head and patted Angus's hand, the short contact annoying Callum. "No need to apologize. Unless you move within archeological circles, you wouldn't have heard." She sat back and then turned her attention to Fletcher, who had taken the seat next to hers. "Thank you once again for retrieving me from the airport."

The smile Fletcher offered oozed charm and seduction. "It was definitely my pleasure, lass."

When she didn't do more than return the pleasant expression and then direct her attention to Callum, Fletcher frowned. Callum bit back a chuckle. Fletcher wasn't accustomed to women ignoring his charm, and it was damned refreshing to meet a woman who was immune to it.

When he turned back to Dr. Chilton, her practiced, professional smile was back in place. Frustration crawled through him until he stopped himself. Why should he care if she didn't give him a warm smile? He didn't, not when she was destined to be another disappointment.

When he said nothing, that damn eyebrow rose again. "Since you seem a bit anxious, why don't you tell me what you want, and we can get down to business."

* * * *

Phoebe Chilton didn't get flustered easily. Her life had never allowed for that. Starting college at the age of thirteen and earning her second doctorate by twenty-two, not to mention the constant lectures she gave, supplied the experience needed to think on her feet, even when males outnumbered her three to one.

In her field, she was accustomed to men, but nothing in her experience even came close to the masculine beauty surrounding her now. The testosterone filling the office was enough to make her dissolve into a puddle of very feminine lust.

When Fletcher Lennon had met her at the airport, she'd had a hard enough time not drooling. At least six feet tall, blue eyed with brown hair tipped in bronze from the sun, he turned the head of every woman between the ages between two and ninety-two. There was a rugged appeal to his face, with the strong jaw and wide, thick shoulders. Not to mention the outfit: a chambray shirt, worn, butt-hugging jeans, and cowboy boots. Cowboy boots on a bloody Scot!

Unlike many other handsome men, he didn't make her nervous. Oh, at first her tongue had been double-tied in knots. With the ease of a longtime friend, he'd joked with her on their trip to the Lennon house, and before she knew it, she found herself relaxing. It was a pleasant surprise when he made the pretext of flirting with her. For him, it was second nature, she understood. But there was no way she would ever be seriously interested in a man who was more beautiful than she. Besides that, she could never take a man who wore cowboy boots in Edinburgh seriously.

She turned her attention to Angus, whose jade green eyes sparkled behind his glasses. Where Fletcher was all practiced seduction, Angus held an air of forgetful genius. She'd talked with him on the phone, never realizing he would be so scrumptious.

His face was lean, as was his body, but not skinny. Sandy blond hair, a bit overgrown, kept falling into his face, which he absentmindedly brushed out of his eyes every few minutes. As he studied her, she sensed deliberate calculation. It didn't bother her, as she tended to study people and situations in the same manner. And though his voice was gentle, there was an underlying strength beneath that calm. His solicitous behavior reminded her of many research assistants she'd encountered over the years.

Callum Lennon was another story altogether.

Before coming to Scotland, she had researched the Lennon family, especially their leader. It was her way. Any smart woman would do the same before embarking alone on a mysterious trip like this. Other than the fact that he headed up one of the most successful corporations in the UK—if not the whole bloody world—Phoebe found precious little else. No pictures, no personal information. A man with this sort of money usually took pains to be seen out, a beauty on his arm, attending benefits, galas and whatnot. Truthfully, though, she doubted any photo could have lived up to the flesh-and-blood man standing before her. And what beautiful flesh it was.

From his expression to his dress, black suited him. Ebony hair, peppered with bits of gray, was cut ruthlessly short. Like his office, he was dour, and more than likely as predictable as a schedule. Where his cousins seemed approachable, Callum's demeanor was a red light.

The only thing appealing about him, other than the fact that he possessed one of the best bodies she'd ever seen, was his eyes. The shape of them would be considered bedroom sleepy, seemingly half-closed. The lazy sensuality was belied by the vigilant alertness she sensed in his study. This man missed nothing, but that wasn't their most amazing quality.

The color held her almost mesmerized. Blue, a completely boring description, would not do justice to their beauty. Flecks of gold lightened the dark, sapphire hue. And when light struck them in just the right manner, there was a hint of green. She'd sigh over them, if it wasn't a completely adolescent thing to do. She'd just have to wait until she was in her room alone. With the lights turned out.

"First, we need to talk contracts." The burr in his voice had thickened since she'd first heard him speak, making her belly flutter. When his words registered, she sighed in regret. Such a beautiful man, completely out of her league, but she'd hoped they'd work on friendly terms.

"No. First, we need to talk about what you want me to do."

He didn't respond for a moment, clearly taken aback by the fact someone disagreed so openly with him. There was a flash of irritation and something akin to admiration—which was an odd combination, to be sure—in his gaze.

"There is no discussion of anything until you sign a contract. We, meaning Lennon Enterprises, must protect our name."

He crossed his arms over his broad chest and gave her what she was sure was his most intimidating stare. Silly man, didn't he know anything about her? She was handling professors who were just as intimidating when she was barely thirteen. And nothing would stand between her and the grant she needed to complete her most important work ever.

"No. As I discussed at length with Angus before I traveled here, I made it very clear that once I arrived, I wanted information up front. I will sign a confidentiality agreement, but I will not sign a binding contract. I understand the need for secrecy, but I assure you there is no problem. I have a reputation that far exceeds even your valued standing in the business community." One ebony brow rose in aggravation—or respect?—for her snooping. "All I know is that it's a serious matter dealing with an artifact you found and need help translating. We will work much better together if I understand what I am dealing with." She offered him her best business smile, the one she used on interviewers and donors.

"I'll no' risk my family name, our honor, to be sold to the highest bidder. The information you could gather would be more valuable on the open market."

She could tell he was angry. His brogue had thickened to the point that she could barely understand him. But she was irritated too. Her temper wasn't quick to ignite, but was a dangerous thing once it did. And Callum Lennon was perilously close to burning.

She took a deep breath. Then another. "Are you questioning my integrity? That something in your twisted logic thinks I would take what information you give me and sell it, my reputation be damned, is an insult to me!"

By the time she finished, her voice had risen almost to a shout, but the moment she stopped talking, deadly silence filled the room.

Callum's eyes flashed and narrowed. "I doona know or care about your reputation. I have a policy for dealing with *this* situation. I willna have my family used."

She counted backwards from ten, then did it twice more. Questioning her honor, was he? Granted, she wasn't being completely honest with him, but she knew if she rolled over on this one, he would either be suspicious of her motives or think he would win every argument.

Phoebe pushed herself to her feet even as she told herself smacking a six-and-a-half-foot broody, totally delectable Scotsman wasn't a good idea.

"Phoebe." She didn't even flinch when Angus tried to interrupt. "Dr. Chilton."

She ignored the worry in the younger cousin's tone. Locked into a stare down with Callum, Angus's voice didn't completely register. The room, and everything in it, faded away until only she and Callum remained. Fire leapt in his eyes, showing his barely-controlled temper. His rigid stance bespoke his command over his emotions. He probably hadn't said even a tenth of what he was thinking, and she was already offended.

She was no coward, but she tended to work with people, negotiate. Her parents had taught her from an early age to be diplomatic. So, it was a complete surprise that the urge to push him further, question *his* integrity and make him slip over the edge of control, almost overwhelmed her.

Before she could stop herself, she stepped closer to the desk. His expression shifted, turning from anger to something that resembled...lust? Her heart tripped over itself, and her nipples tightened against her cotton bra. His nostrils flared. A charge filled the air, drifting over her, heating her. Bloody hell, every drop of moisture in her mouth evaporated.

Something primal that she'd never experienced before leapt in her blood. Her breath tangled in her throat. All she could think of was touching him, moving her hand over his flesh. Bare flesh. Thankfully, before she could embarrass herself, Angus interrupted her thoughts.

"*Callum.*"

The rebuke in his cousin's voice reached the dark leader. He shook his head as if to clear it, and that was enough to bring Phoebe to her senses. She needed to keep her head straight or she would surely give herself away.

Drawing in a deep breath, she dropped back into the chair, her body still humming from the confrontation. Callum abruptly turned to face the window.

"Since Phoebe is here for at least a week, why don't we get her settled in her room? She can freshen up and then we can discuss the particulars of our working relationship," Angus offered.

Her unprofessional behavior shamed her. She could blame it on Callum Lennon, but she knew better. Shaken to her core, Phoebe nodded. Unwilling to make eye contact with Angus, her gaze drifted to Callum. He nodded, once.

Fletcher stepped in, trying to ease over the tense moment. His voice was gentle when he spoke. "I'd be more than happy to show you to your room, Dr. Chilton."

Fletcher offered her his arm. Releasing a breath she

didn't know she'd been holding, she accepted and rose from the chair. Unable to meet the gaze of either of his cousins, she said nothing more before leaving the room.

Once Fletcher closed the door, he motioned with his hand down the hall. Without a word, she stepped forward, losing herself in her thoughts. She needed to recoup, pull herself together for her next confrontation. And there *would* be one. Callum Lennon struck her as a man who wouldn't give an inch unless forced to. She admired that, even though it irritated her. It wasn't a situation from which she would shy away.

As they walked, their footsteps against the polished wooden floor were the only sounds echoing down the hallway. No servants or workers peeked out of doorways. It reminded her of a museum. The atmosphere would have been oppressive to some, but she took comfort in it.

As she mentally put aside her confrontation with Callum Lennon, she noticed artifacts hanging on the walls she had missed on her way in. There was a magnificent collection of weaponry that looked to be from the eighteenth century, not to mention a multitude of oil paintings depicting what she assumed where Lennon family ancestors. She'd love to get her hands on several of the pieces, including the jeweled dirk she spied. It was a testament to just how harried her trip to Edinburgh had been that she hadn't noticed them.

"I hope you won't worry about my cousin." Fletcher's relaxed tone soothed her.

She glanced at him. "I'll let you in on a little secret. I've been handling domineering men most my life. Your cousin doesn't worry me."

"So you like domineering men?" he teased, gesturing to a staircase that led up.

She started to climb the stairs. "No. In fact, I have a feeling I was seen as a bit of a 'fish wife' when I was married."

Simon had loved using that term for her, and it still

bothered her. He'd employed it whenever he sought to make her feel guilty, which was often. Of course, at the time, it had worked. Now…it no longer had the power to hurt her.

After stepping up on the last step, she moved aside to wait for Fletcher. "But in my academic career and line of work, I've become familiar with men like your cousin."

Fletcher stepped up then edged closer, smiling down at her. There was a hint of approval in his gaze, along with a dash of sexual interest. *Oh, bother.* She was sure he didn't fancy himself in love with her. And he probably wasn't even interested in her. Men like him flirted as easily as they breathed. They weren't interested in her—not without another reason.

"I don't think Callum has had someone stand up to him like that in...well, ever. Not since he took over the family business." He gestured with his hand to the right. "Your room is this way."

"I can't believe that you and your other cousins don't give him a hard time about other matters. From what I understand, all of you have some say in the company."

He tossed her a smile that would likely melt most women. "There is that, but family is different." He shrugged. "We all know that when it comes down to it, Callum will do what is best for the company."

"How long has he been running Lennon Enterprises?"

His shoulders tensed ever so slightly, the only indication she had tread on hallowed ground. Curious. It fit right into the strange absence of information on the Internet about the family. In all the research she'd done on the Lennons, Phoebe had not been able to find out how the company had been started. Stranger still, there hadn't been one news story outlining when Callum Lennon took up the reins.

She knew from Fletcher's reaction that she wouldn't get much information from him. It was only a moment or two before the lazy sensuality returned to his face again, like a smoke screen.

"For too long, if you ask me," Fletcher finally answered. "But it's what drives him, what he craves."

"I take it he had a lot to live up to?"

He looked at her blankly.

"With it being a family company, I assumed that he'd been trained by his father or maybe an uncle?"

"From birth, Callum always seemed to be ready to take control."

Which wasn't an answer. "I just thought it odd that you didn't have any pictures of board members or of Callum out and about at charity events."

Fletcher shrugged. "Callum isn't that photogenic."

He slowed down and opened the door to a room, his gaze roaming down her body, then back up. Instead of arousal, a dash of irritation, along with a helping of amusement, stole through her. That he thought he could flirt with her and make her stop sniffing around their company was both insulting and funny.

"Is this my room?"

He blinked, his smile dimming just a bit. Poor Fletcher wasn't accustomed to a woman ignoring his ploys. If she wasn't sure he'd take it the wrong way, she'd kiss him.

"Uh, yes, this is your room. Your bags have already been brought up."

She brushed past him and stepped over the threshold. Before he could follow her in, she placed a hand on his chest and smiled. "Thank you so much for escorting me."

He looked down at her hand and frowned. "I can show you around your room."

She laughed. "I can handle it myself. I'm used to travel. Thank you once again."

Before he could argue with her, she closed the door directly in his face. She needed a break from the testosterone of all the Lennon men for a few minutes. If she didn't get it, there was a good chance she would faint from the overload—if not the embarrassment of her behavior.

She took a good look at the room. She stood in a small sitting room that opened up into the larger room. As she stepped into the bedroom itself, she sighed. A massive bed, with a mattress so thick there was a step stool beside it for her use, dominated the room. When she stepped further into the room, she noticed the high vaulted ceiling. With it painted in celestial blue, along with the lighter, almost airy quality of the furnishings and bed linens, it felt as if she were walking through the heavens. Still agitated with Callum, not to mention with herself, the atmosphere was a calming influence, bringing her back to her goal at hand.

Phoebe approached the bureau and noticed that her bags were indeed sitting by the foot of the bed. When she looked up, she saw herself in the mirror and groaned. No wonder Callum Lennon had thought she was an idiot. Her suit was a mess, wrinkled and still damp from the rain. Half of her hair was still piled on top of her head, while the other half hung down in a mess of tangled curls. What makeup she had worn was now either smudged on her face or was gone. Good God, she looked like she'd rolled through a ditch before coming to meet them.

Knowing there was nothing she could do about it now, she grabbed her toiletry bag and headed to the bathroom to clean herself up. At least when she met the remaining two cousins, she would look professional, and with her armor back in place, she could better deal with Callum Lennon.

Before she could start cleaning up, her mobile buzzed. The familiar number made her groan. She'd forgotten to contact Kenneth McWalton, the head of the grant board, after she arrived. She wasn't in the mood to deal with him. However, his say would carry a lot of weight when the grant she needed was given out, so she'd best put up with his blustery impatience and answer. Besides, he would continue to ring her until she did. This was inconvenient enough, but she definitely didn't want him to ring her when she was with the Lennons.

"Hello."

"Dr. Chilton. I thought you said you would ring me up when you landed," McWalton chastised.

Phoebe took a deep breath before answering. She hadn't had to answer to anyone for over eighteen months, and she refused to do it now.

She kept her voice calm and businesslike. "We were fogged in and took off later than usual."

There was a pause, as if he were weighing her every word, trying to decide if she were telling the truth.

"Hmm. Well, I was worried." His tone had turned solicitous enough to agitate her. "I thought you might have had second thoughts."

"I haven't even had time to freshen up, let alone look over whatever artifact they have for me."

Another pause. "You *are* going to try for the grant, aren't you?"

"As I told you before, I'll make that decision when I have a chance to evaluate what this is."

"I was just wondering because Sir Wendell Farthington has contacted me about the grant. Seems he has something he thinks might win over the committee."

A wave of apprehension washed over her at the mention of her arch rival from college. Whiney Wendell was still annoyed she'd beat him out for valedictorian—especially since he had ten years on her. If he'd contacted McWalton, there was a good chance he knew she was interested.

"I'll let you know as soon as I can be certain if I'm onto something that will fit what the grant committee is looking for."

As soon as she reassured McWalton twice more, she rung off and sighed. She'd felt more than a little twinge of guilt for being a bit deceptive. Okay, she felt a lot. She'd built a reputation on being fair and honest. This could tarnish that image. Greatly. But, this was the most important leap of faith in her career, one that could leave her reputation in tatters or give her the recognition, independent of her parents, she had always craved.

Before she could get back into the bathroom, her mobile rang again. When she noticed Isabel Totaro's number, she immediately answered.

"Where the hell are you?" her former assistant asked.

"Hello, Isabel. How are you?" She laughed.

"I'm fine. I'm always fine. You, on the other hand, were supposed to have lunch with me tomorrow and your new assistant—who has the manners of a goat—called me to cancel." All of this was delivered in a mixture of heavily accented English and Spanish. When irritated, Isabel had a habit of slipping in and out of different languages.

"She doesn't have the manners of a goat. She's efficient. Besides, you quit."

"She was rude and wouldn't tell me where you were. I was worried you went back to Egypt with Barbie and Ken."

Phoebe sighed. She wasn't used to this, although she should be after three years. Isabel had bounced into her life during the horrific last months of Simon's illness. Five-foot two of dynamite that one was. She'd refused to allow Phoebe to wallow in self-pity. Her resignation last month had been bittersweet, but she'd fallen in love with an Italian businessman and they were moving back to the continent. It was hard to lose your only friend.

Phoebe smiled, but she still felt she should admonish her friend. "I wish you wouldn't call my parents names."

"You know you like it. So, tell me where you are."

"Scotland."

"What the bloody hell are you doing there?"

"I've thrown caution to the wind, and I'm having a mad affair with four Scotsmen."

"About damned time."

Phoebe laughed. "No, I have a chance to look at an artifact from the Lennon family."

"Lennon Enterprises? Hold on." Phoebe heard a deep

murmur in the background before Izzy came back. "Roberto wants to know if you met Callum Lennon."

Just hearing his name sent a shiver of awareness across her nerve endings.

"Yes, in fact, I've met two of the others also."

More murmuring, then Izzy giggled. "Roberto said he's a real bastard."

"He's met Callum Lennon?"

"Roberto negotiated a deal with them a few years ago. They want you to look at an artifact? What is it?"

"I haven't heard, but apparently it might work for that grant I wanted to go after."

Izzy said nothing for a moment. "Don't do this."

"What?"

"Poppet, I love you. You know I do. So I'm saying this for your own good. Your parents aren't worth it."

"Izzy—"

"They will never accept you."

A sharp shard of pain stabbed her heart. Izzy was right. They both knew it.

"I don't give a damn about them accepting me." She drew in an unsteady breath. It was the truth, even if it took her almost thirty years to accept that. "What I want is to study Celtic myths full time."

"Then do it. You have enough money."

"I can't...well, I can. It's just..." How did she say she wanted to stick their noses in her success without sounding like a horrible daughter? She would never be free of their shadows if she couldn't make it on her own without their help. They would always try to influence her career unless she made a clean break.

"You want to say shove it to Barbie and Ken." Amusement infused Izzy's voice. "I wholly approve."

Phoebe chuckled. "I thought you might. They won't say a word if I get a reputable historical society to back me. But none of that is going to happen until I get a look at what the

Lennons have. I can't do that until I negotiate the terms with Callum Lennon."

"What was that?"

"I said, I can't—"

"No. There was something in your voice. You...oh, my. You're attracted to him."

Phoebe swallowed. "Him?"

"Callum Lennon."

Bugger. Izzy always could tell what Phoebe was feeling even before Phoebe knew. "You can tell that all from the tone in my voice?"

"Yes. There was a little heat in your voice when you talked about him."

"It's because he's a pompous ass."

Izzy laughed. "You are attracted." Phoebe opened her mouth to lie, but her friend was too fast for her. "Don't even fib to me. I'll let you go, but I want regular updates."

Phoebe sighed. As if she could talk Izzy out of it... "You got it."

After ringing off, Phoebe looked at her reflection in the mirror. Her hair was still a mess, her makeup still streaked her skin. This was not the most auspicious of beginnings.

* * * *

As soon as Fletcher escorted Dr. Chilton from the room, Callum shifted weight from one foot to the other, trying to calm his body's reaction to her. Bloody hell, he'd practically jumped over the desk and kissed her, not caring who was there to witness.

Be truthful, Callum. You wanted to do a whole lot more than kiss the lass.

Aye, he did. She made his blood pump, and he wanted to know if she'd look as heated when she moaned his name.

"Just what the fucking hell was that?"

Angus's cursing wasn't normal. Callum knew he

deserved the rebuke, but it didn't mean he cared for his younger cousin's tone.

"Nothing."

"*Nothing?*"

"You willna question me on this, Angus. Nothing happened and nothing will."

Callum turned and watched the younger man approach him. As leader, Callum allowed discussion, but with his body still aroused, any debate was like pouring salt into the wound. Not only was he angry with himself for the desire still curling in his belly, but he'd shown disrespect to a woman by showing such blatant lust, not to mention giving her a way to use him. If she had any idea how much he wanted her, she could get just about anything she wanted. He never bedded women who worked for him. *Ever.*

Dr. Chilton had been attractive in a rumpled sort of way. He had a feeling that under the ill-fitting jacket, she had curves he couldn't find on women today—ones he thirsted to explore. He still didn't trust her. Not many people would turn down money just because of a simple contract. Callum couldn't put his finger on it, but something about the woman bothered him. Other than the fact he wanted her beneath him, digging her nails into his back.

Sweet Jesus, when she'd stood up to him, mild interest had shot to heated desire in the blink of an eye. The force of it had left him shaken to his soul.

"We can't have you tupping the help, Callum."

He smiled, knowing it was all teeth and no humor. "Have you ever known me to?"

"No." Angus looked out the window, and Callum could almost hear his mind turning over the problem. When he met his cousin's gaze, Callum realized he wasn't angry but worried. "But I've also never seen you act like that."

"I'm hardly a virgin."

Angus smiled, but it didn't reach his eyes, a hint of sadness darkening his gaze. "I know that. Seriously, if it were anyone else, I would say take her to bed for a week—even if I think you two are completely wrong for each other. You have a business mind, she has a scientific mind and you would never—"

"Sweet Jesus, Angus, just get on with it."

He sighed. "This is too important."

Guilt, familiar and uncomfortable, had the muscles in his gut clenching. He knew he'd failed before when it had counted the most. But he refused to let his emotions get the better of him again. Even for a woman with the fire Phoebe Chilton showed—especially when she held their future in her hands.

"Doona fash yourself."

Before Angus could reply, Fletcher returned, Anice following close behind him. A frown puckered her brow as she kept darting nasty looks at Fletcher.

Without preamble, Fletcher said, "I think we need to be careful of Dr. Chilton."

"You have no basis for that." Anice had crossed her arms which was a sure sign she was ready to fight.

"For the love of Christ, you haven't even met the woman. I have, and she was asking too many questions about us and the company."

"The company?" Callum asked, his suspicion rising.

"She wanted to know when you took over Lennon Enterprises and who was in charge before you. I tried to dissuade her, but she kept on it until we reached the room."

"I'm sure she forced you to answer her." Disgust ripened Anice's voice. "You're over six feet tall, and she is barely five and a half feet."

"I'm not saying she forced me but that she was persistent."

"I think—"

"Enough!" Callum shouted. When brother and sister got going, they could make him barmy.

He thought of her refusal to sign the contract, possibly

turning down a healthy amount of euros. People just didn't do that without cause. Now she was asking about them. She was insistent enough to make Fletcher question her motives, and he rarely thought straight when a woman was involved.

"I want you to check out her background."

Angus studied him with a frown. "I did. I double-checked it, in fact. There is nothing to indicate she would sell out."

Callum gritted his teeth and then blew out an aggravated breath. "Triple check. I want to know everything there is to know about Phoebe Chilton, especially if this turns out to be the cure we've been searching for."

Angus nodded.

"Since I missed my meeting, I need to ring up the supplier and set a new one. I'll be having dinner by myself with her tonight," Callum said.

All three cousins looked at each other. Angus, the one who had always been their spokesperson said, "I don't think that is a good idea."

"I didn't ask."

Callum sensed that Angus wanted to say more, but nodded instead.

"I need some privacy to get this done so I can meet Dr. Chilton for dinner. The sooner she gets it translated and decoded, the sooner she is gone."

Anice, the peacemaker, stepped in. "And the sooner we will be able to start working on a resolution to our problem. Come on, boys."

Fletcher curled his lip. "I take offense to being called 'boys,' especially at my advanced age."

But he followed his sister just the same. Angus looked to argue again, but Anice said, "Come on, cuz. We have a meeting with department heads, and we're already late."

When the door shut and Callum was blessedly alone, some of his tension eased. He stared out at the garden again, watching the wind blow the naked limbs this way and that.

He knew the feeling, the loss of control to outside forces—the impotence over the failure to shape your own destiny. He'd sworn never to feel that way again.

If it meant he had to resist a golden-haired angel with the temper of the devil, so be it. He would ignore the momentary loss of control and find another woman to satisfy his needs. Angus was right. Tupping the help would not only be bad for business, it could dash any hopes the other four had. That and he still didn't trust her. This diary could hold the secrets that could save them—or doom them to the hell they now suffered. He couldn't chance it. Regret shifted through him when he realized he would enjoy sparring with the woman and slowly conquering her. But even as a surge of fire lit through his blood, Callum ordered his body and soul to ignore it.

The clan was all that mattered.

www.ingramcontent.com/pod-product-compliance
Lightning Source LLC
Chambersburg PA
CBHW022023240626
47154CB00007B/2241